# Disney Princess

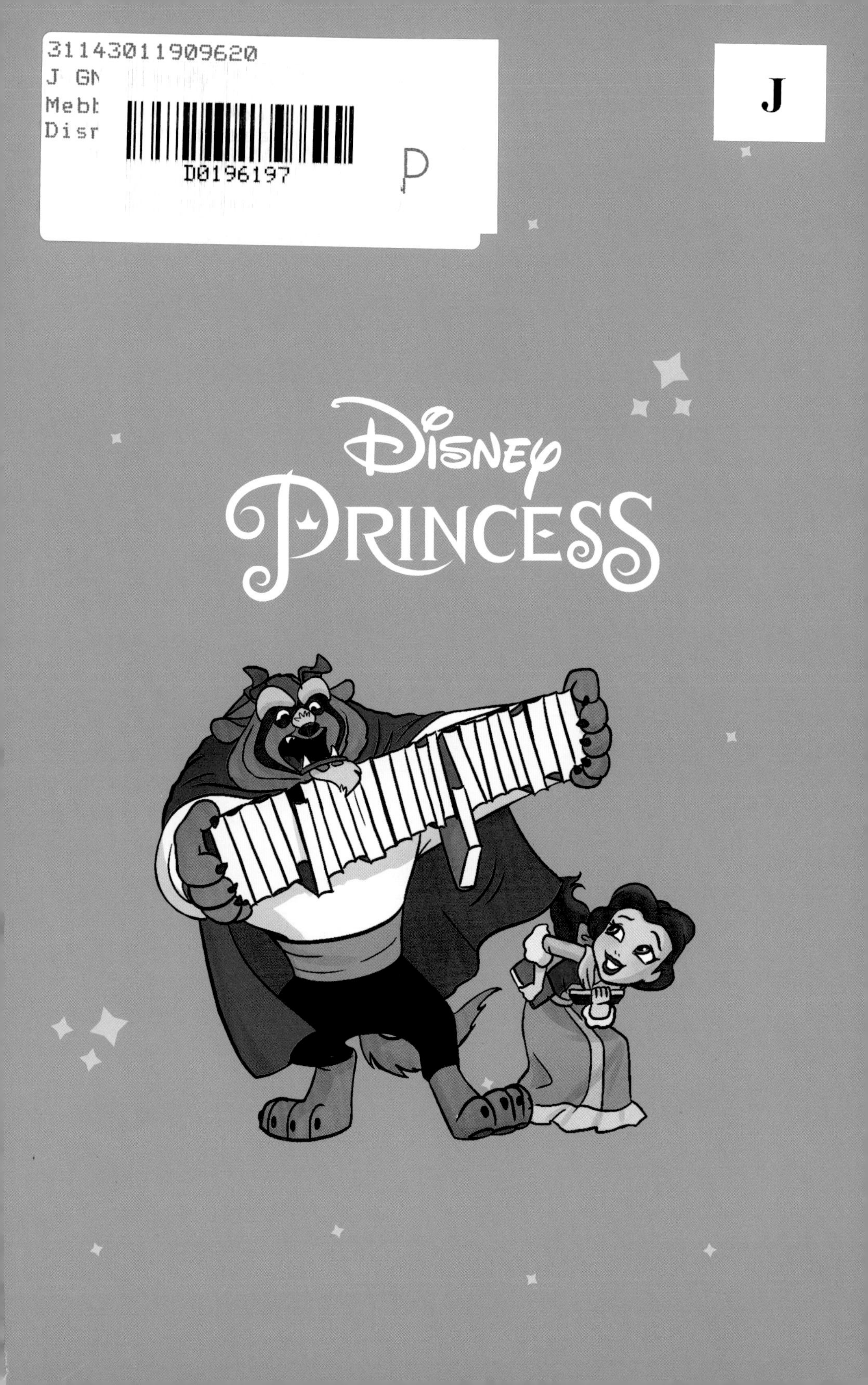

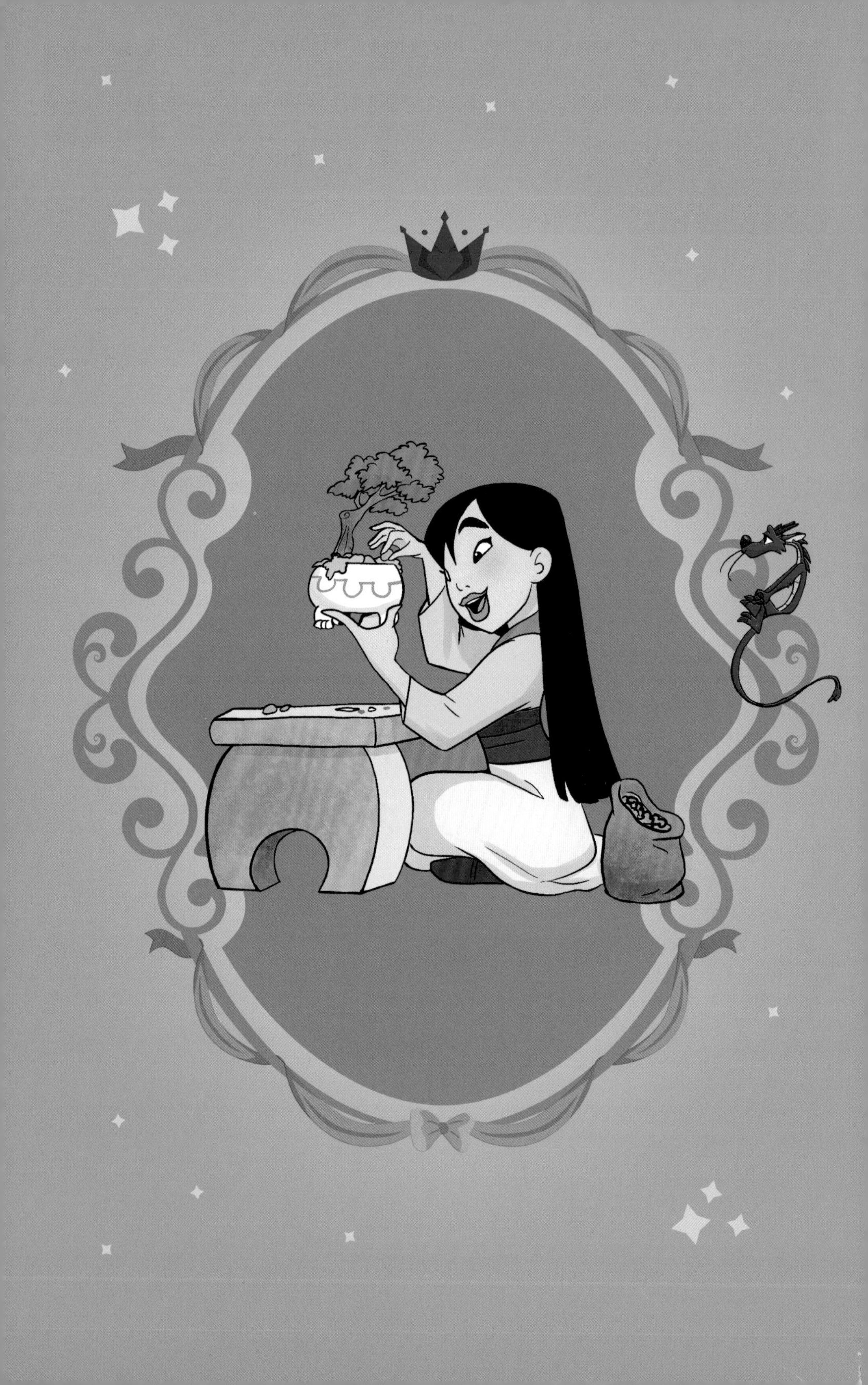

# DISNEY PRINCESS

## Follow Your Heart

*Script by*
**Amy Mebberson**
**Georgia Ball**
**Patrick Storck**
**Pat Shand**
**Geoffrey Golden**
**Caleb Goellner**

*Illustration by*
**Amy Mebberson**

*Lettering by*
**AndWorld Design**

*Cover Art by*
**Amy Mebberson**

**Dark Horse Books**

Before we jump into stories with the Disney Princesses, let's take a moment to learn some *quick key details* about a few of them with these very informative *infographics*!

**Presenting, Belle, Mulan, and Cinderella . . .**

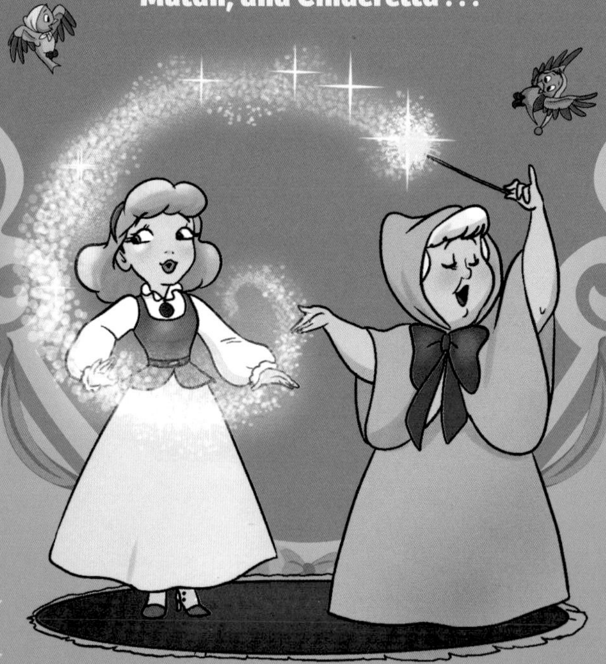

# Meet the Princesses
# Belle

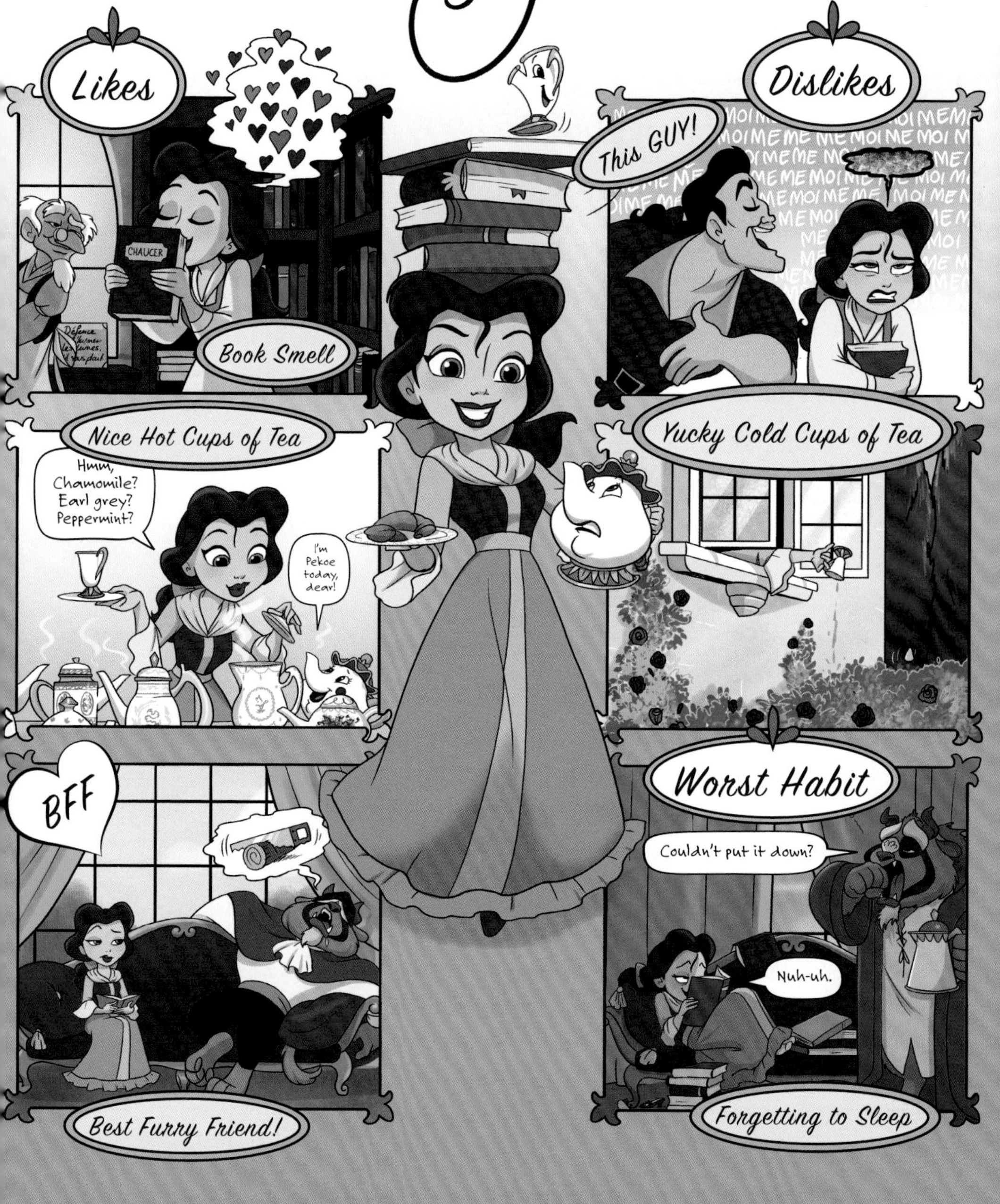

Likes
CHAUCER
Book Smell
Dislikes
This GUY!
Nice Hot Cups of Tea
Hmm, Chamomile? Earl grey? Peppermint?
I'm Pekoe today, dear!
Yucky Cold Cups of Tea
BFF
Best Furry Friend!
Worst Habit
Couldn't put it down?
Nuh-uh.
Forgetting to Sleep

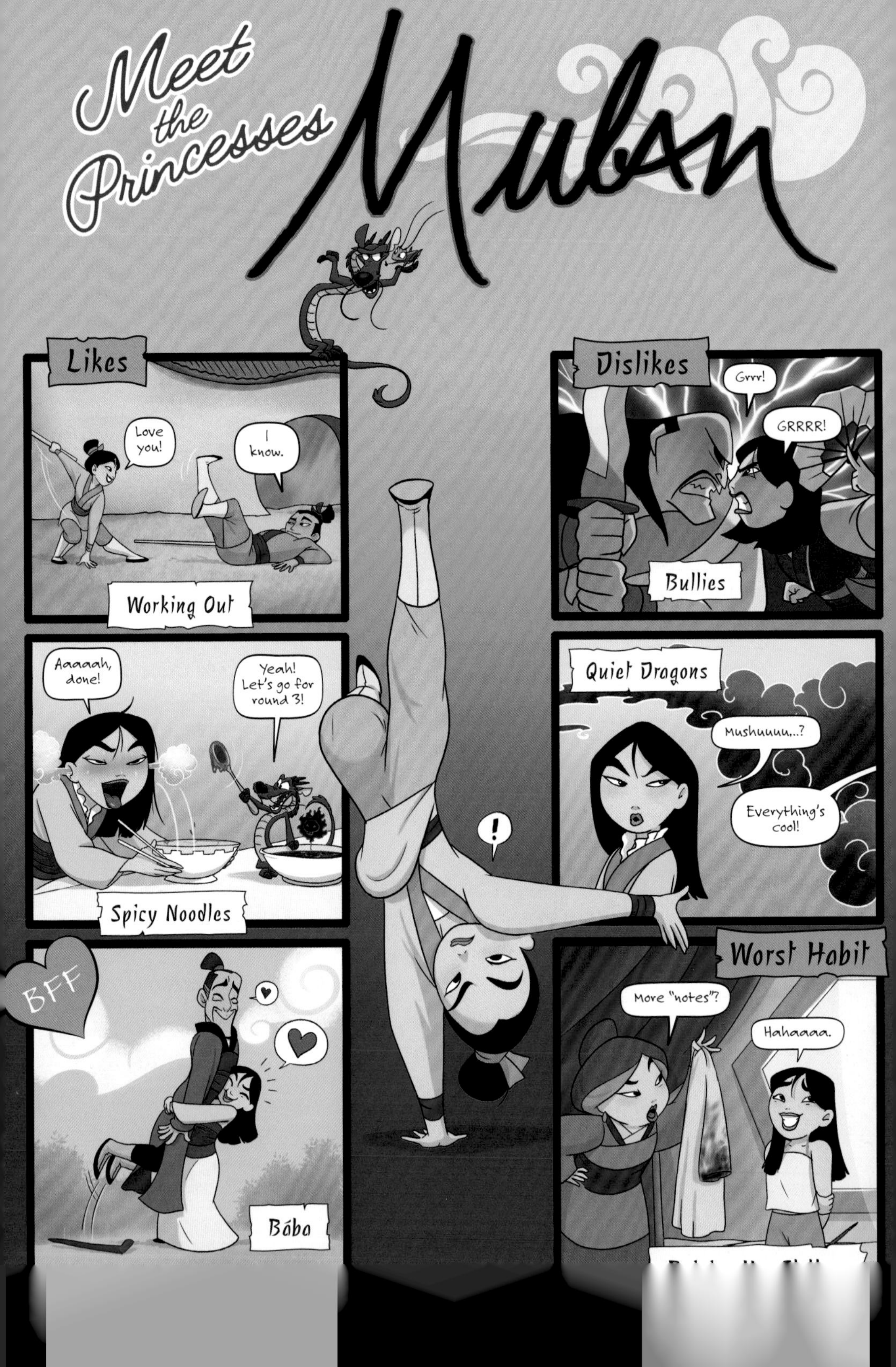
Meet the Princesses
Mulan
Likes
Love you!
I know.
Working Out
Dislikes
Grrr!
GRRRR!
Bullies
Aaaaah, done!
Yeah! Let's go for round 3!
Spicy Noodles
Quiet Dragons
Mushuuuu...?
Everything's cool!
!
BFF
Bába
Worst Habit
More "notes"?
Hahaaaa.

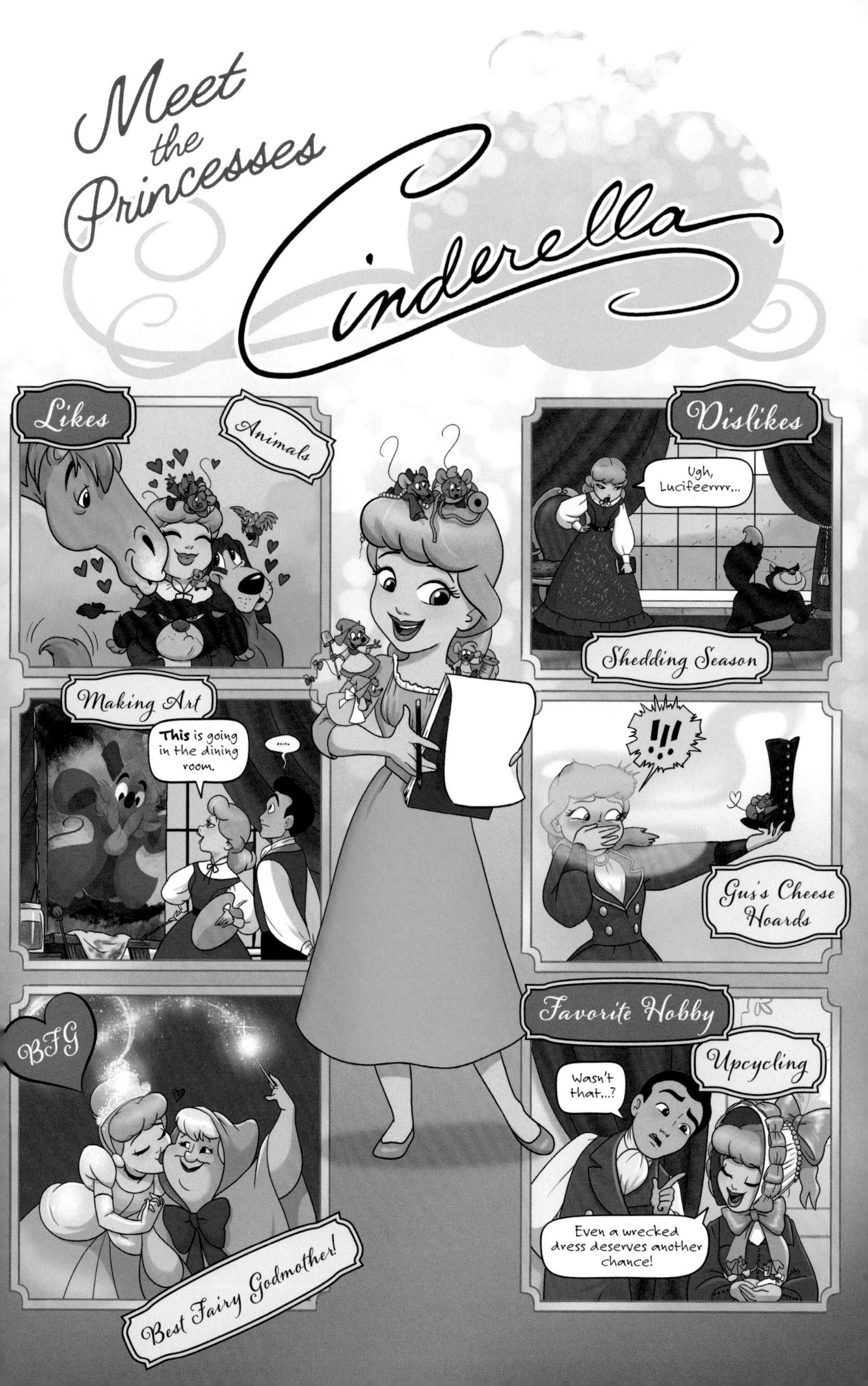
Meet the Princesses
Cinderella
Likes
Animals
Dislikes
Ugh, Lucifeerrrr...
Shedding Season
Making Art
This is going in the dining room.
!!!
Gus's Cheese Hoards
BFG
Favorite Hobby
Upcycling
Wasn't that...?
Even a wrecked dress deserves another chance!
Best Fairy Godmother!

# "TOUGH CHOICES"

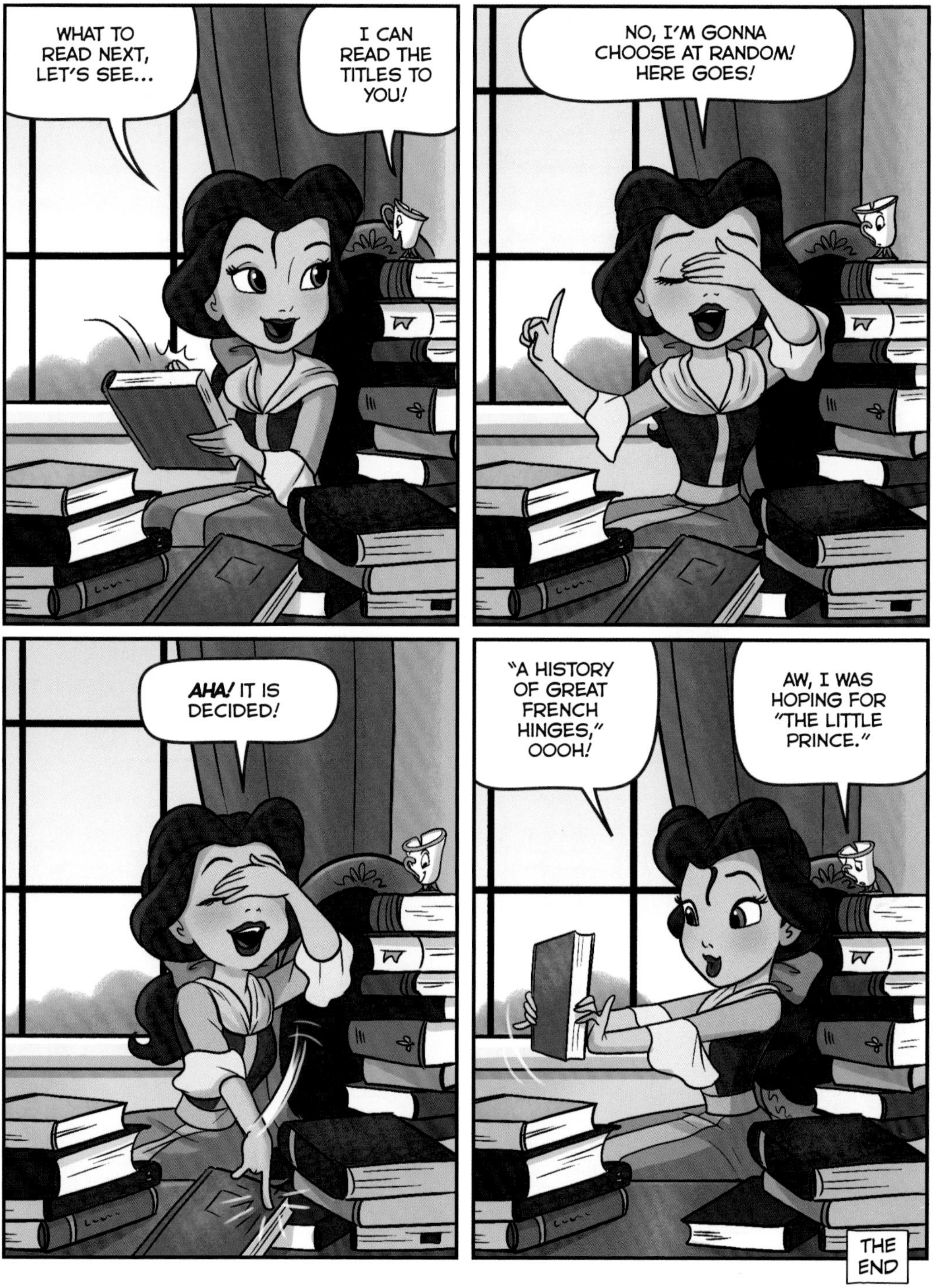
WHAT TO READ NEXT, LET'S SEE...
I CAN READ THE TITLES TO YOU!
NO, I'M GONNA CHOOSE AT RANDOM! HERE GOES!
AHA! IT IS DECIDED!
"A HISTORY OF GREAT FRENCH HINGES," OOOH!
AW, I WAS HOPING FOR "THE LITTLE PRINCE."
THE END

# "HOW TO SLEEP" by Rapunzel

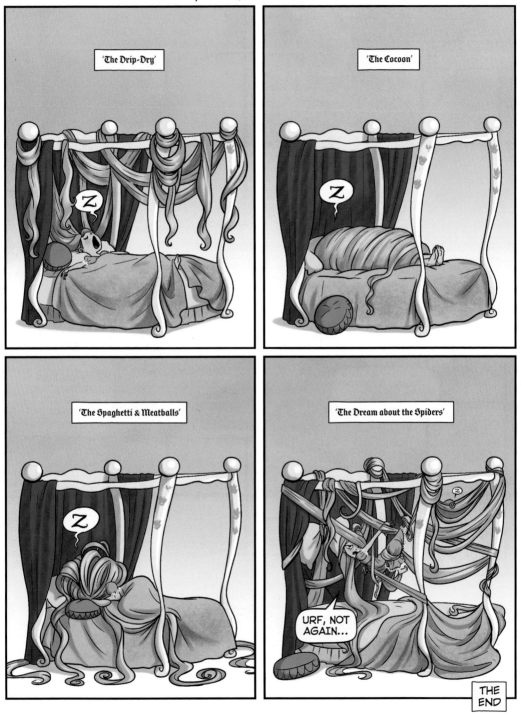

'The Drip-Dry'

'The Cocoon'

'The Spaghetti & Meatballs'

'The Dream about the Spiders'

URF, NOT AGAIN...

THE END

# "ROCK DRAWINGS"

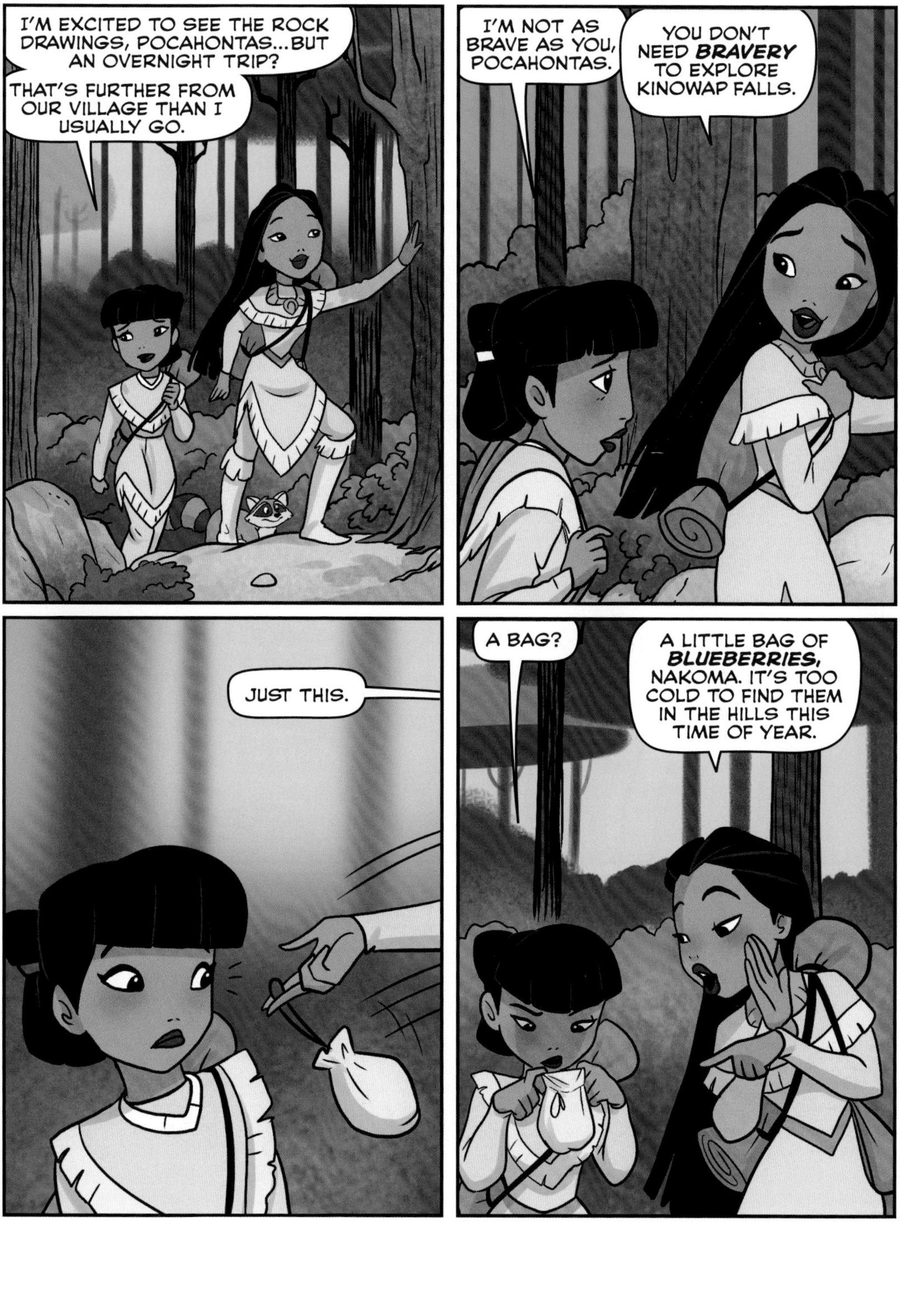
I'M EXCITED TO SEE THE ROCK DRAWINGS, POCAHONTAS...BUT AN OVERNIGHT TRIP?
THAT'S FURTHER FROM OUR VILLAGE THAN I USUALLY GO.
I'M NOT AS BRAVE AS YOU, POCAHONTAS.
YOU DON'T NEED *BRAVERY* TO EXPLORE KINOWAP FALLS.
JUST THIS.
A BAG?
A LITTLE BAG OF *BLUEBERRIES,* NAKOMA. IT'S TOO COLD TO FIND THEM IN THE HILLS THIS TIME OF YEAR.

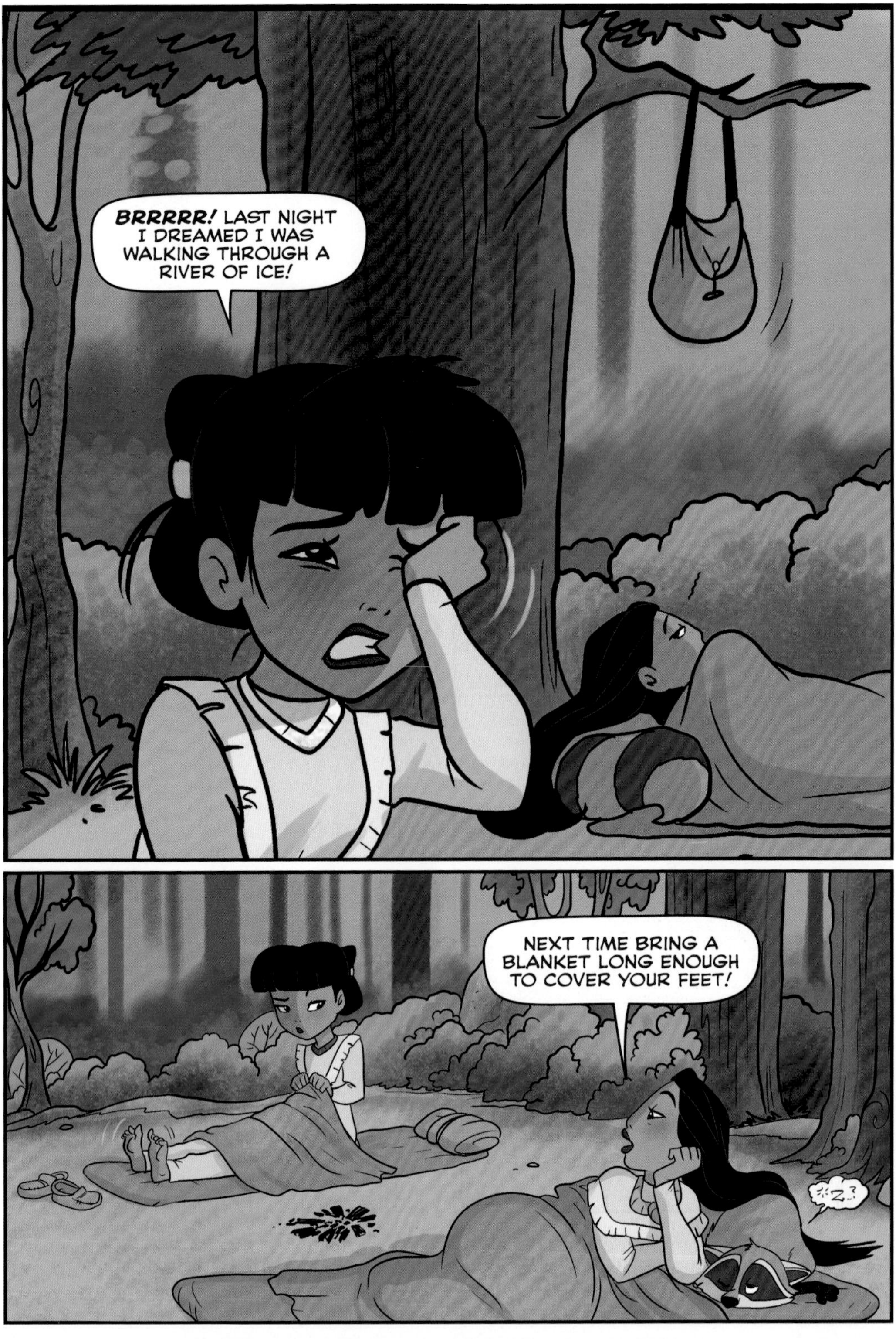
BRRRRR! LAST NIGHT I DREAMED I WAS WALKING THROUGH A RIVER OF ICE!
NEXT TIME BRING A BLANKET LONG ENOUGH TO COVER YOUR FEET!

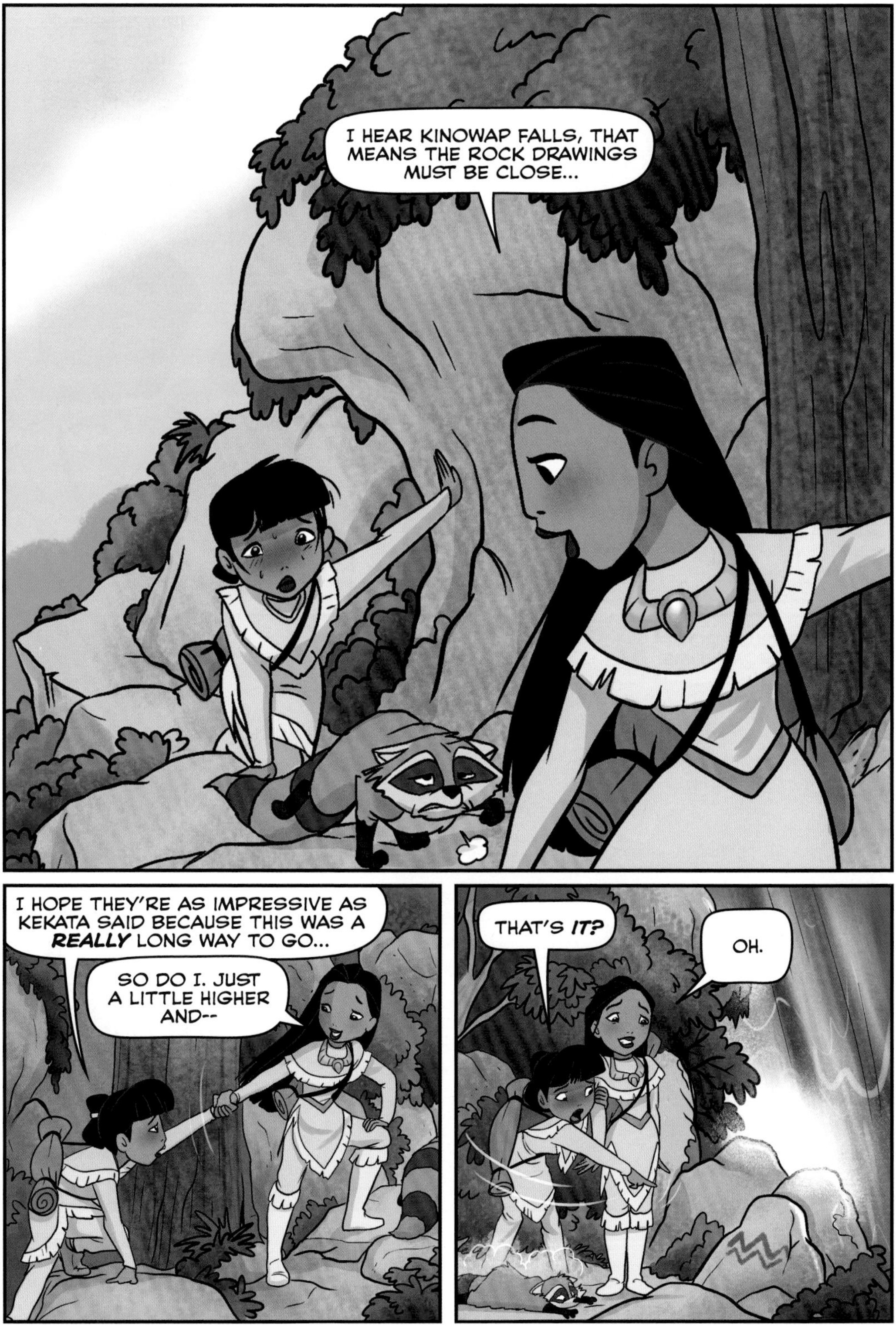

I HEAR KINOWAP FALLS, THAT MEANS THE ROCK DRAWINGS MUST BE CLOSE...
I HOPE THEY'RE AS IMPRESSIVE AS KEKATA SAID BECAUSE THIS WAS A *REALLY* LONG WAY TO GO...
SO DO I. JUST A LITTLE HIGHER AND--
THAT'S *IT?*
OH.

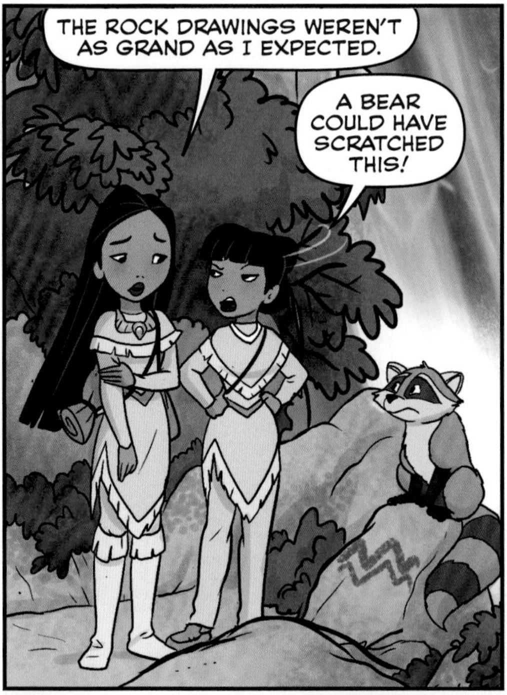
THE ROCK DRAWINGS WEREN'T AS GRAND AS I EXPECTED.
A BEAR COULD HAVE SCRATCHED THIS!

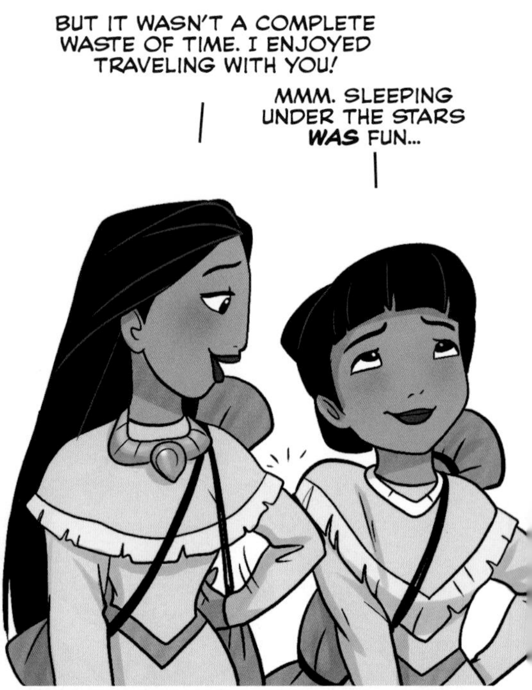
BUT IT WASN'T A COMPLETE WASTE OF TIME. I ENJOYED TRAVELING WITH YOU!
MMM. SLEEPING UNDER THE STARS *WAS* FUN...

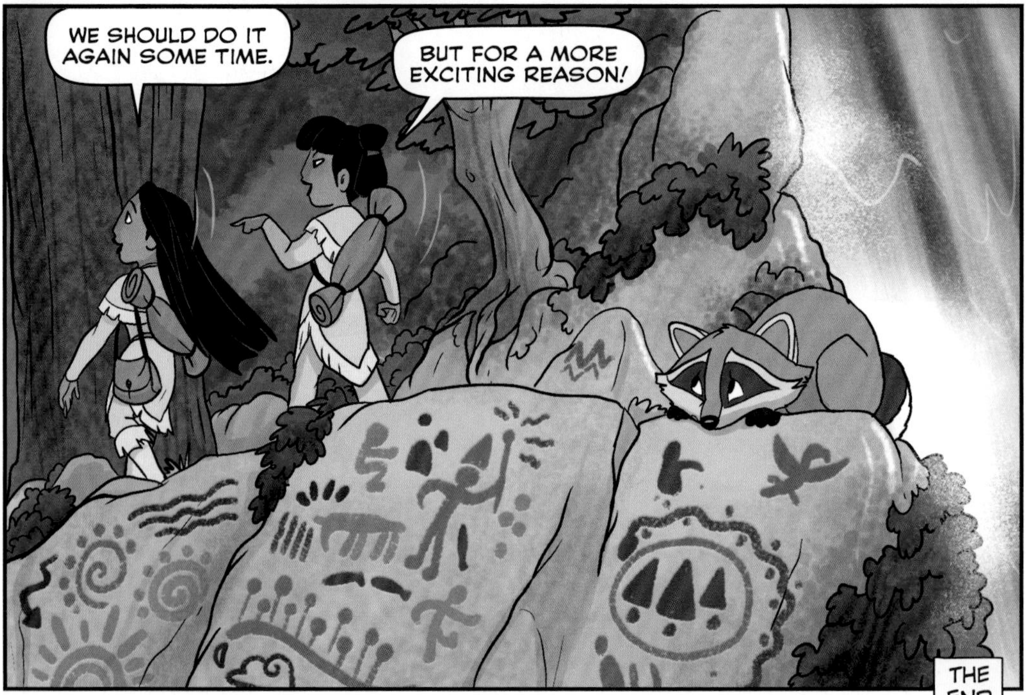
WE SHOULD DO IT AGAIN SOME TIME.
BUT FOR A MORE EXCITING REASON!
THE END

# "SOME LIKE IT HOTTER"

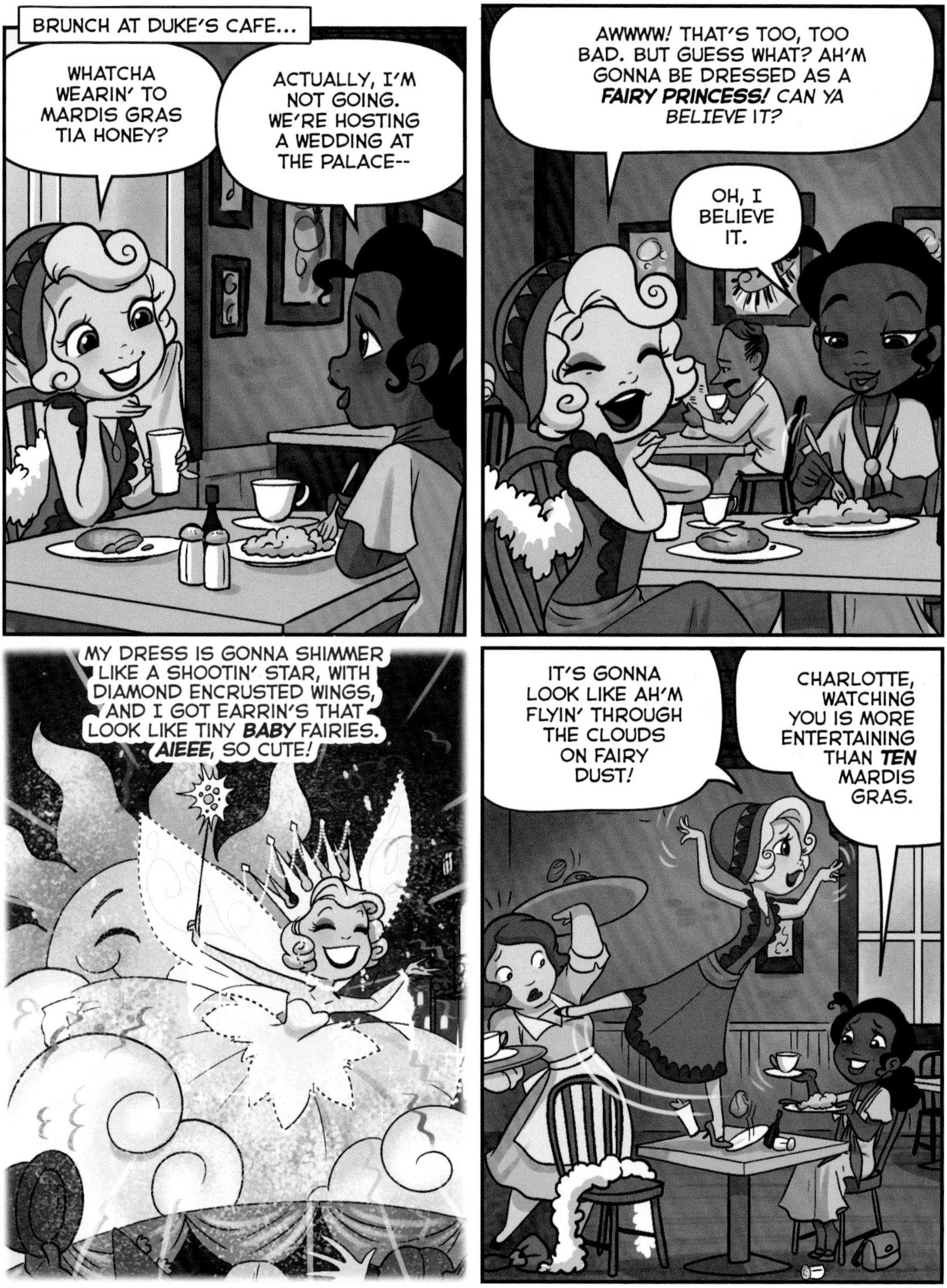
BRUNCH AT DUKE'S CAFE...
WHATCHA WEARIN' TO MARDIS GRAS TIA HONEY?
ACTUALLY, I'M NOT GOING. WE'RE HOSTING A WEDDING AT THE PALACE--
AWWWW! THAT'S TOO, TOO BAD. BUT GUESS WHAT? AH'M GONNA BE DRESSED AS A *FAIRY PRINCESS!* CAN YA *BELIEVE* IT?
OH, I BELIEVE IT.
MY DRESS IS GONNA SHIMMER LIKE A SHOOTIN' STAR, WITH DIAMOND ENCRUSTED WINGS, AND I GOT EARRIN'S THAT LOOK LIKE TINY *BABY* FAIRIES. *AIEEE*, SO CUTE!
IT'S GONNA LOOK LIKE AH'M FLYIN' THROUGH THE CLOUDS ON FAIRY DUST!
CHARLOTTE, WATCHING YOU IS MORE ENTERTAINING THAN *TEN* MARDIS GRAS.

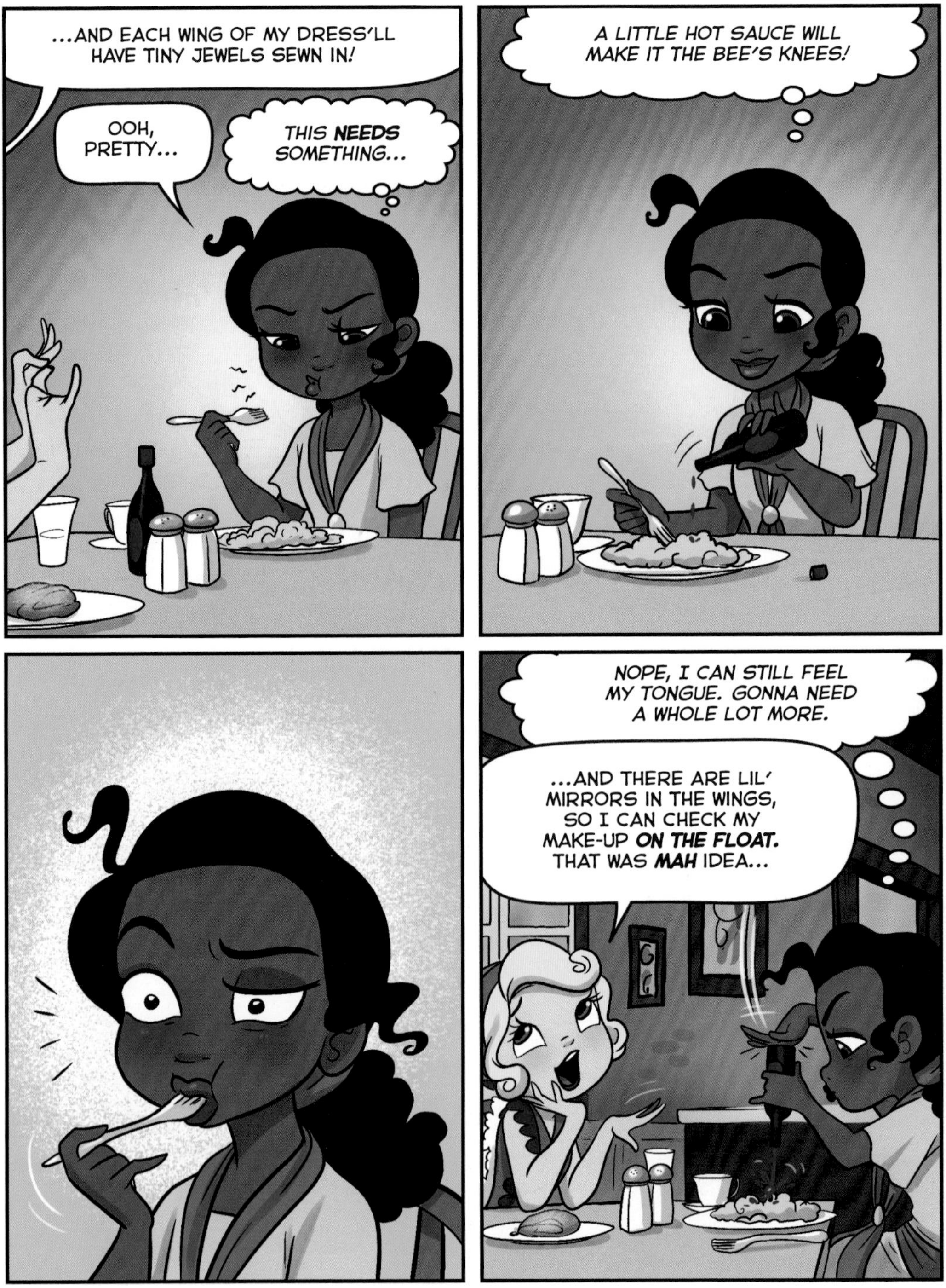
...AND EACH WING OF MY DRESS'LL HAVE TINY JEWELS SEWN IN!
OOH, PRETTY...
THIS **NEEDS** SOMETHING...
A LITTLE HOT SAUCE WILL MAKE IT THE BEE'S KNEES!
NOPE, I CAN STILL FEEL MY TONGUE. GONNA NEED A WHOLE LOT MORE.
...AND THERE ARE LIL' MIRRORS IN THE WINGS, SO I CAN CHECK MY MAKE-UP **ON THE FLOAT.** THAT WAS **MAH** IDEA...

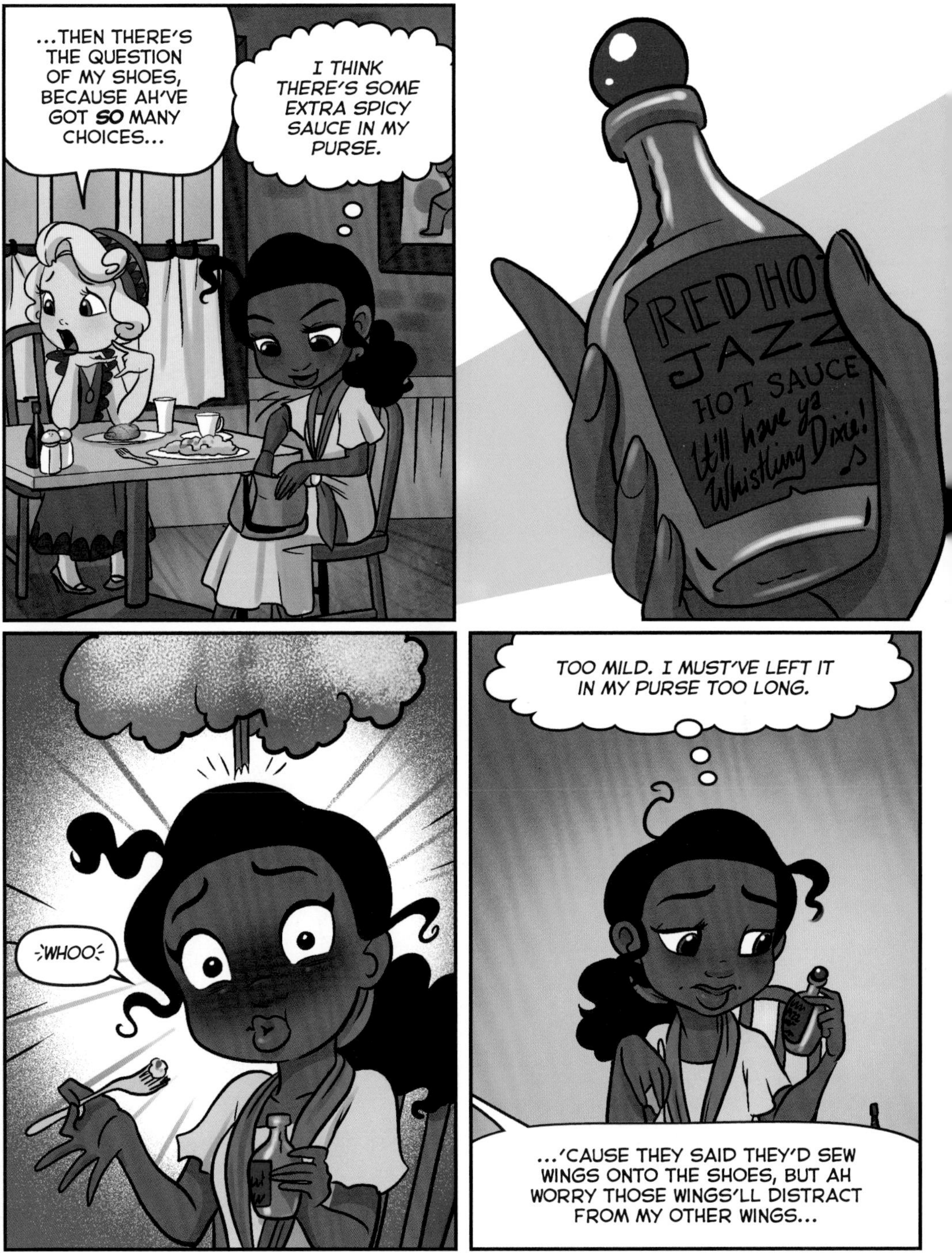
...THEN THERE'S THE QUESTION OF MY SHOES, BECAUSE AH'VE GOT **SO** MANY CHOICES...
I THINK THERE'S SOME EXTRA SPICY SAUCE IN MY PURSE.
RED HOT JAZZ HOT SAUCE It'll have ya Whistling Dixie!
WHOO
TOO MILD. I MUST'VE LEFT IT IN MY PURSE TOO LONG.
...'CAUSE THEY SAID THEY'D SEW WINGS ONTO THE SHOES, BUT AH WORRY THOSE WINGS'LL DISTRACT FROM MY OTHER WINGS...

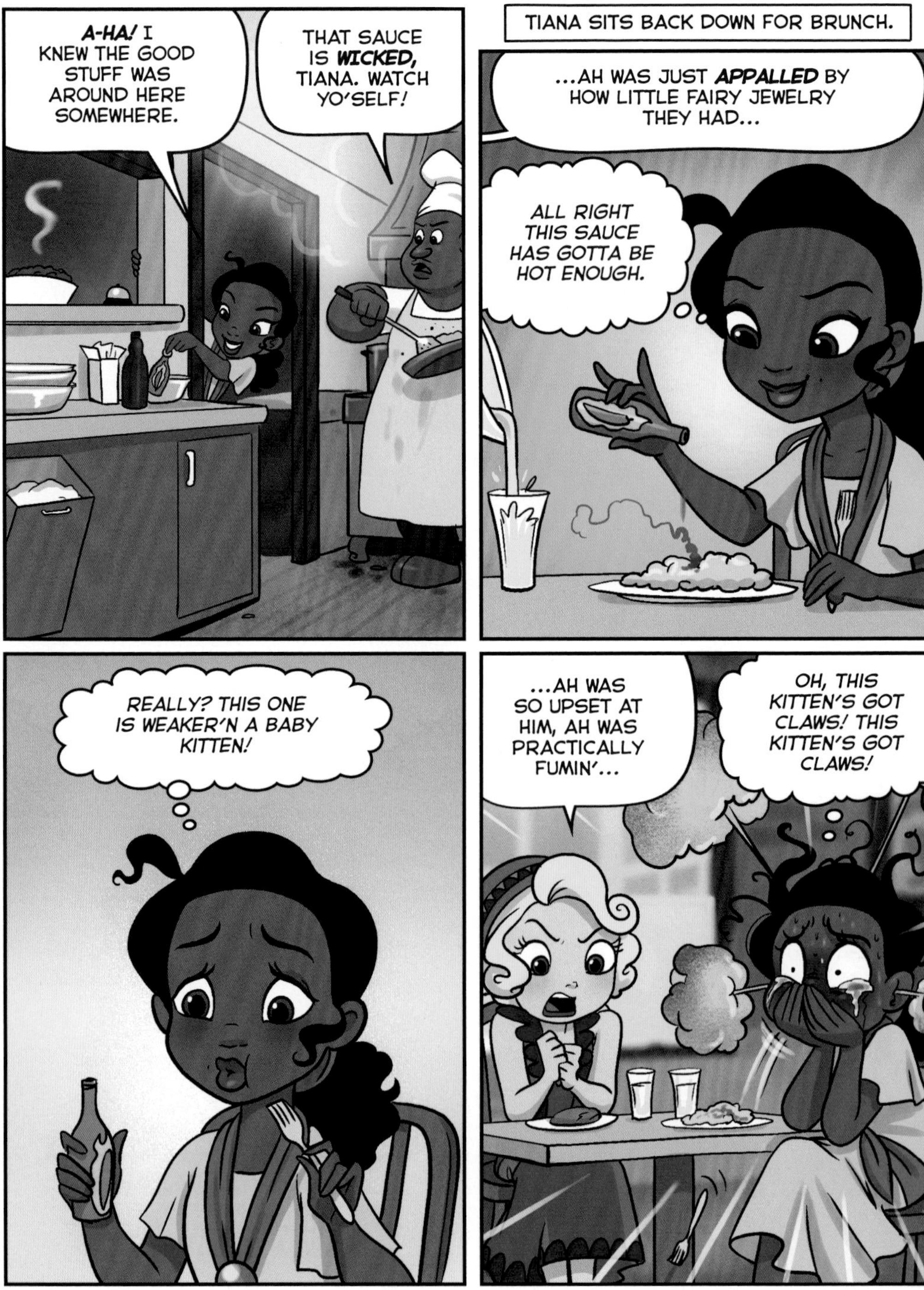
A-HA! I KNEW THE GOOD STUFF WAS AROUND HERE SOMEWHERE.
THAT SAUCE IS WICKED, TIANA. WATCH YO'SELF!
TIANA SITS BACK DOWN FOR BRUNCH.
...AH WAS JUST APPALLED BY HOW LITTLE FAIRY JEWELRY THEY HAD...
ALL RIGHT THIS SAUCE HAS GOTTA BE HOT ENOUGH.
REALLY? THIS ONE IS WEAKER'N A BABY KITTEN!
...AH WAS SO UPSET AT HIM, AH WAS PRACTICALLY FUMIN'...
OH, THIS KITTEN'S GOT CLAWS! THIS KITTEN'S GOT CLAWS!

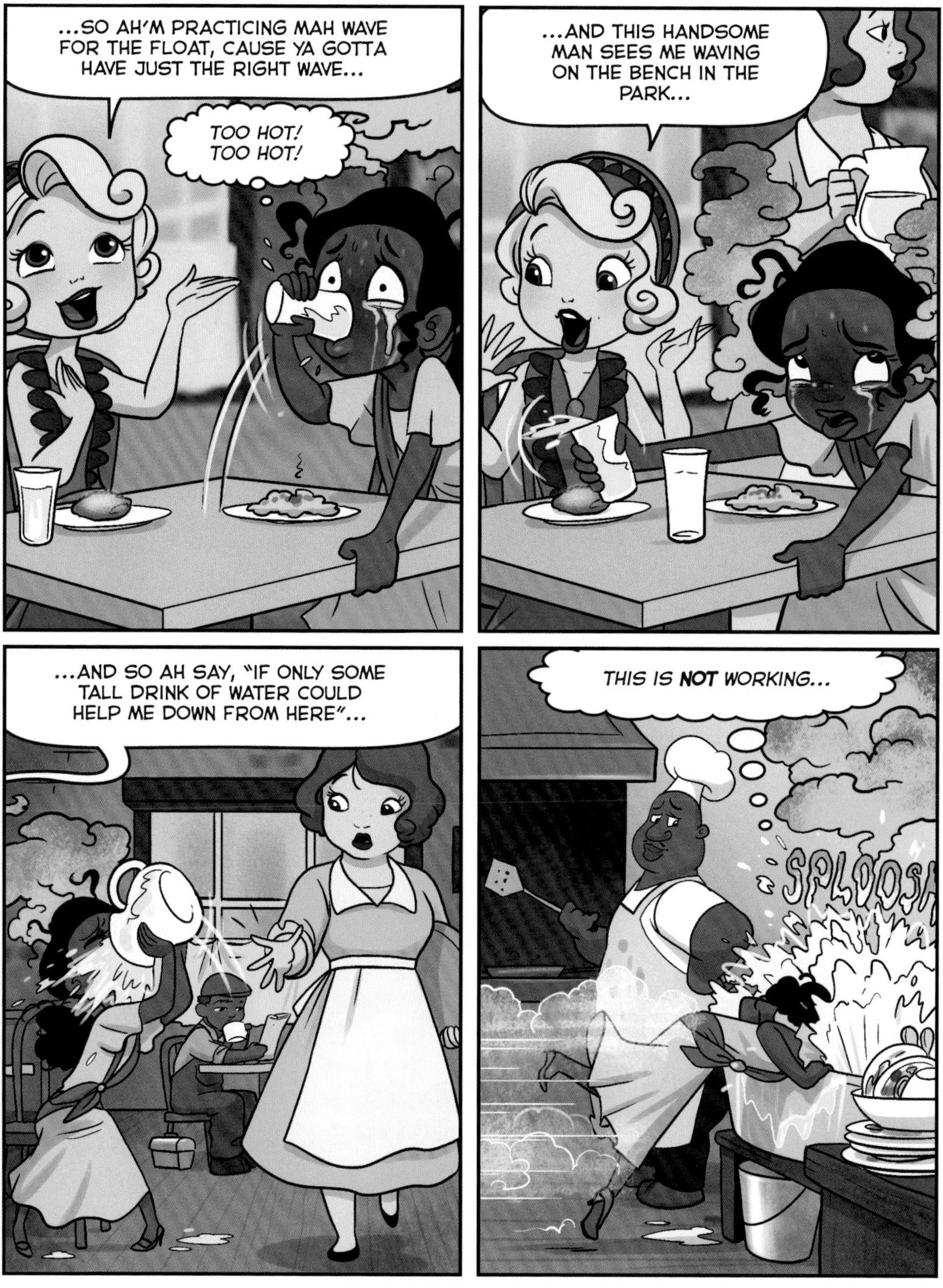
...SO AH'M PRACTICING MAH WAVE FOR THE FLOAT, CAUSE YA GOTTA HAVE JUST THE RIGHT WAVE...
TOO HOT! TOO HOT!
...AND THIS HANDSOME MAN SEES ME WAVING ON THE BENCH IN THE PARK...
...AND SO AH SAY, "IF ONLY SOME TALL DRINK OF WATER COULD HELP ME DOWN FROM HERE"...
THIS IS **NOT** WORKING...
SPLOOSH

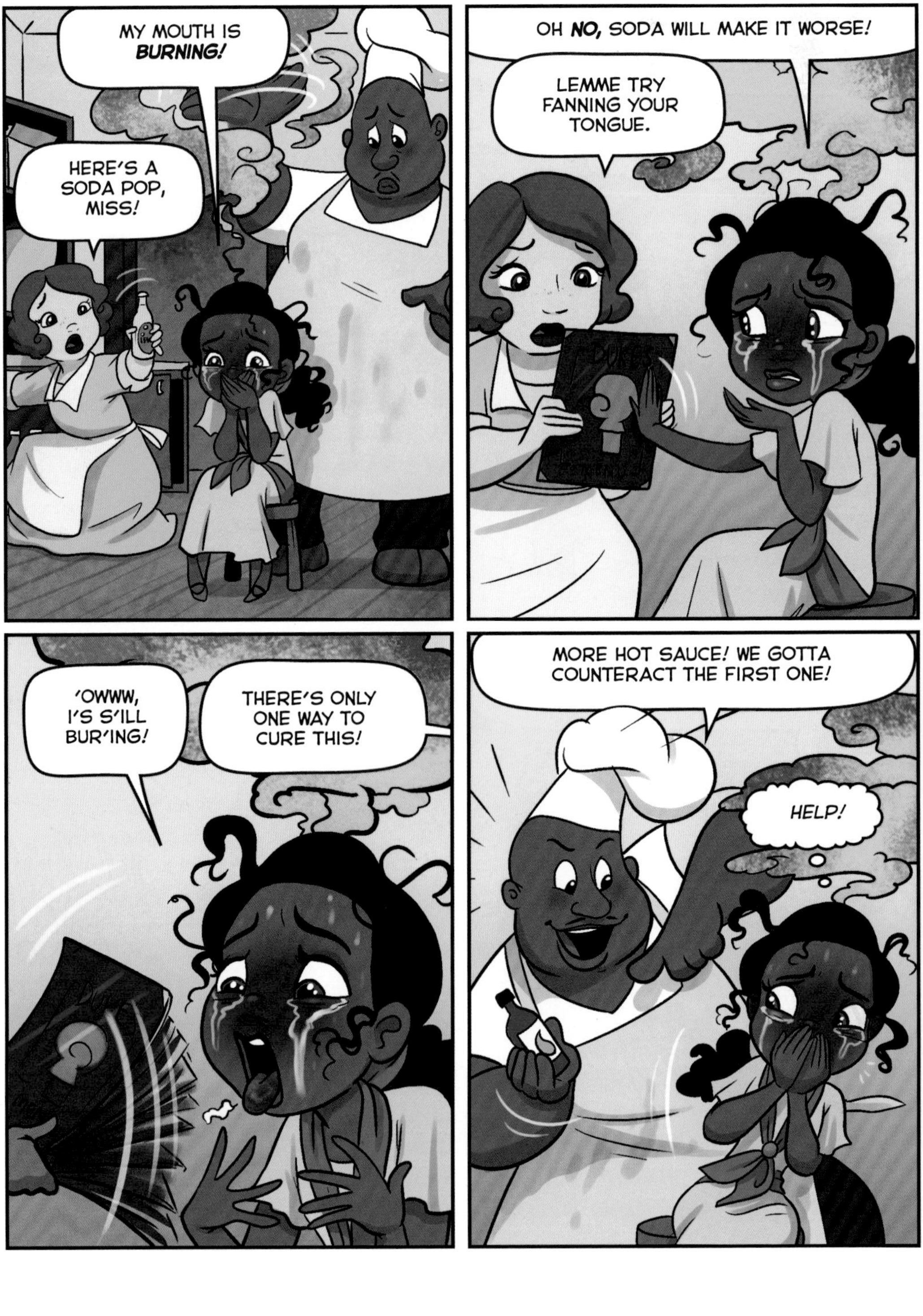
MY MOUTH IS BURNING!
HERE'S A SODA POP, MISS!
OH NO, SODA WILL MAKE IT WORSE!
LEMME TRY FANNING YOUR TONGUE.
'OWWW, I'S S'ILL BUR'ING!
THERE'S ONLY ONE WAY TO CURE THIS!
MORE HOT SAUCE! WE GOTTA COUNTERACT THE FIRST ONE!
HELP!

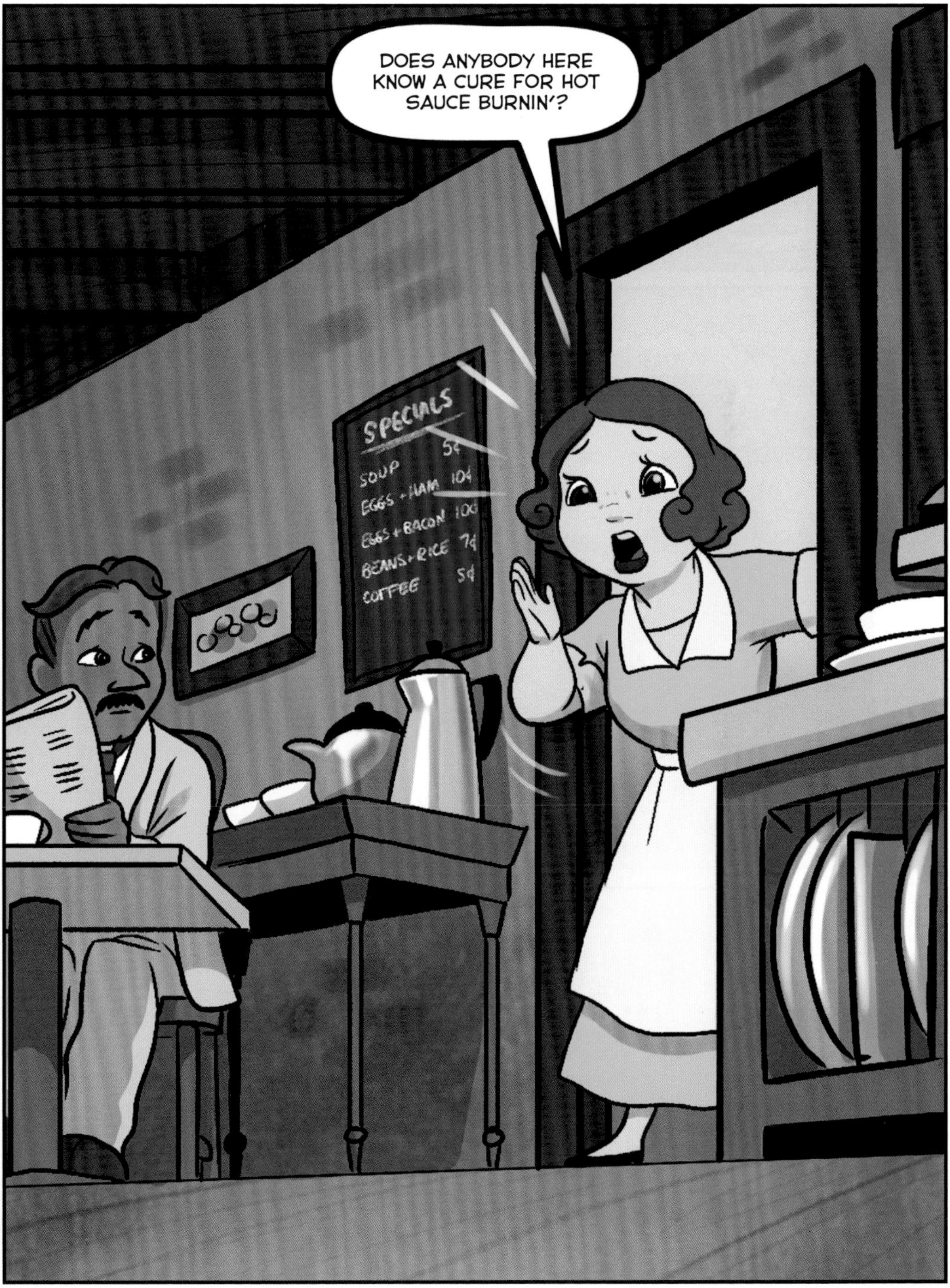
DOES ANYBODY HERE KNOW A CURE FOR HOT SAUCE BURNIN'?
SPECIALS
SOUP 5¢
EGGS + HAM 10¢
EGGS + BACON 10¢
BEANS + RICE 7¢
COFFEE 5¢

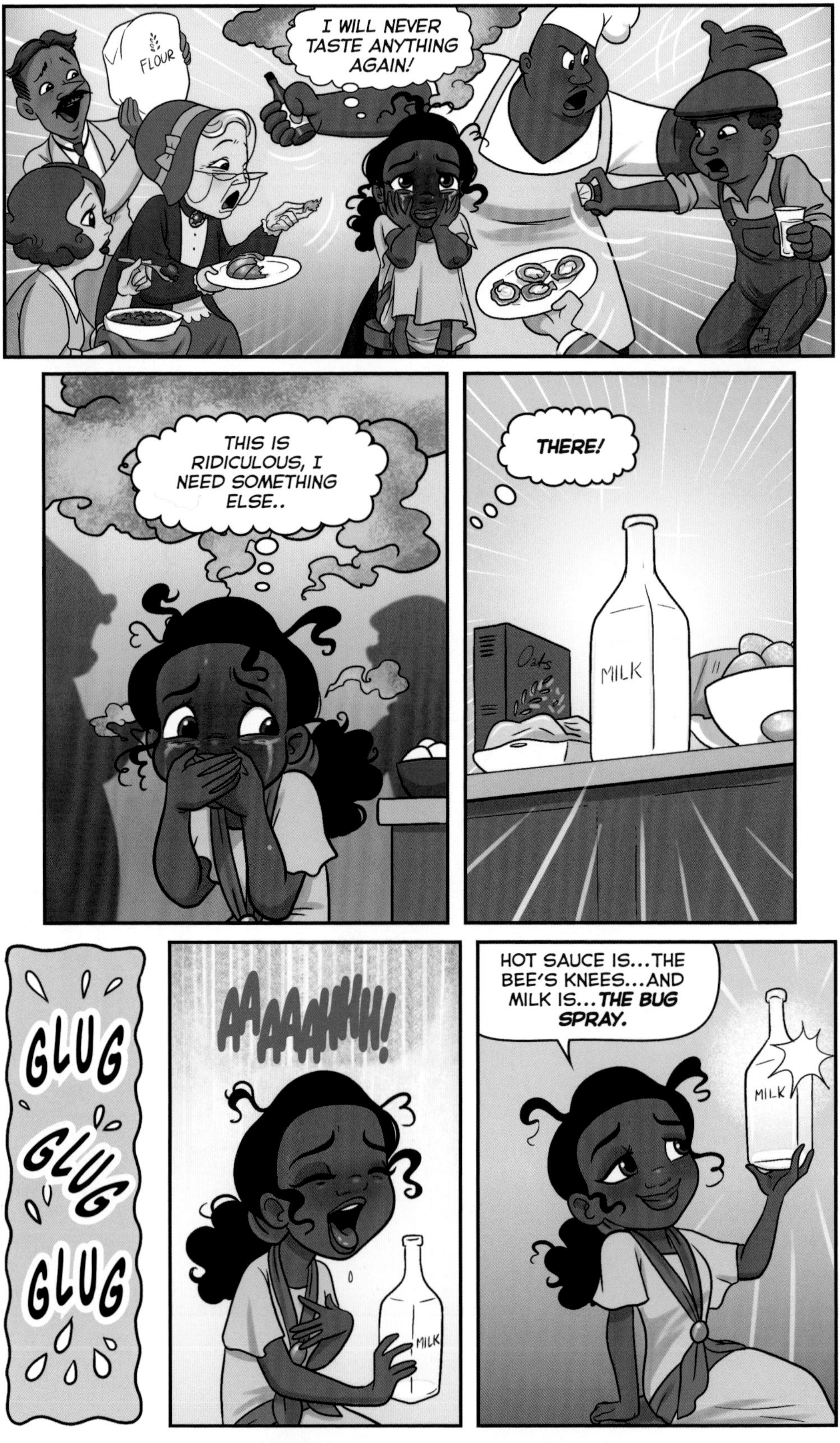
FLOUR
I WILL NEVER TASTE ANYTHING AGAIN!
THIS IS RIDICULOUS, I NEED SOMETHING ELSE..
THERE!
Oats
MILK
GLUG GLUG GLUG
AAAAAHHH!
MILK
HOT SAUCE IS...THE BEE'S KNEES...AND MILK IS...**THE BUG SPRAY.**
MILK

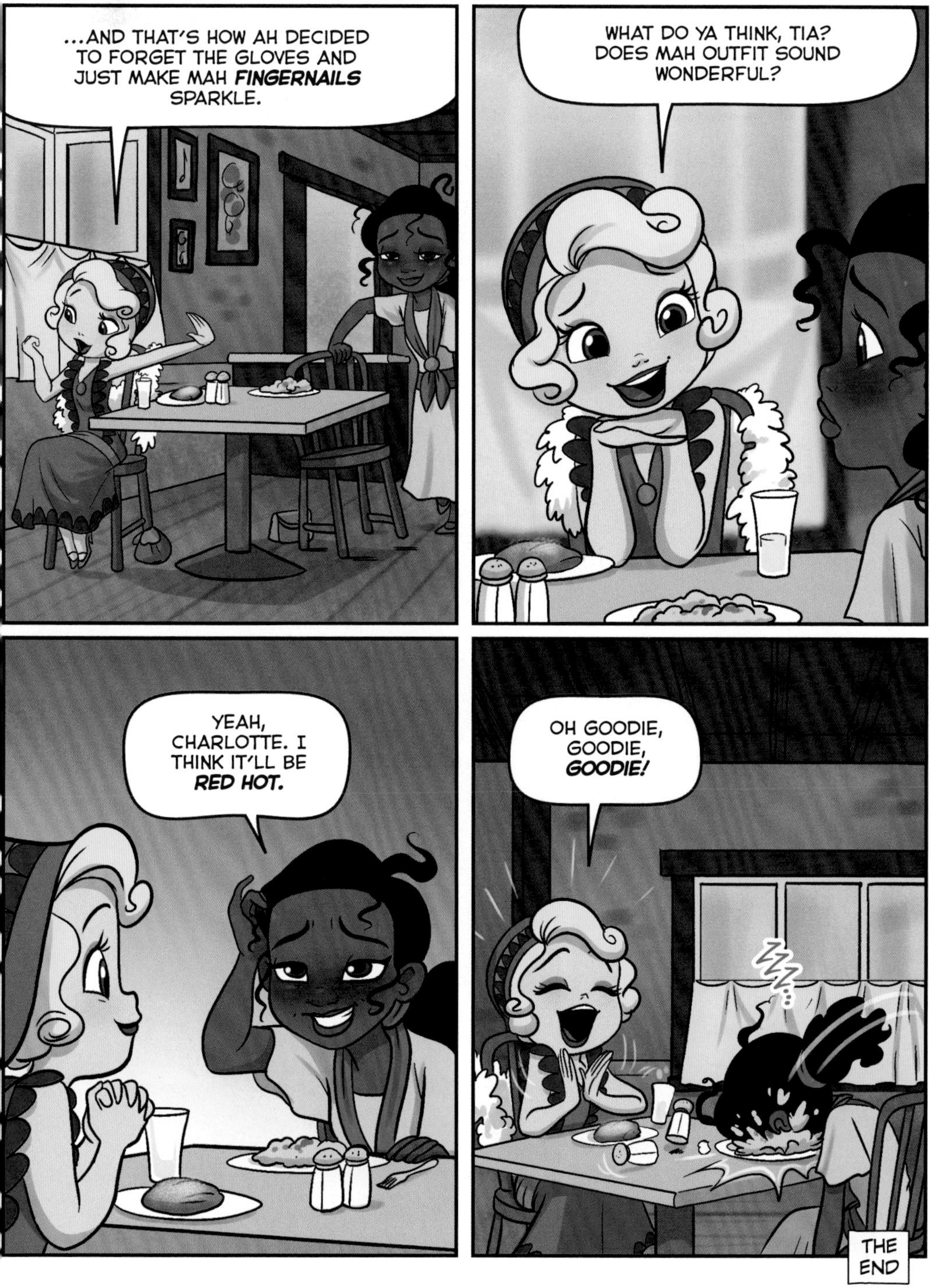
...AND THAT'S HOW AH DECIDED TO FORGET THE GLOVES AND JUST MAKE MAH FINGERNAILS SPARKLE.
WHAT DO YA THINK, TIA? DOES MAH OUTFIT SOUND WONDERFUL?
YEAH, CHARLOTTE. I THINK IT'LL BE RED HOT.
OH GOODIE, GOODIE, GOODIE!
ZZZ...
THE END

# "WORLD OF RAIN"

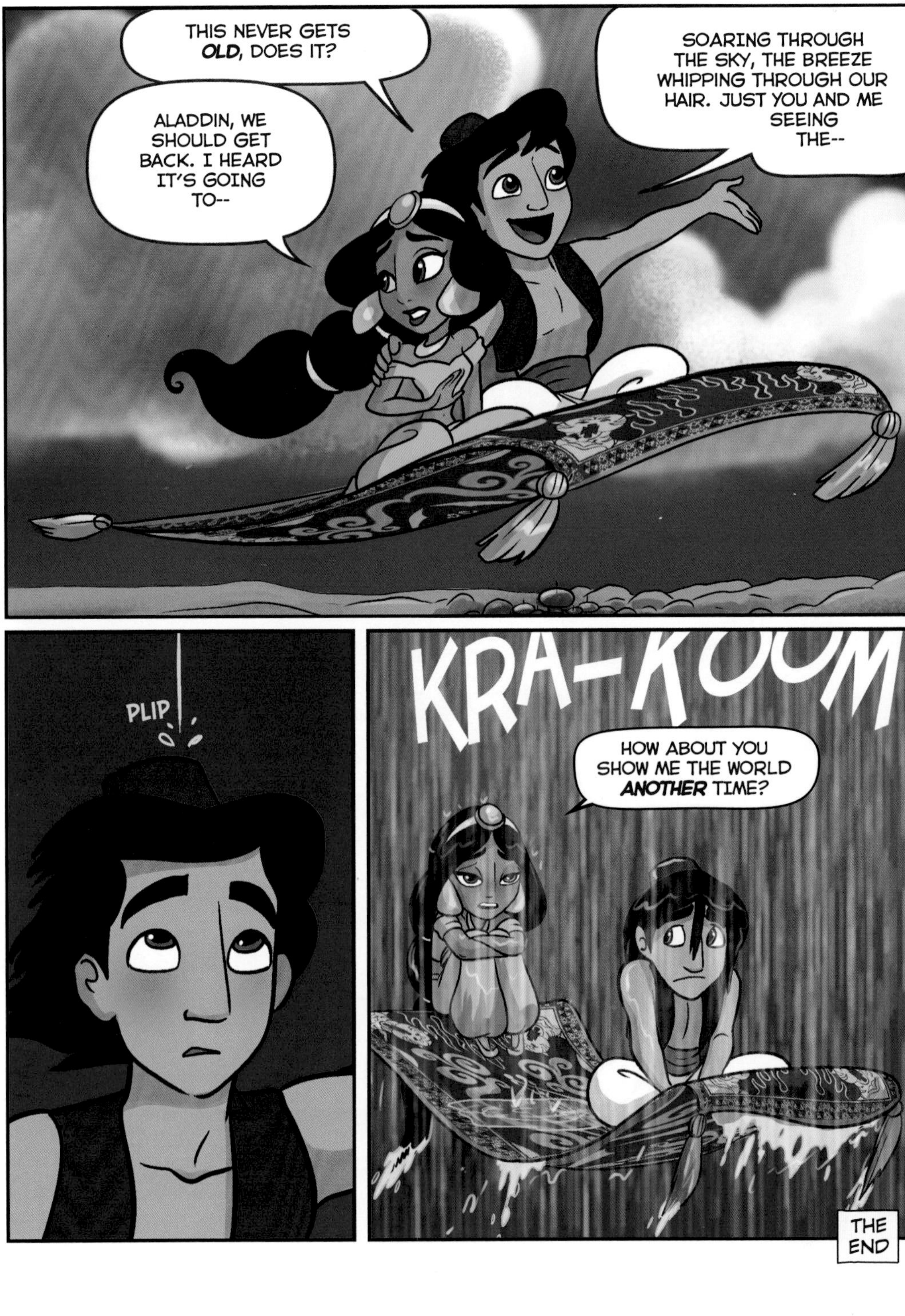

THIS NEVER GETS OLD, DOES IT?
SOARING THROUGH THE SKY, THE BREEZE WHIPPING THROUGH OUR HAIR. JUST YOU AND ME SEEING THE--
ALADDIN, WE SHOULD GET BACK. I HEARD IT'S GOING TO--
PLIP
KRA-KOOM
HOW ABOUT YOU SHOW ME THE WORLD ANOTHER TIME?
THE END

# "MY FAIR ROYAL HIGHNESS"

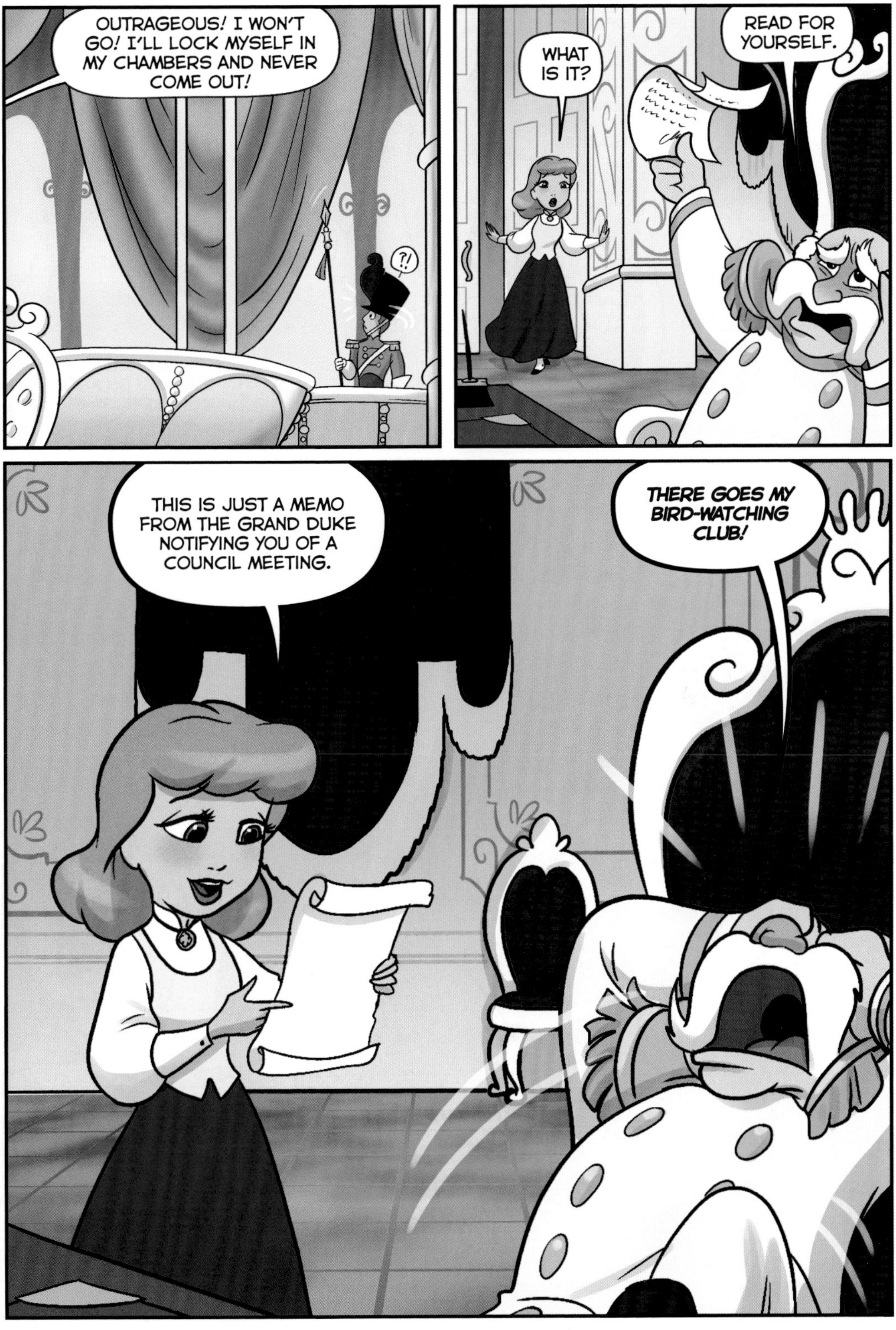
OUTRAGEOUS! I WON'T GO! I'LL LOCK MYSELF IN MY CHAMBERS AND NEVER COME OUT!
?!
WHAT IS IT?
READ FOR YOURSELF.
THIS IS JUST A MEMO FROM THE GRAND DUKE NOTIFYING YOU OF A COUNCIL MEETING.
THERE GOES MY BIRD-WATCHING CLUB!

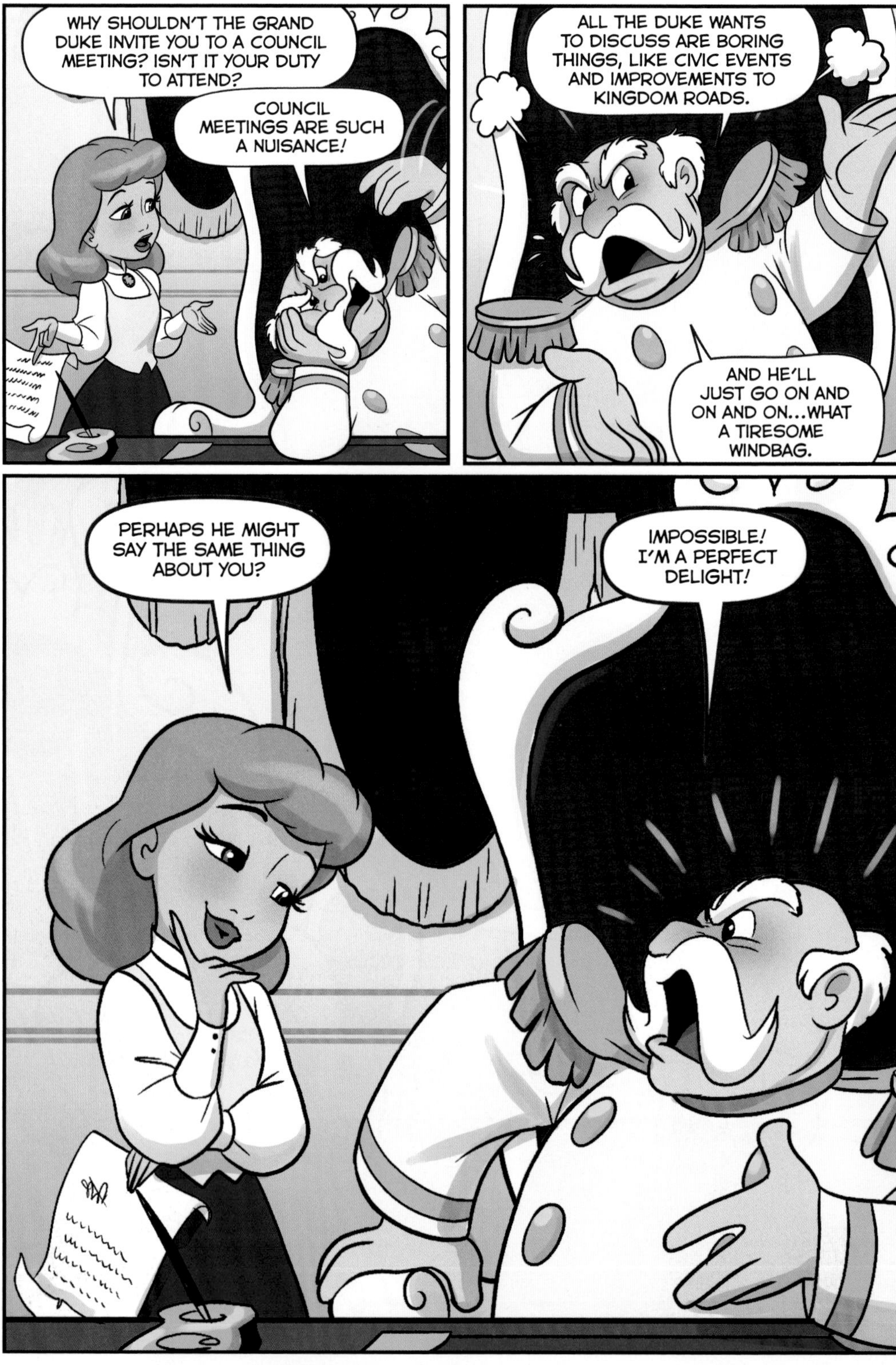
WHY SHOULDN'T THE GRAND DUKE INVITE YOU TO A COUNCIL MEETING? ISN'T IT YOUR DUTY TO ATTEND?
COUNCIL MEETINGS ARE SUCH A NUISANCE!
ALL THE DUKE WANTS TO DISCUSS ARE BORING THINGS, LIKE CIVIC EVENTS AND IMPROVEMENTS TO KINGDOM ROADS.
AND HE'LL JUST GO ON AND ON AND ON...WHAT A TIRESOME WINDBAG.
PERHAPS HE MIGHT SAY THE SAME THING ABOUT YOU?
IMPOSSIBLE! I'M A PERFECT DELIGHT!

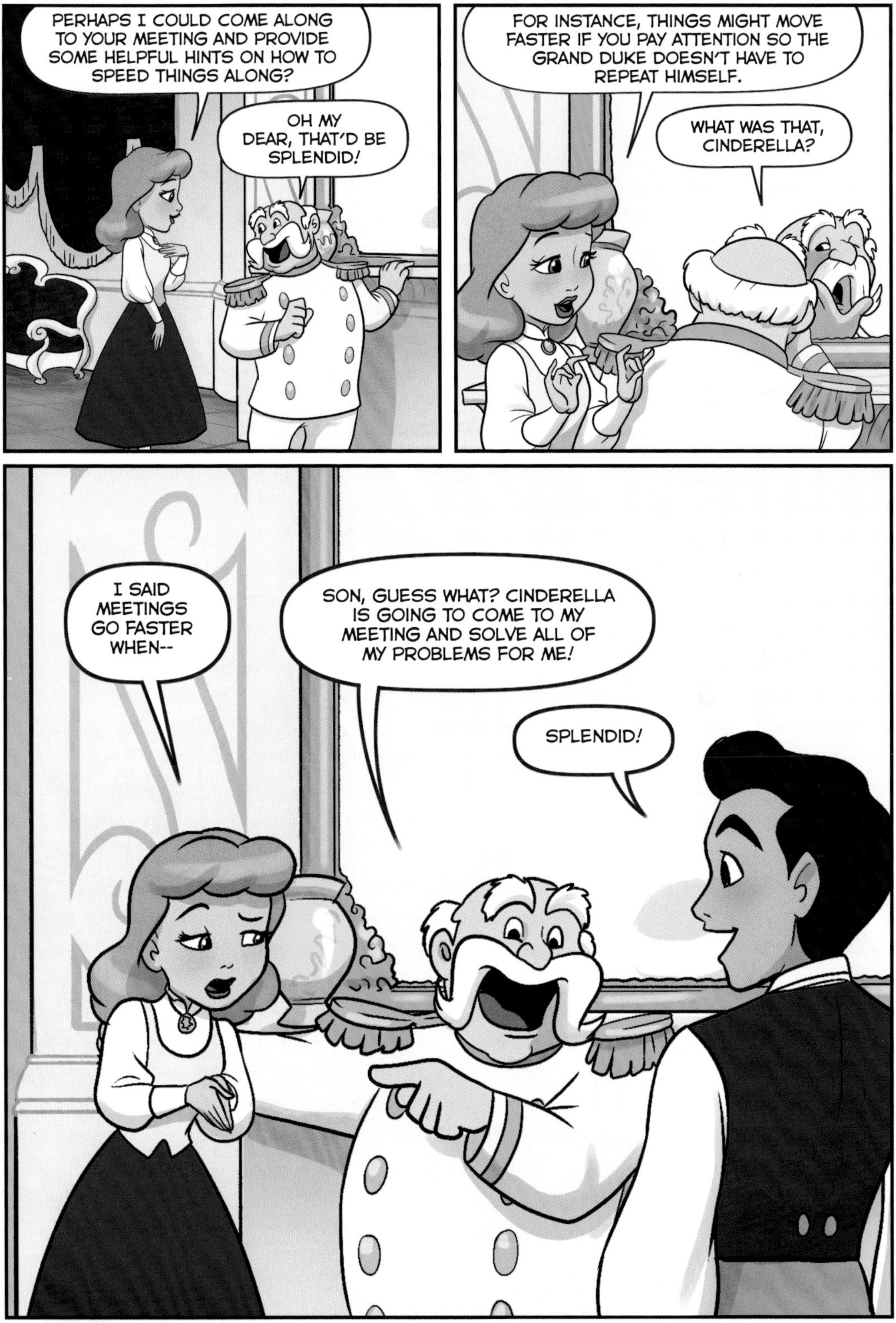
PERHAPS I COULD COME ALONG TO YOUR MEETING AND PROVIDE SOME HELPFUL HINTS ON HOW TO SPEED THINGS ALONG?
OH MY DEAR, THAT'D BE SPLENDID!
FOR INSTANCE, THINGS MIGHT MOVE FASTER IF YOU PAY ATTENTION SO THE GRAND DUKE DOESN'T HAVE TO REPEAT HIMSELF.
WHAT WAS THAT, CINDERELLA?
I SAID MEETINGS GO FASTER WHEN--
SON, GUESS WHAT? CINDERELLA IS GOING TO COME TO MY MEETING AND SOLVE ALL OF MY PROBLEMS FOR ME!
SPLENDID!

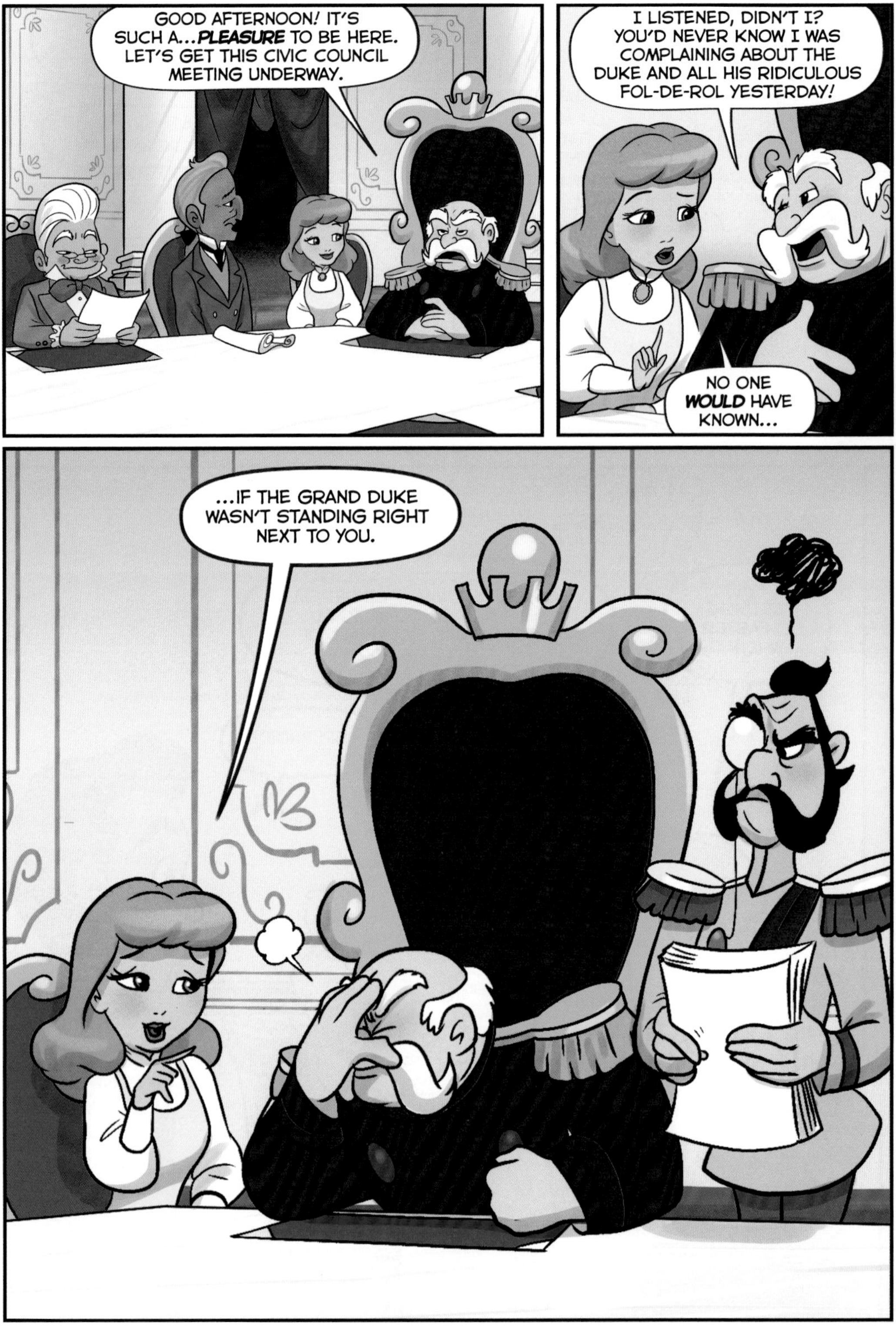
GOOD AFTERNOON! IT'S SUCH A...PLEASURE TO BE HERE. LET'S GET THIS CIVIC COUNCIL MEETING UNDERWAY.
I LISTENED, DIDN'T I? YOU'D NEVER KNOW I WAS COMPLAINING ABOUT THE DUKE AND ALL HIS RIDICULOUS FOL-DE-ROL YESTERDAY!
NO ONE WOULD HAVE KNOWN...
...IF THE GRAND DUKE WASN'T STANDING RIGHT NEXT TO YOU.

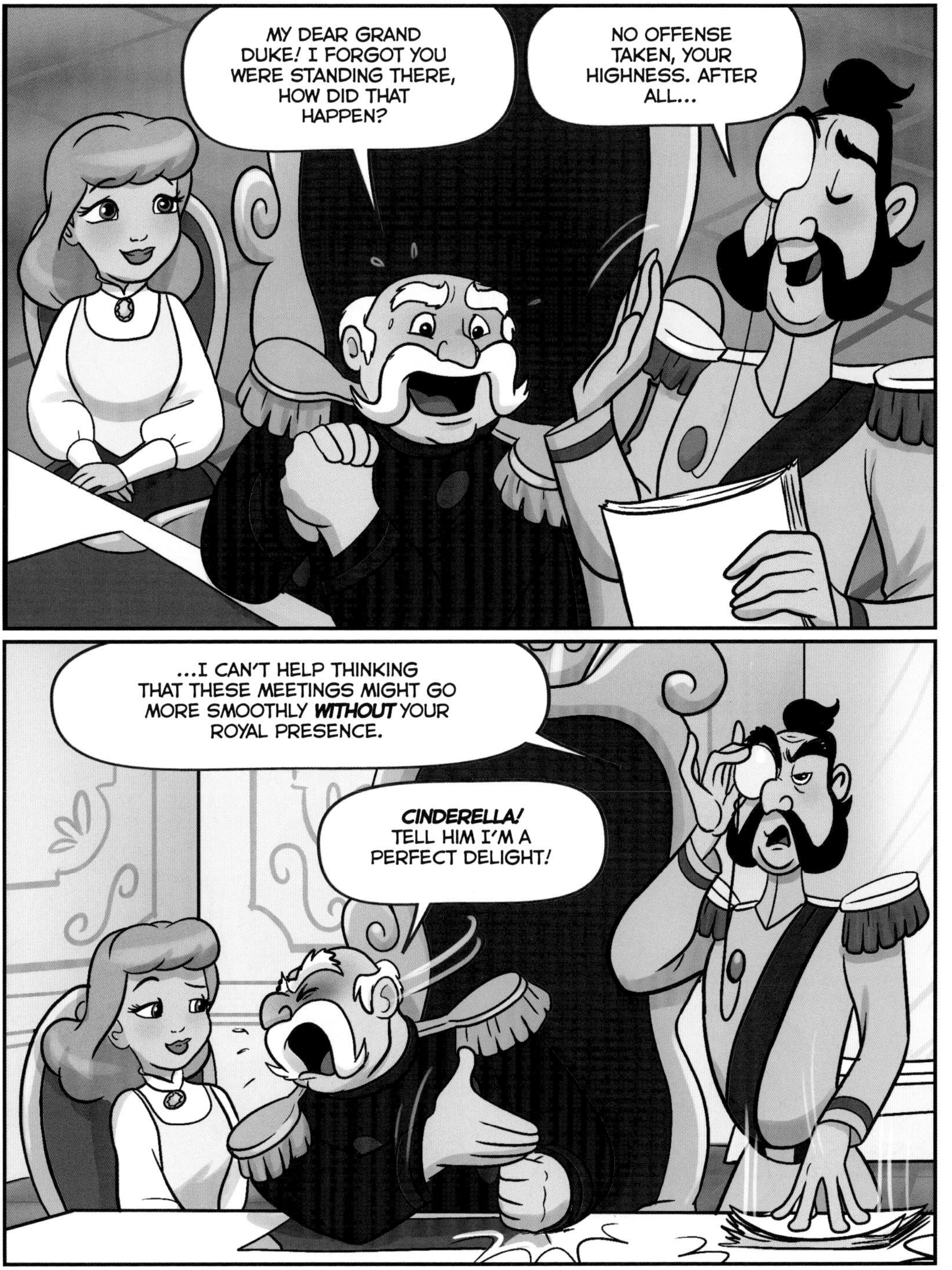
MY DEAR GRAND DUKE! I FORGOT YOU WERE STANDING THERE, HOW DID THAT HAPPEN?
NO OFFENSE TAKEN, YOUR HIGHNESS. AFTER ALL...
...I CAN'T HELP THINKING THAT THESE MEETINGS MIGHT GO MORE SMOOTHLY WITHOUT YOUR ROYAL PRESENCE.
CINDERELLA! TELL HIM I'M A PERFECT DELIGHT!

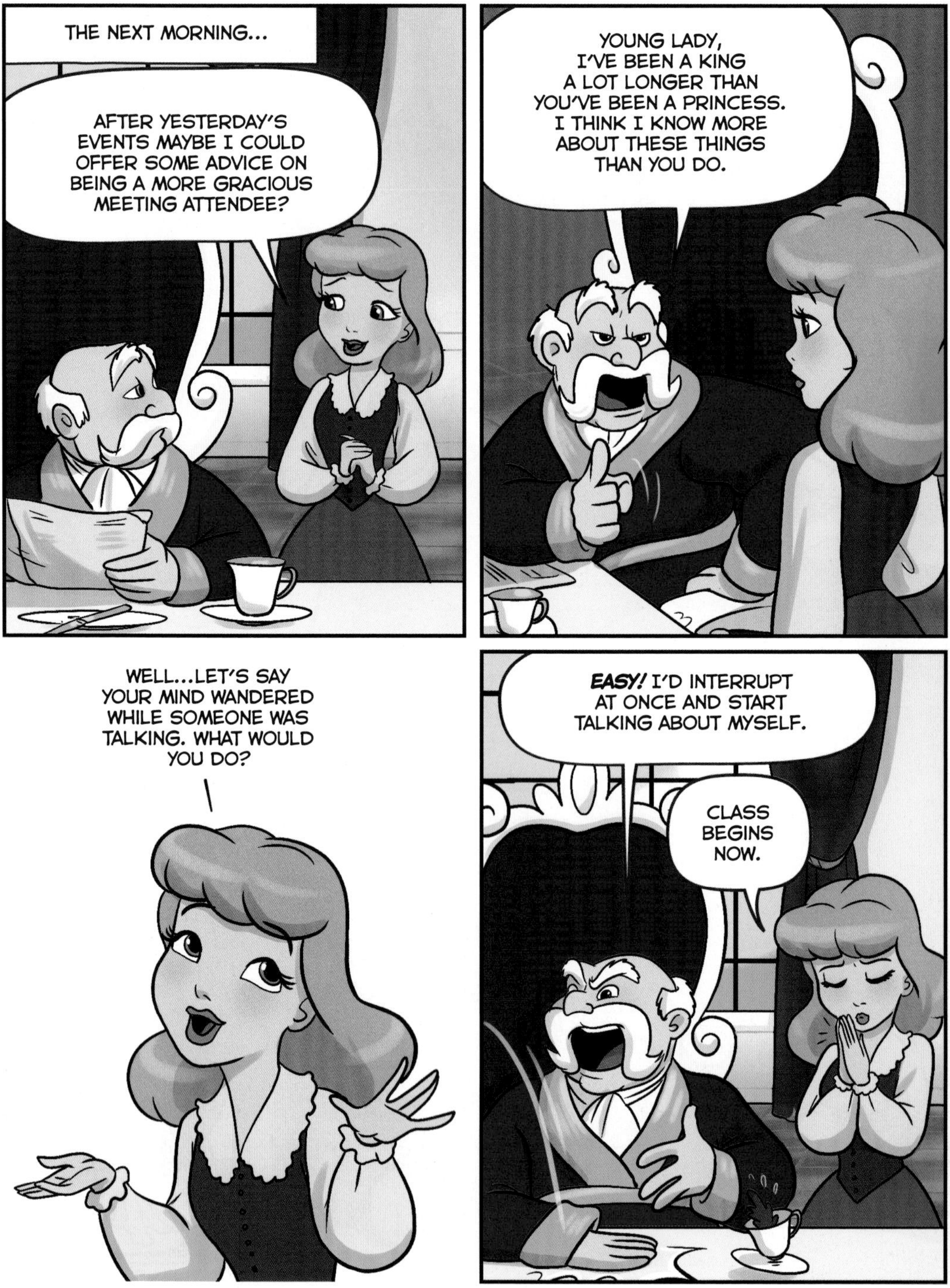
THE NEXT MORNING...
AFTER YESTERDAY'S EVENTS MAYBE I COULD OFFER SOME ADVICE ON BEING A MORE GRACIOUS MEETING ATTENDEE?
YOUNG LADY, I'VE BEEN A KING A LOT LONGER THAN YOU'VE BEEN A PRINCESS. I THINK I KNOW MORE ABOUT THESE THINGS THAN YOU DO.
WELL...LET'S SAY YOUR MIND WANDERED WHILE SOMEONE WAS TALKING. WHAT WOULD YOU DO?
*EASY!* I'D INTERRUPT AT ONCE AND START TALKING ABOUT MYSELF.
CLASS BEGINS NOW.

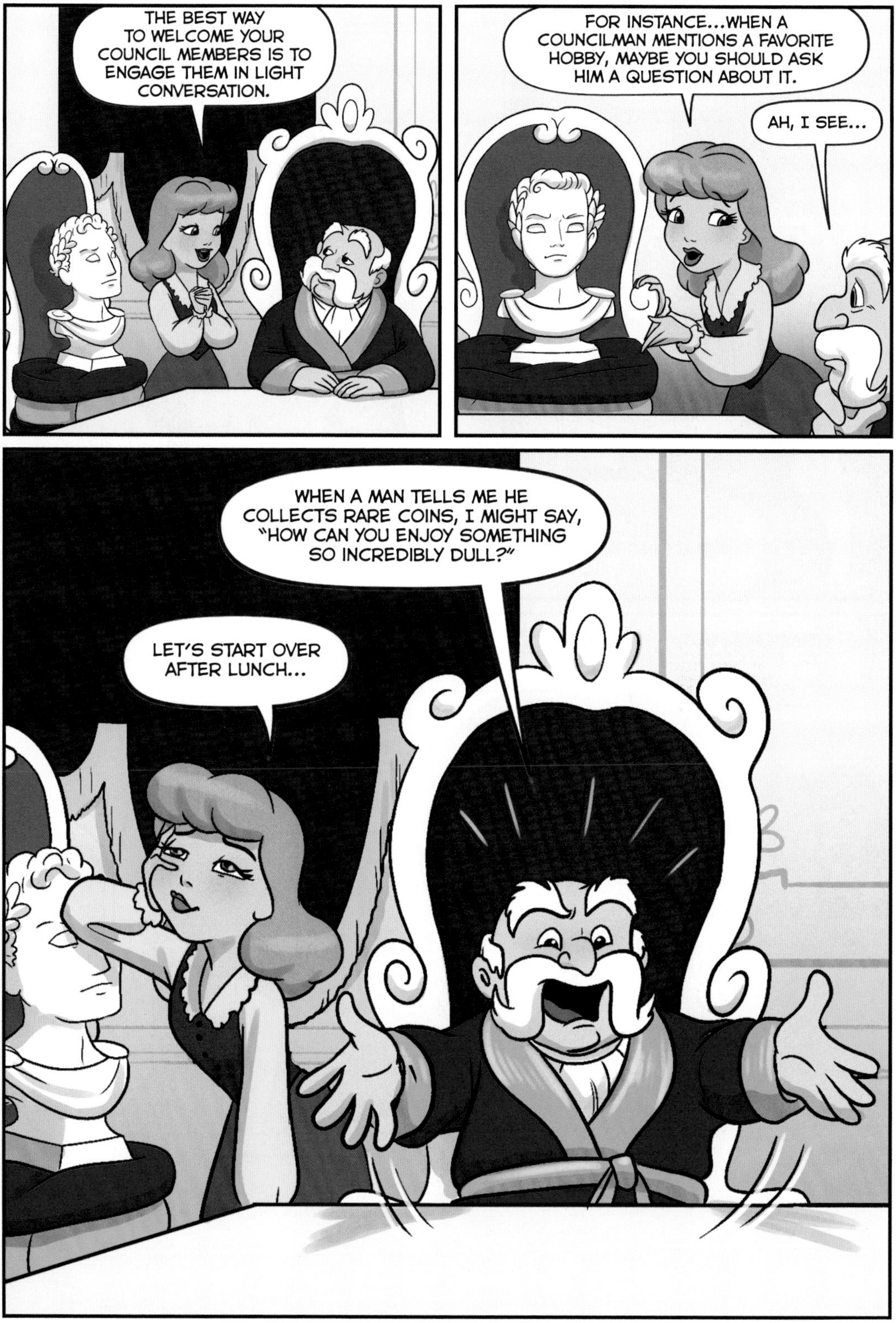
THE BEST WAY TO WELCOME YOUR COUNCIL MEMBERS IS TO ENGAGE THEM IN LIGHT CONVERSATION.
FOR INSTANCE...WHEN A COUNCILMAN MENTIONS A FAVORITE HOBBY, MAYBE YOU SHOULD ASK HIM A QUESTION ABOUT IT.
AH, I SEE...
WHEN A MAN TELLS ME HE COLLECTS RARE COINS, I MIGHT SAY, "HOW CAN YOU ENJOY SOMETHING SO INCREDIBLY DULL?"
LET'S START OVER AFTER LUNCH...

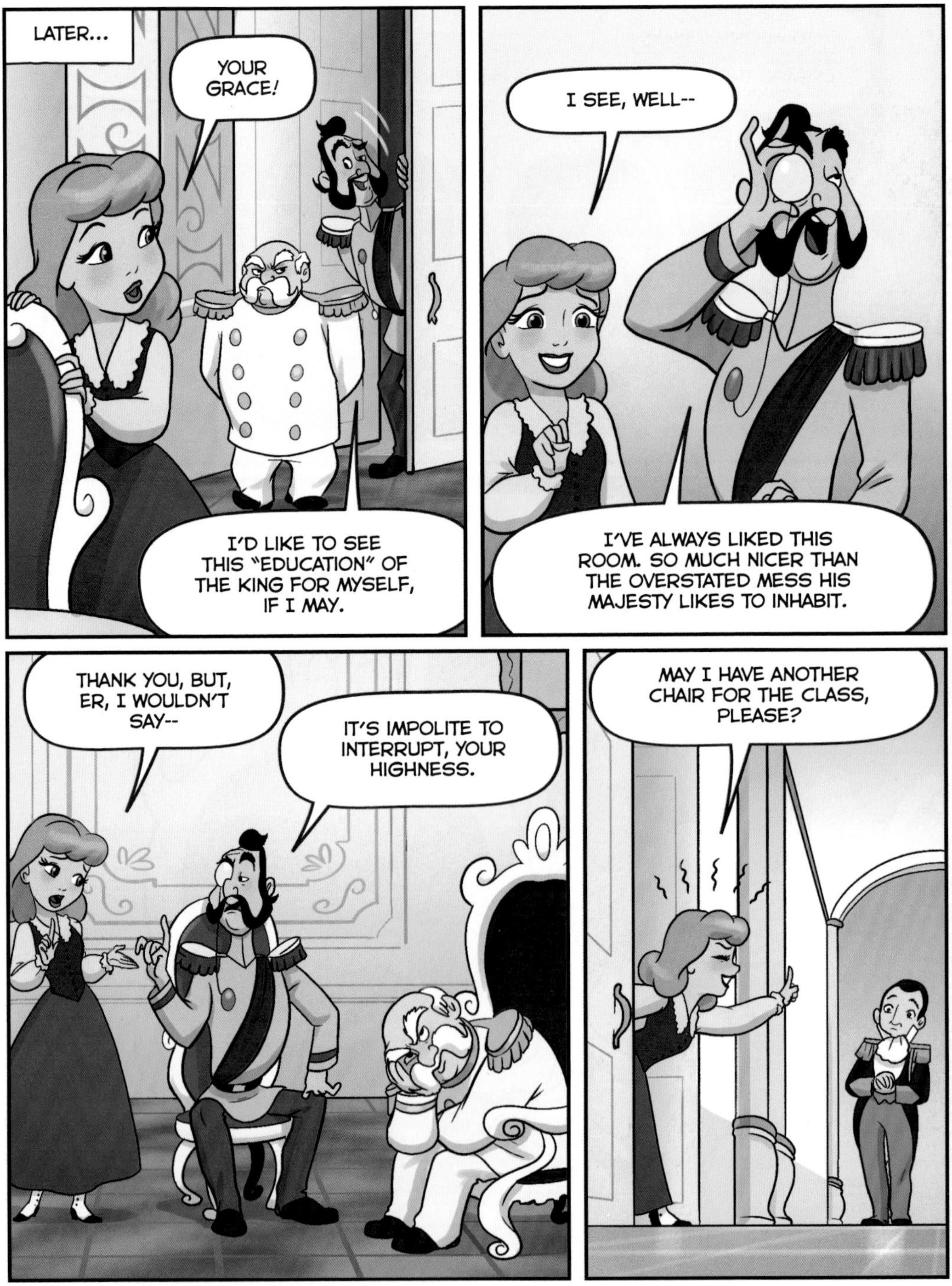
LATER...
YOUR GRACE!
I'D LIKE TO SEE THIS "EDUCATION" OF THE KING FOR MYSELF, IF I MAY.
I SEE, WELL--
I'VE ALWAYS LIKED THIS ROOM. SO MUCH NICER THAN THE OVERSTATED MESS HIS MAJESTY LIKES TO INHABIT.
THANK YOU, BUT, ER, I WOULDN'T SAY--
IT'S IMPOLITE TO INTERRUPT, YOUR HIGHNESS.
MAY I HAVE ANOTHER CHAIR FOR THE CLASS, PLEASE?

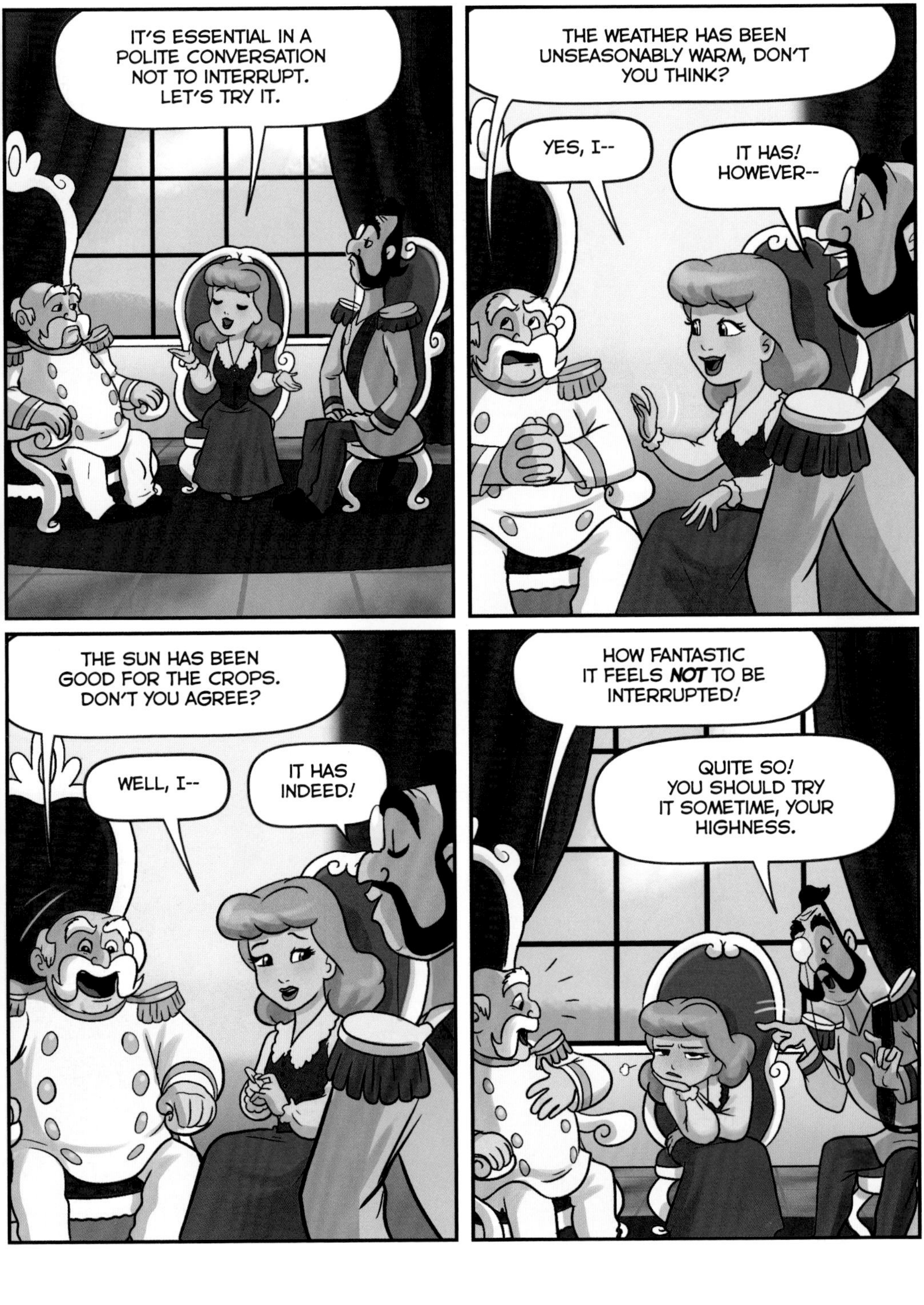
IT'S ESSENTIAL IN A POLITE CONVERSATION NOT TO INTERRUPT. LET'S TRY IT.
THE WEATHER HAS BEEN UNSEASONABLY WARM, DON'T YOU THINK?
YES, I--
IT HAS! HOWEVER--
THE SUN HAS BEEN GOOD FOR THE CROPS. DON'T YOU AGREE?
WELL, I--
IT HAS INDEED!
HOW FANTASTIC IT FEELS *NOT* TO BE INTERRUPTED!
QUITE SO! YOU SHOULD TRY IT SOMETIME, YOUR HIGHNESS.

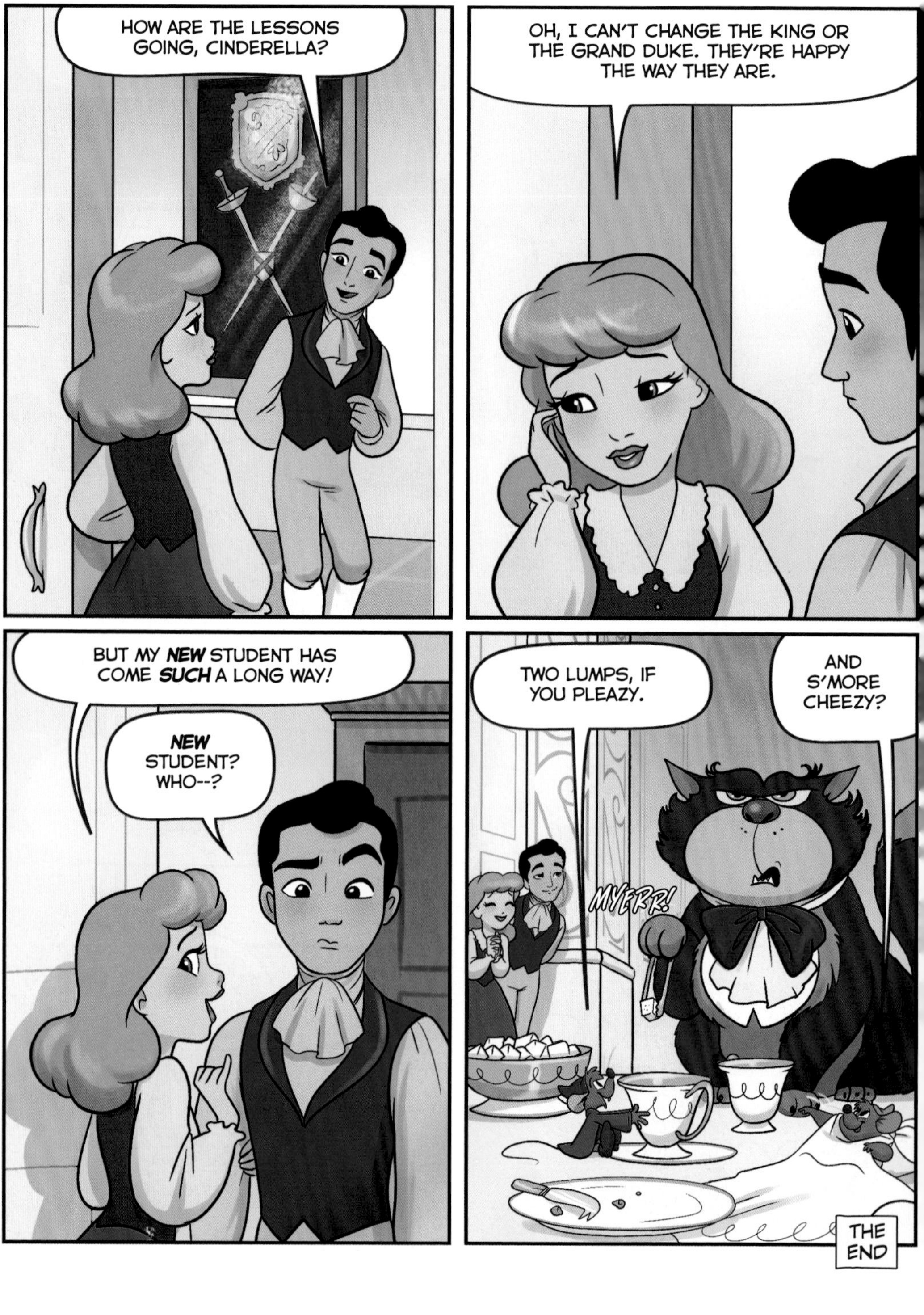
HOW ARE THE LESSONS GOING, CINDERELLA?
OH, I CAN'T CHANGE THE KING OR THE GRAND DUKE. THEY'RE HAPPY THE WAY THEY ARE.
BUT MY **NEW** STUDENT HAS COME **SUCH** A LONG WAY!
**NEW** STUDENT? WHO--?
TWO LUMPS, IF YOU PLEAZY.
AND S'MORE CHEEZY?
MYERR!
THE END

# "DEFENSIVE TRAINING"

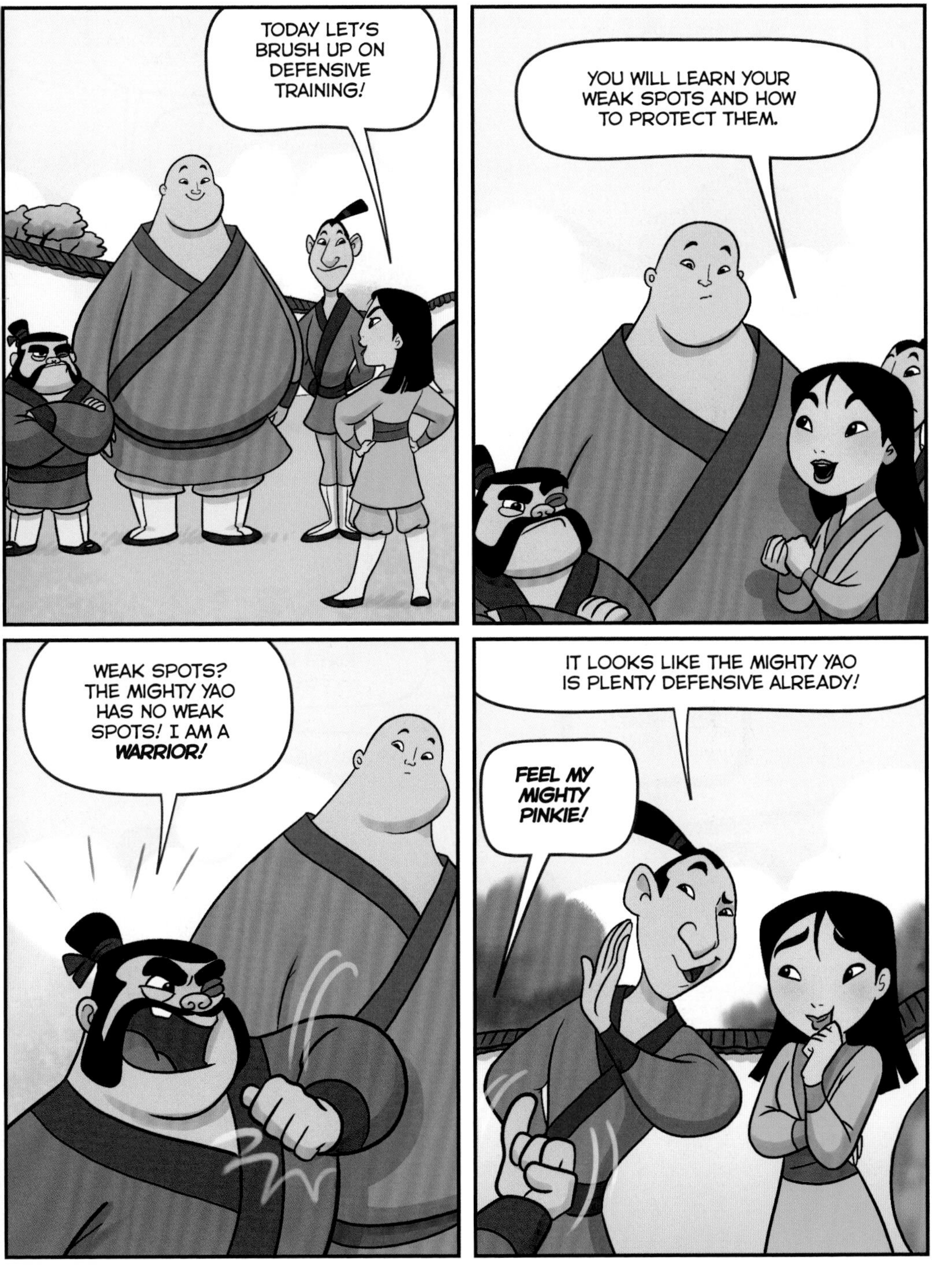
TODAY LET'S BRUSH UP ON DEFENSIVE TRAINING!
YOU WILL LEARN YOUR WEAK SPOTS AND HOW TO PROTECT THEM.
WEAK SPOTS? THE MIGHTY YAO HAS NO WEAK SPOTS! I AM A *WARRIOR!*
IT LOOKS LIKE THE MIGHTY YAO IS PLENTY DEFENSIVE ALREADY!
*FEEL MY MIGHTY PINKIE!*

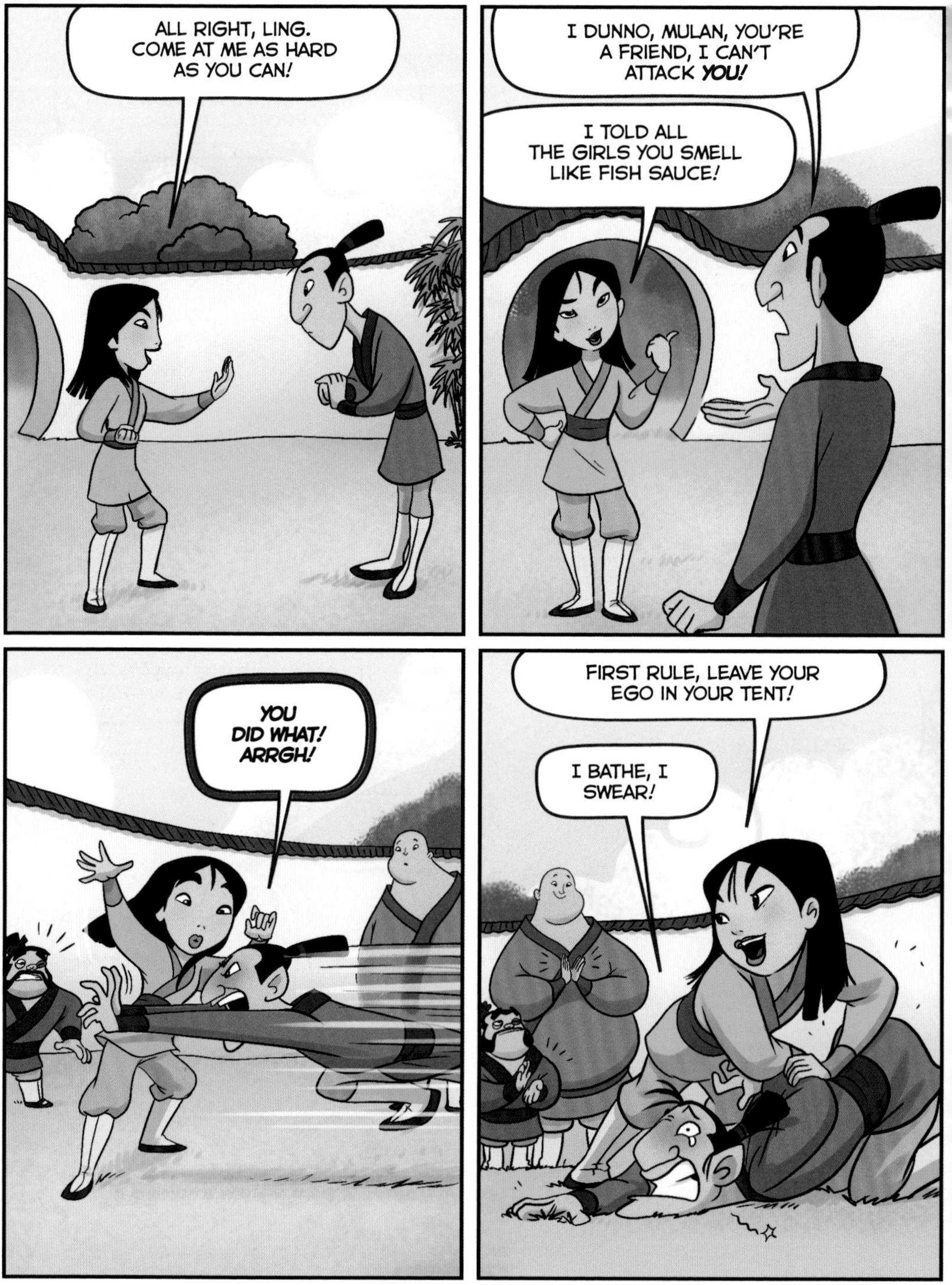
ALL RIGHT, LING. COME AT ME AS HARD AS YOU CAN!
I DUNNO, MULAN, YOU'RE A FRIEND, I CAN'T ATTACK YOU!
I TOLD ALL THE GIRLS YOU SMELL LIKE FISH SAUCE!
YOU DID WHAT! ARRGH!
FIRST RULE, LEAVE YOUR EGO IN YOUR TENT!
I BATHE, I SWEAR!

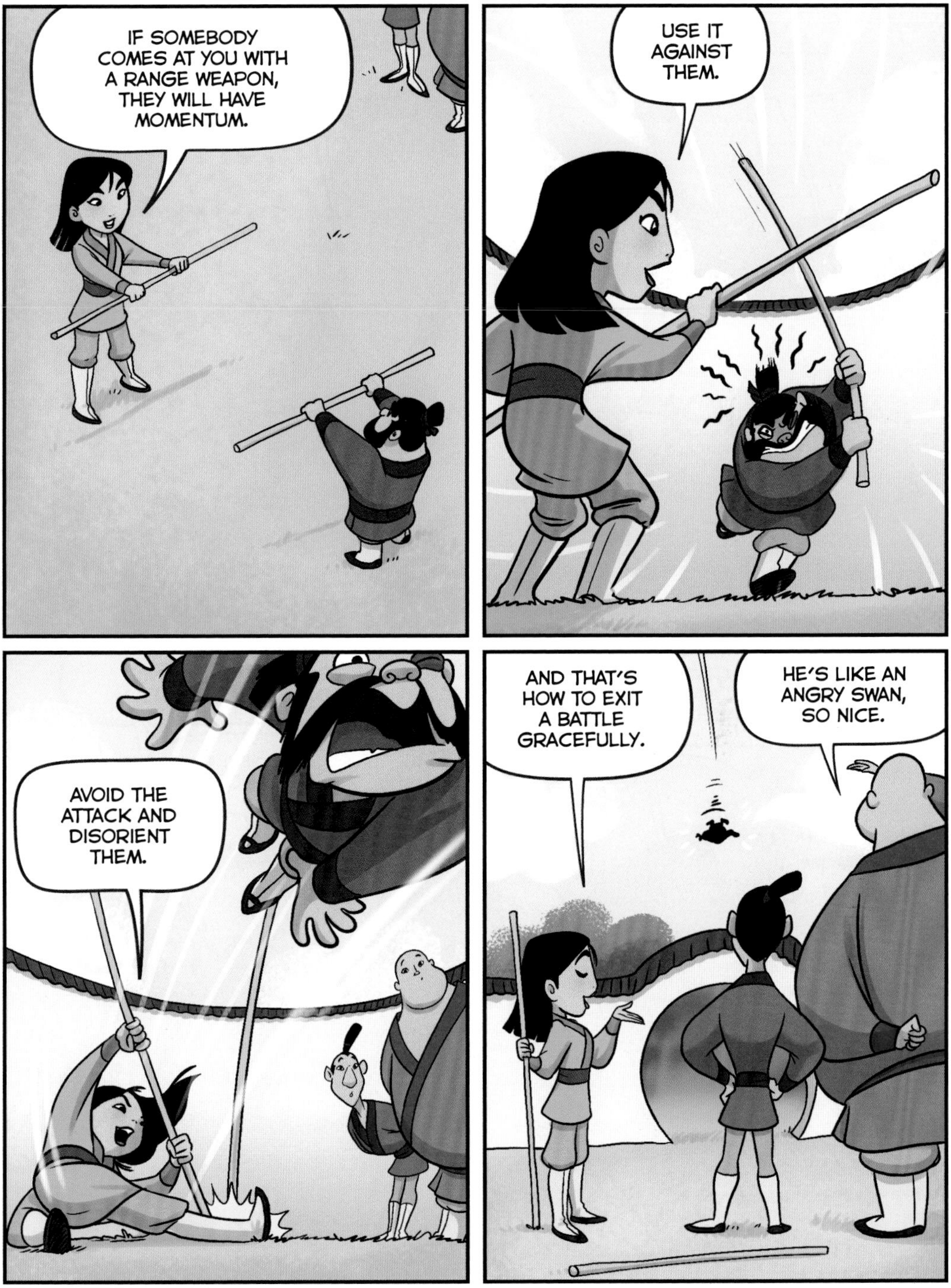
IF SOMEBODY COMES AT YOU WITH A RANGE WEAPON, THEY WILL HAVE MOMENTUM.
USE IT AGAINST THEM.
AVOID THE ATTACK AND DISORIENT THEM.
AND THAT'S HOW TO EXIT A BATTLE GRACEFULLY.
HE'S LIKE AN ANGRY SWAN, SO NICE.

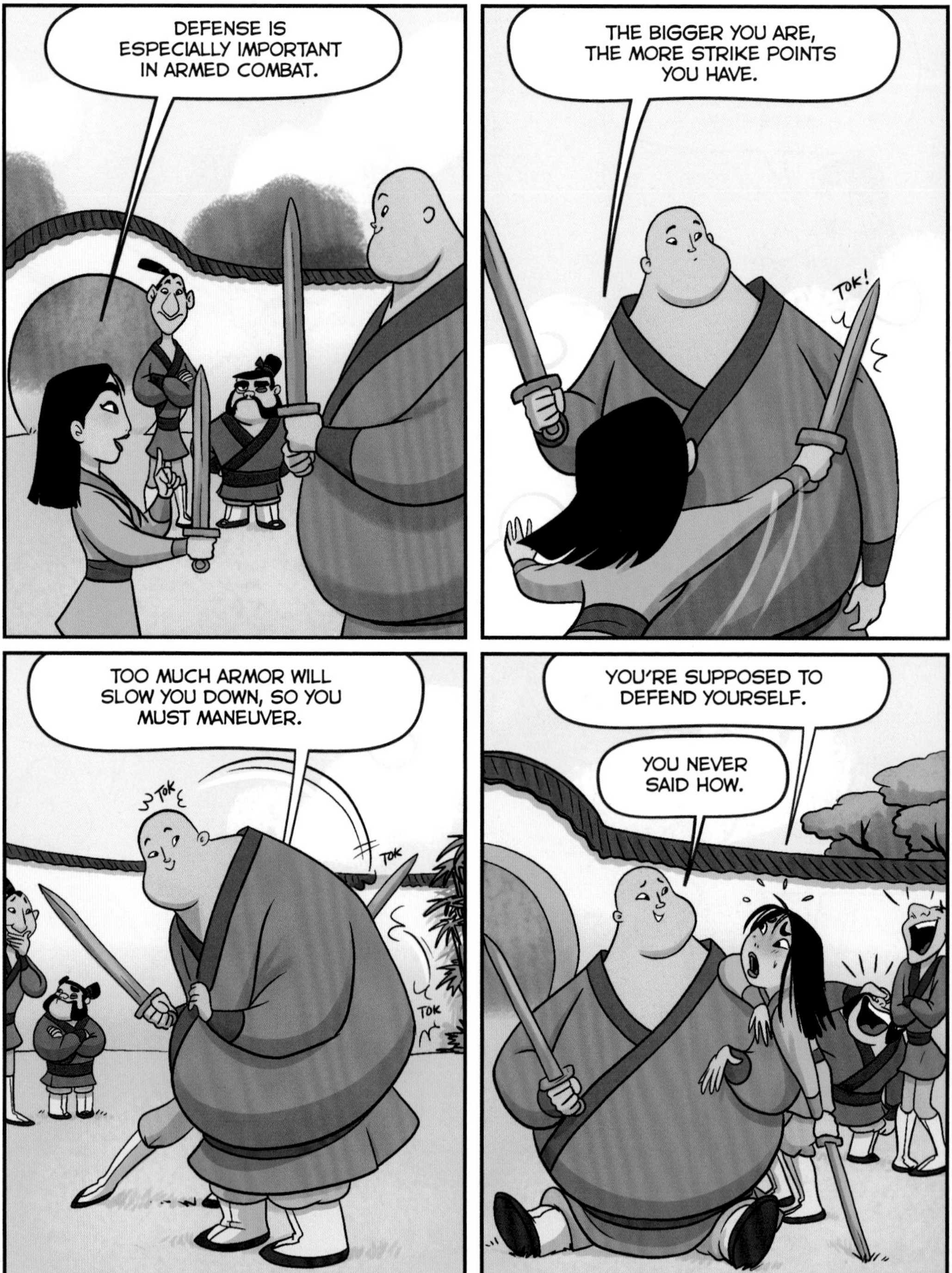
DEFENSE IS ESPECIALLY IMPORTANT IN ARMED COMBAT.
THE BIGGER YOU ARE, THE MORE STRIKE POINTS YOU HAVE.
TOK!
TOO MUCH ARMOR WILL SLOW YOU DOWN, SO YOU MUST MANEUVER.
TOK
TOK
TOK
YOU'RE SUPPOSED TO DEFEND YOURSELF.
YOU NEVER SAID HOW.

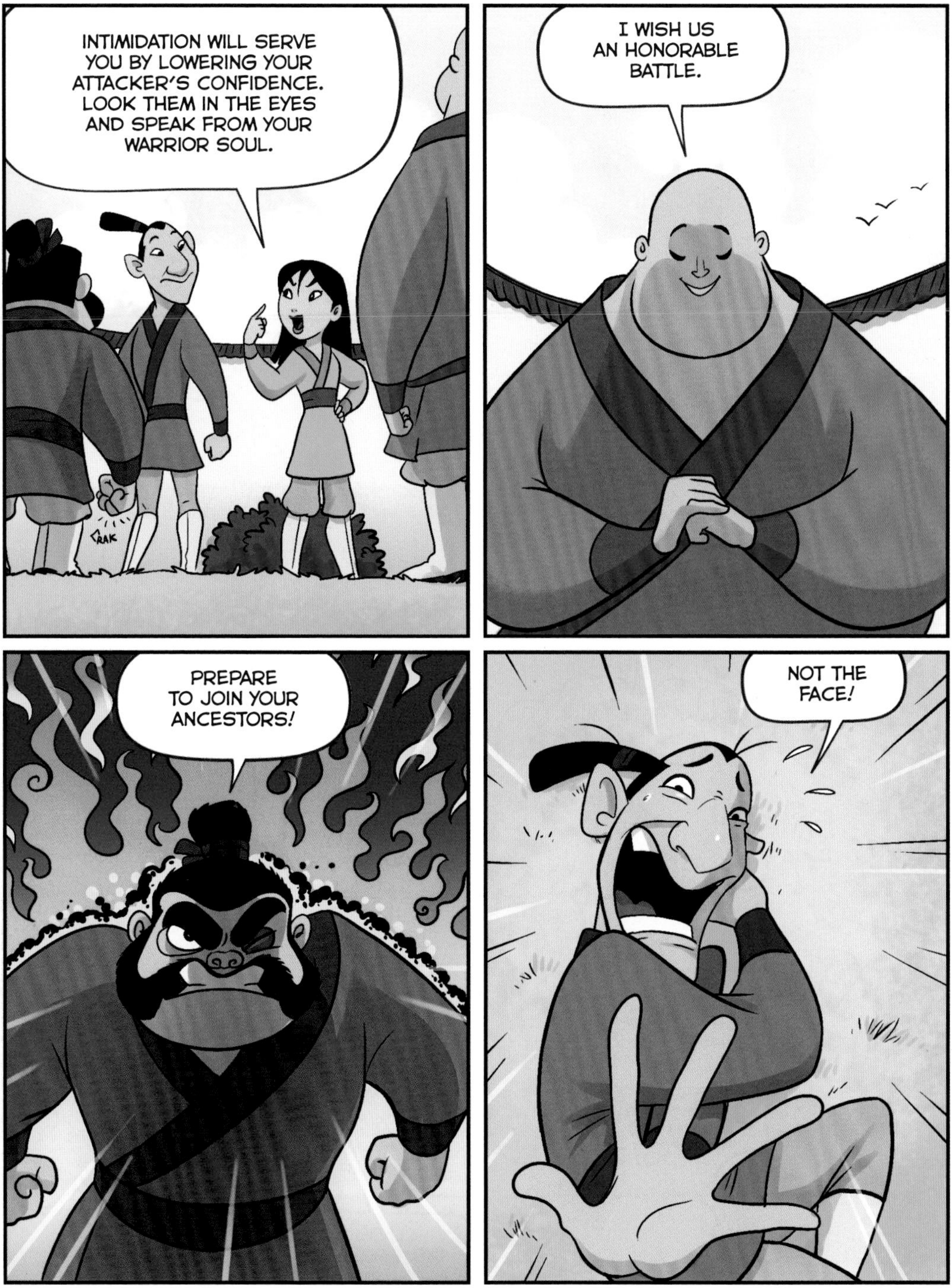
INTIMIDATION WILL SERVE YOU BY LOWERING YOUR ATTACKER'S CONFIDENCE. LOOK THEM IN THE EYES AND SPEAK FROM YOUR WARRIOR SOUL.
CRAK
I WISH US AN HONORABLE BATTLE.
PREPARE TO JOIN YOUR ANCESTORS!
NOT THE FACE!

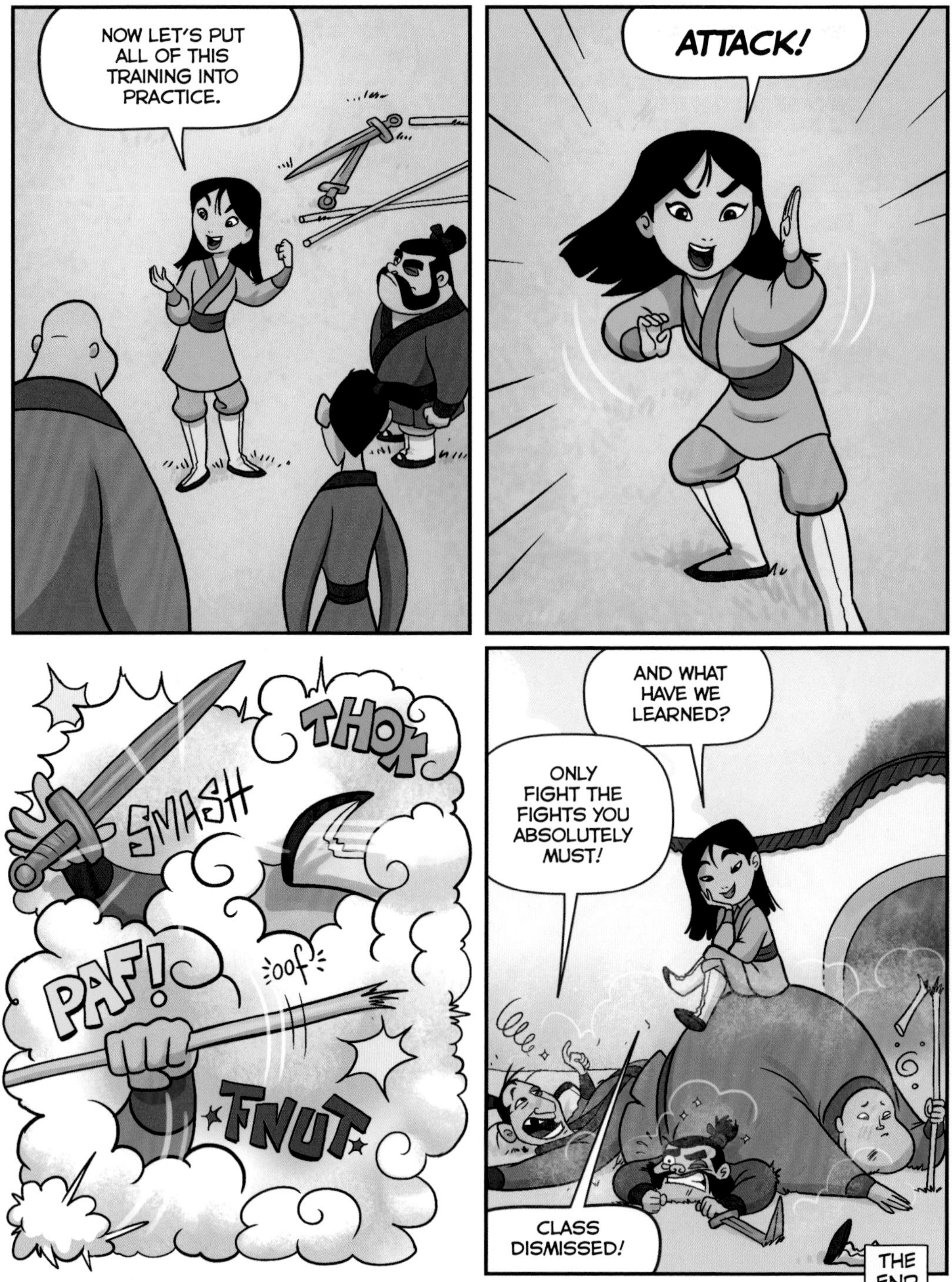
NOW LET'S PUT ALL OF THIS TRAINING INTO PRACTICE.
ATTACK!
THOK
SMASH
PAF!
oof
FNUT
AND WHAT HAVE WE LEARNED?
ONLY FIGHT THE FIGHTS YOU ABSOLUTELY MUST!
CLASS DISMISSED!
THE END

# "MUSIC CLASS"

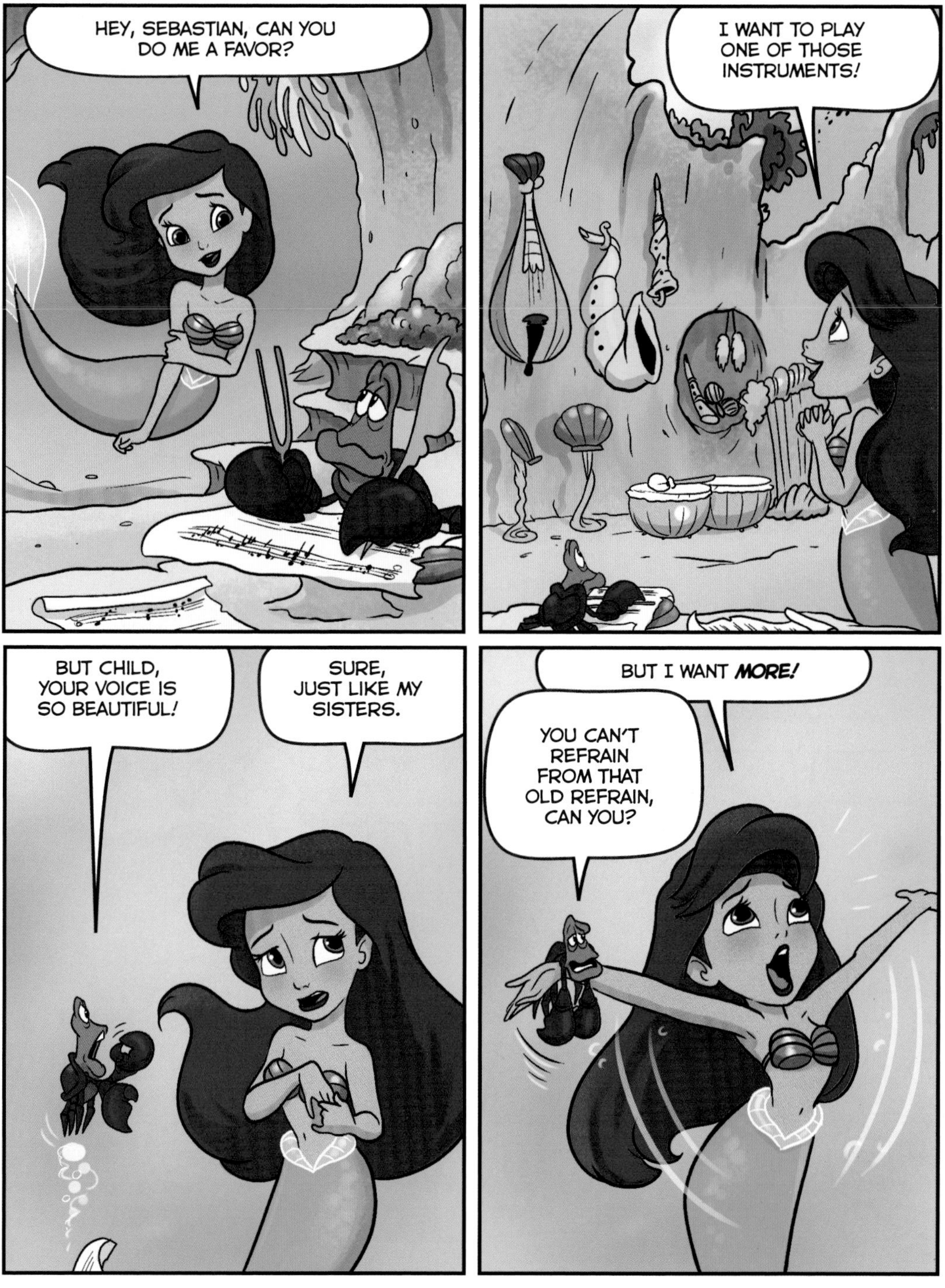
HEY, SEBASTIAN, CAN YOU DO ME A FAVOR?
I WANT TO PLAY ONE OF THOSE INSTRUMENTS!
SURE, JUST LIKE MY SISTERS.
BUT CHILD, YOUR VOICE IS SO BEAUTIFUL!
BUT I WANT MORE!
YOU CAN'T REFRAIN FROM THAT OLD REFRAIN, CAN YOU?

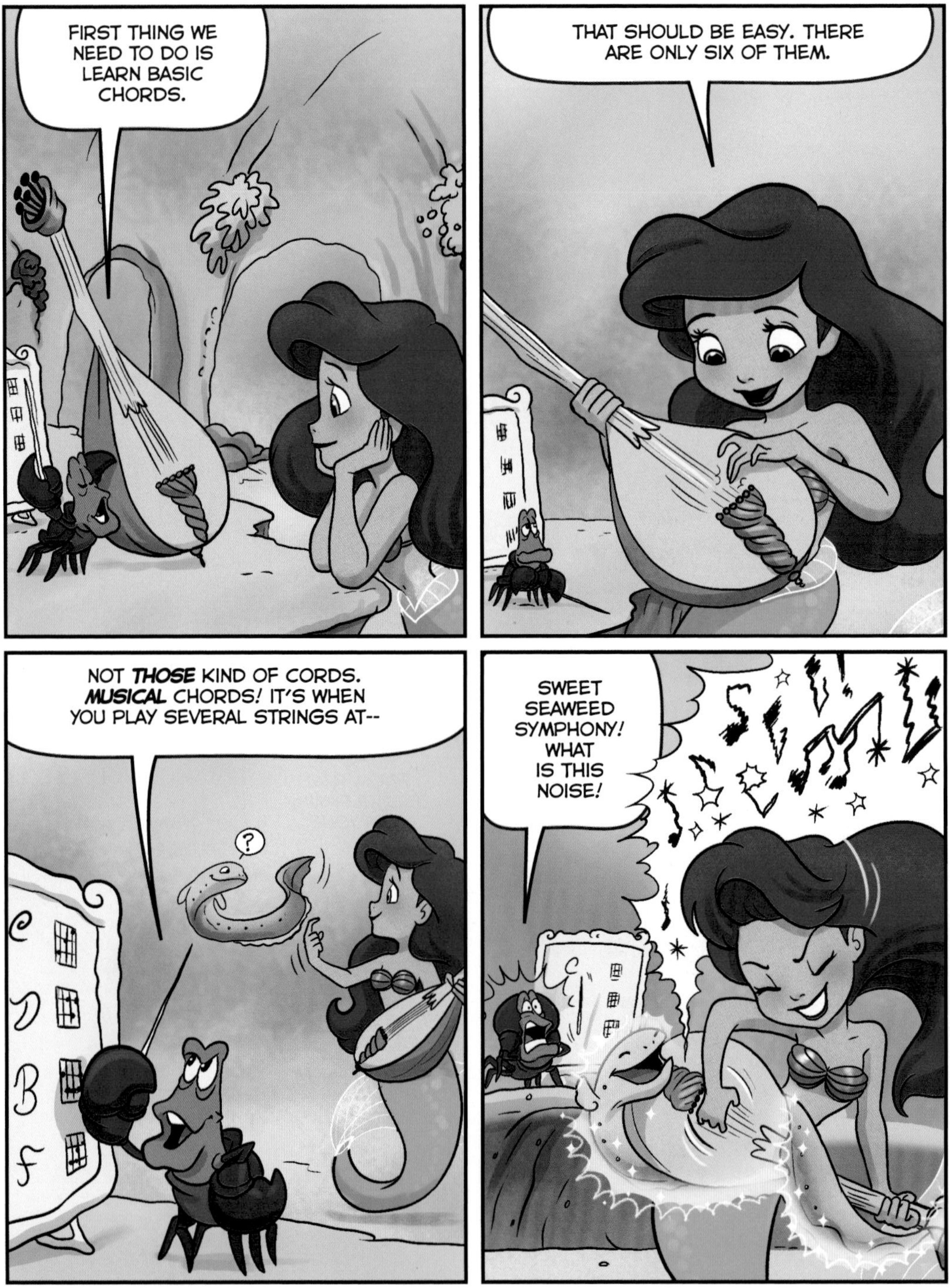
FIRST THING WE NEED TO DO IS LEARN BASIC CHORDS.
THAT SHOULD BE EASY. THERE ARE ONLY SIX OF THEM.
NOT THOSE KIND OF CORDS. MUSICAL CHORDS! IT'S WHEN YOU PLAY SEVERAL STRINGS AT--
?
SWEET SEAWEED SYMPHONY! WHAT IS THIS NOISE!

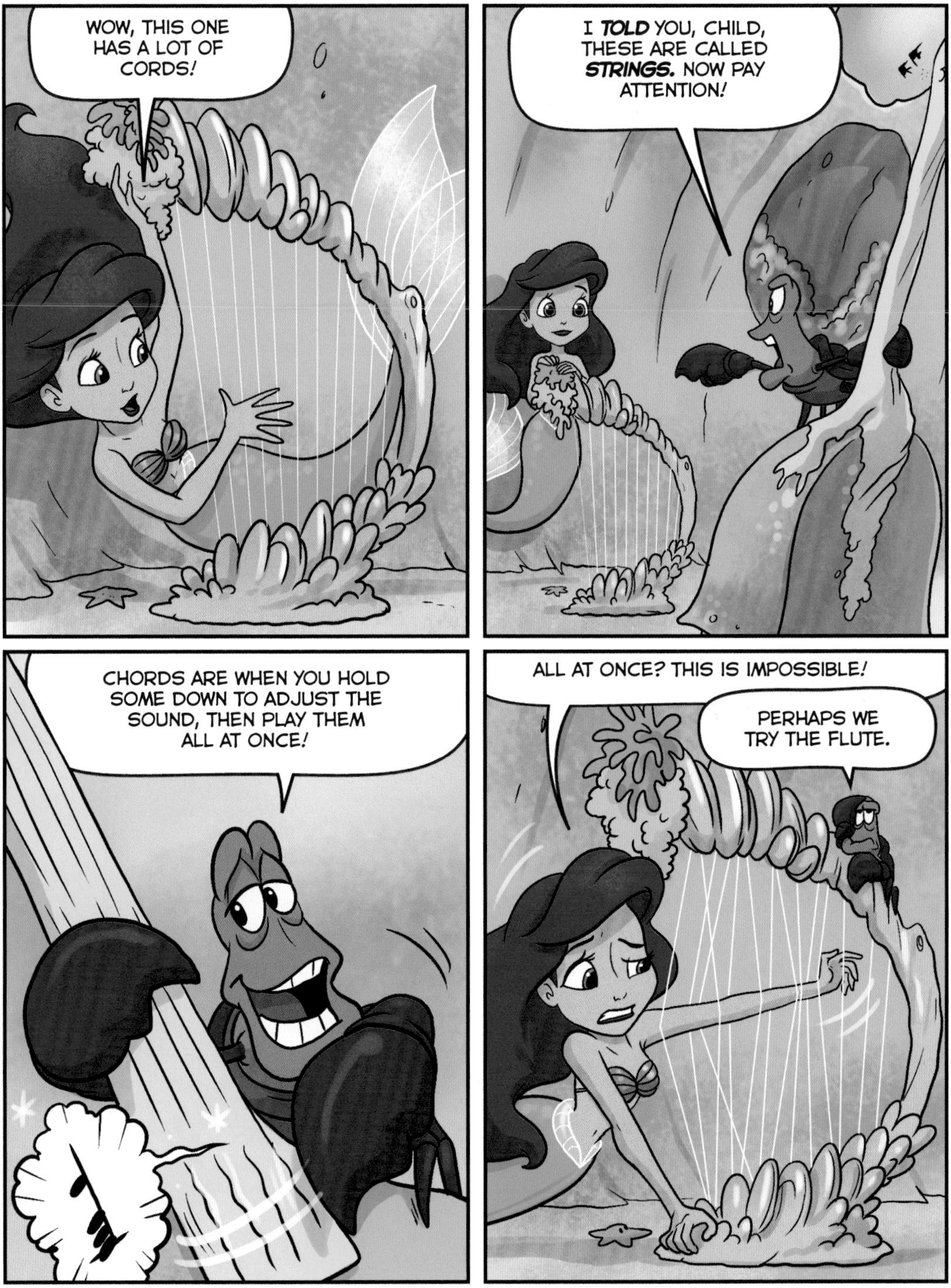
WOW, THIS ONE HAS A LOT OF CORDS!
I *TOLD* YOU, CHILD, THESE ARE CALLED *STRINGS.* NOW PAY ATTENTION!
CHORDS ARE WHEN YOU HOLD SOME DOWN TO ADJUST THE SOUND, THEN PLAY THEM ALL AT ONCE!
ALL AT ONCE? THIS IS IMPOSSIBLE!
PERHAPS WE TRY THE FLUTE.

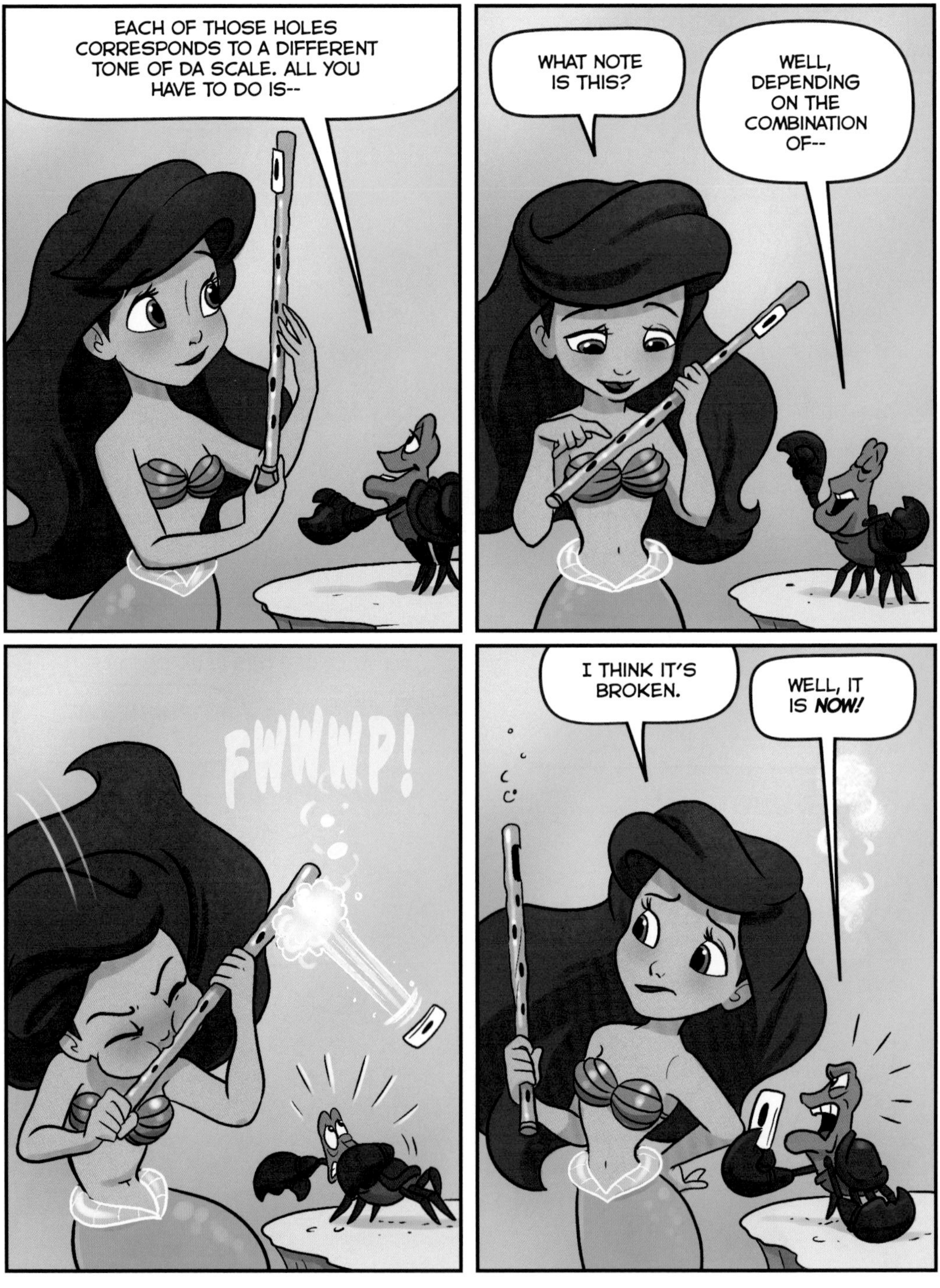

EACH OF THOSE HOLES CORRESPONDS TO A DIFFERENT TONE OF DA SCALE. ALL YOU HAVE TO DO IS--
WHAT NOTE IS THIS?
WELL, DEPENDING ON THE COMBINATION OF--
FWWWP!
I THINK IT'S BROKEN.
WELL, IT IS ***NOW!***

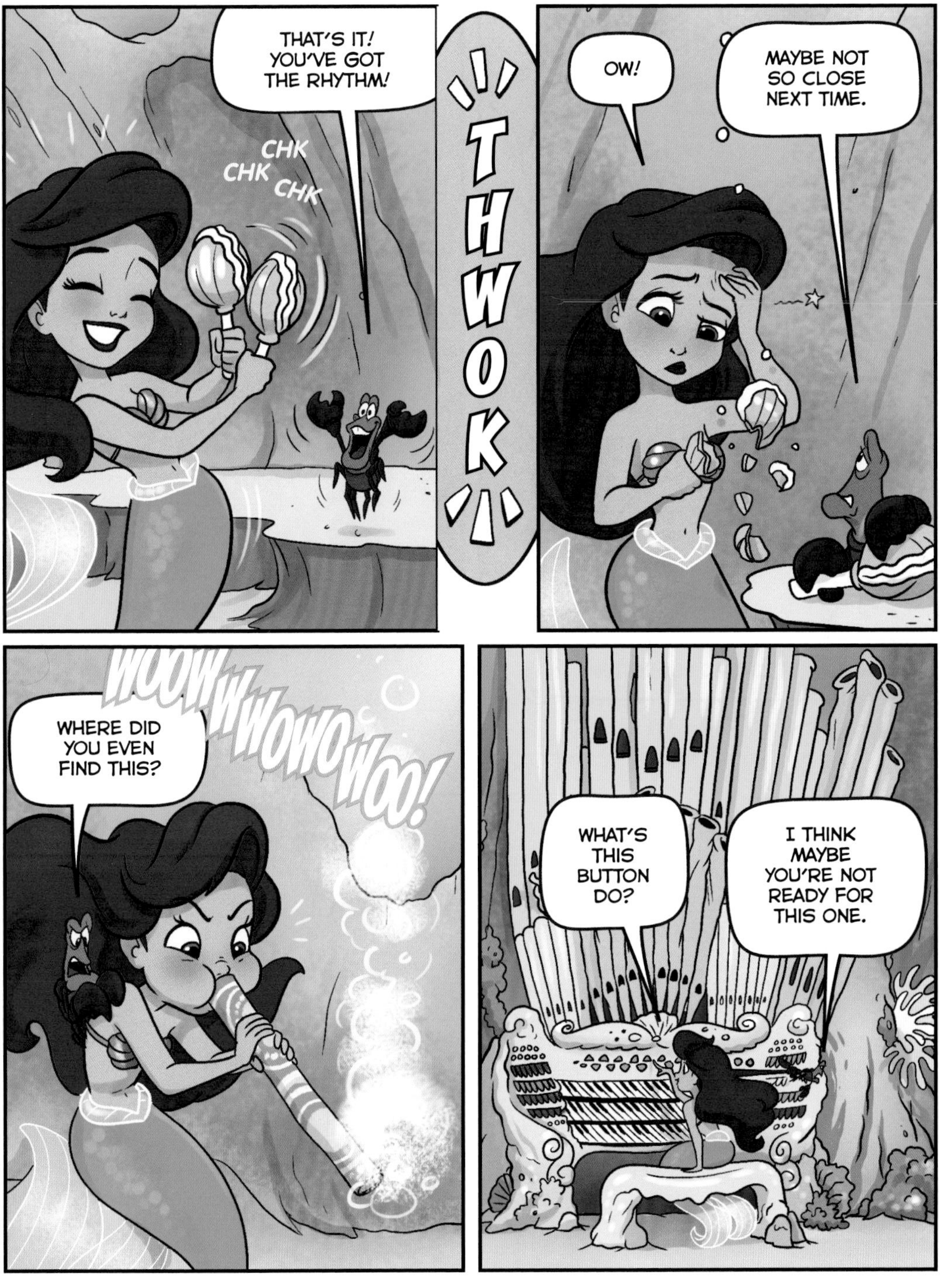
THAT'S IT! YOU'VE GOT THE RHYTHM!
CHK CHK CHK
THWOK
OW!
MAYBE NOT SO CLOSE NEXT TIME.
WHERE DID YOU EVEN FIND THIS?
WOOWWWOWOWOO!
WHAT'S THIS BUTTON DO?
I THINK MAYBE YOU'RE NOT READY FOR THIS ONE.

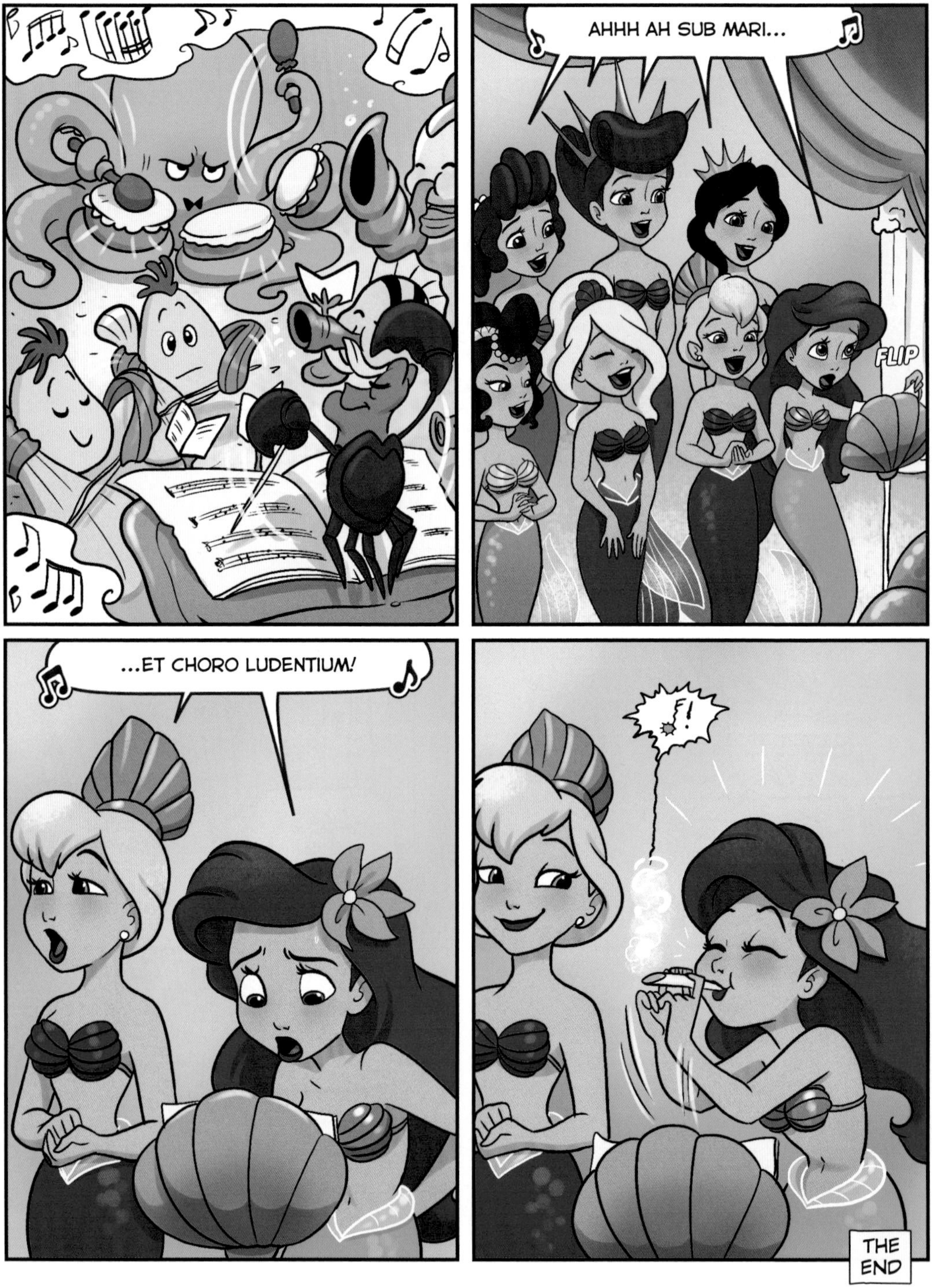
AHHH AH SUB MARI...
FLIP
...ET CHORO LUDENTIUM!
F!
THE END

# "LAUGHING WARRIOR"

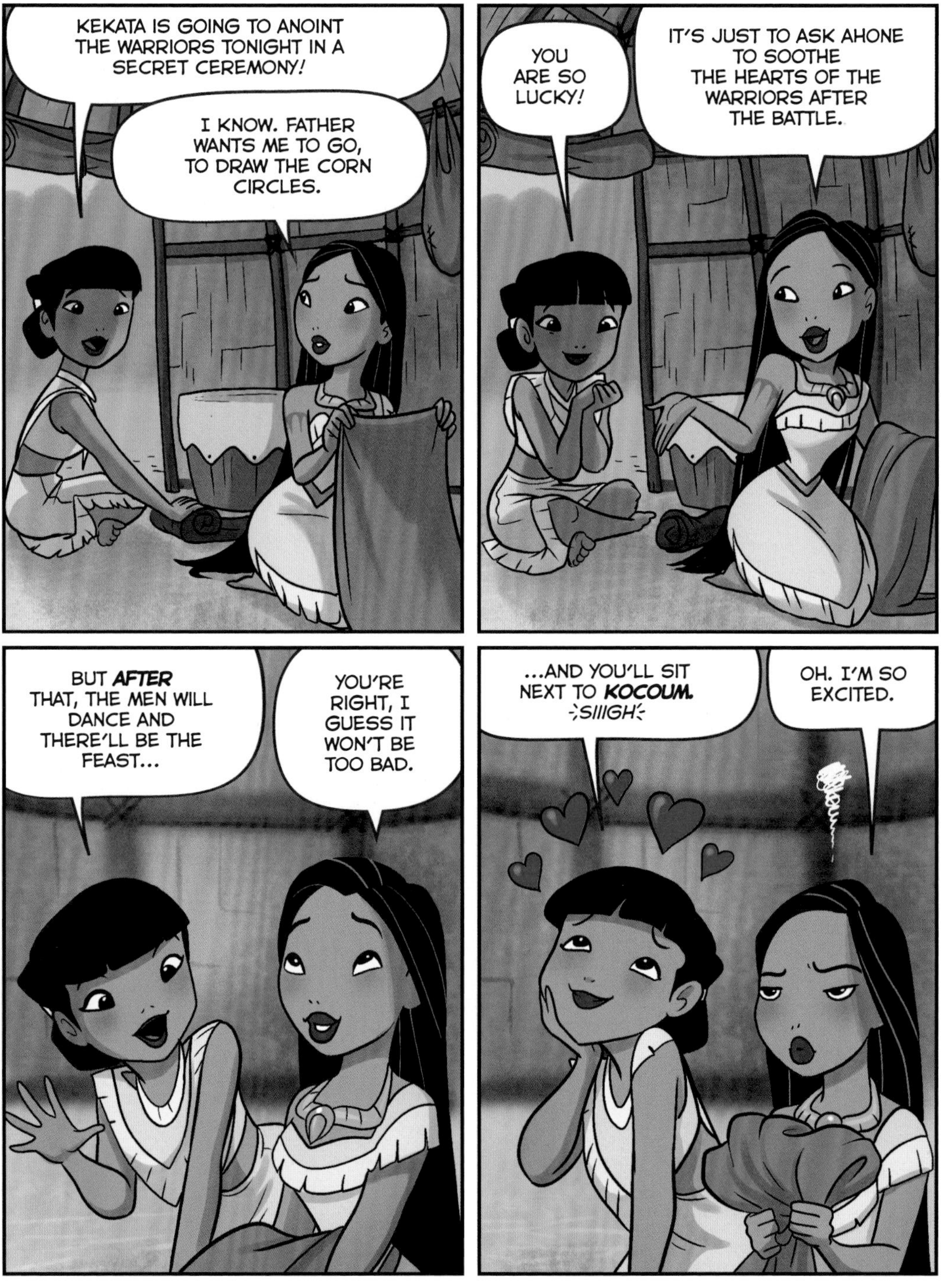
KEKATA IS GOING TO ANOINT THE WARRIORS TONIGHT IN A SECRET CEREMONY!
I KNOW. FATHER WANTS ME TO GO, TO DRAW THE CORN CIRCLES.
YOU ARE SO LUCKY!
IT'S JUST TO ASK AHONE TO SOOTHE THE HEARTS OF THE WARRIORS AFTER THE BATTLE.
BUT AFTER THAT, THE MEN WILL DANCE AND THERE'LL BE THE FEAST...
YOU'RE RIGHT, I GUESS IT WON'T BE TOO BAD.
...AND YOU'LL SIT NEXT TO KOCOUM. SIIIGH
OH. I'M SO EXCITED.

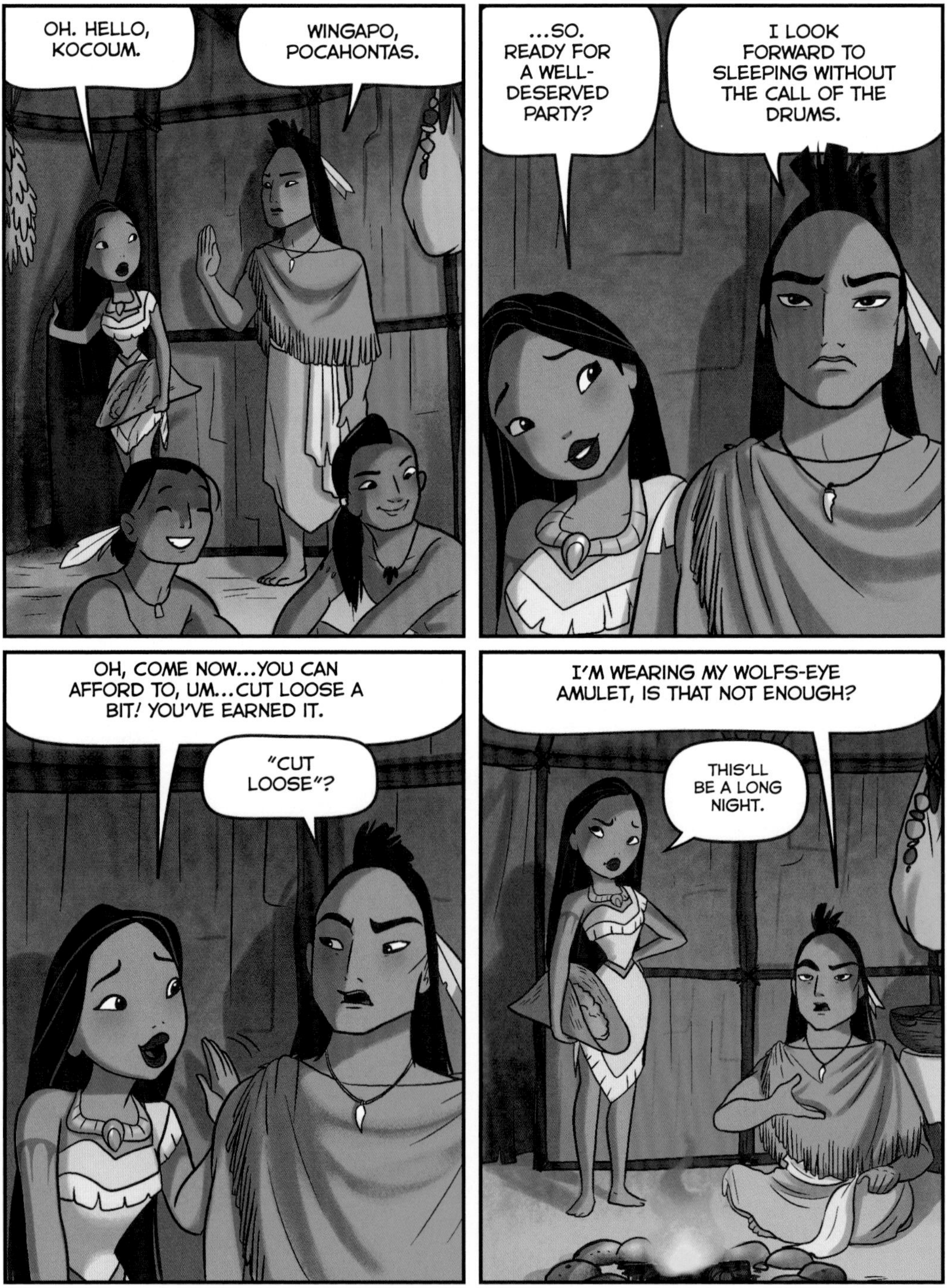
OH. HELLO, KOCOUM.
WINGAPO, POCAHONTAS.
...SO. READY FOR A WELL-DESERVED PARTY?
I LOOK FORWARD TO SLEEPING WITHOUT THE CALL OF THE DRUMS.
OH, COME NOW...YOU CAN AFFORD TO, UM...CUT LOOSE A BIT! YOU'VE EARNED IT.
"CUT LOOSE"?
I'M WEARING MY WOLFS-EYE AMULET, IS THAT NOT ENOUGH?
THIS'LL BE A LONG NIGHT.

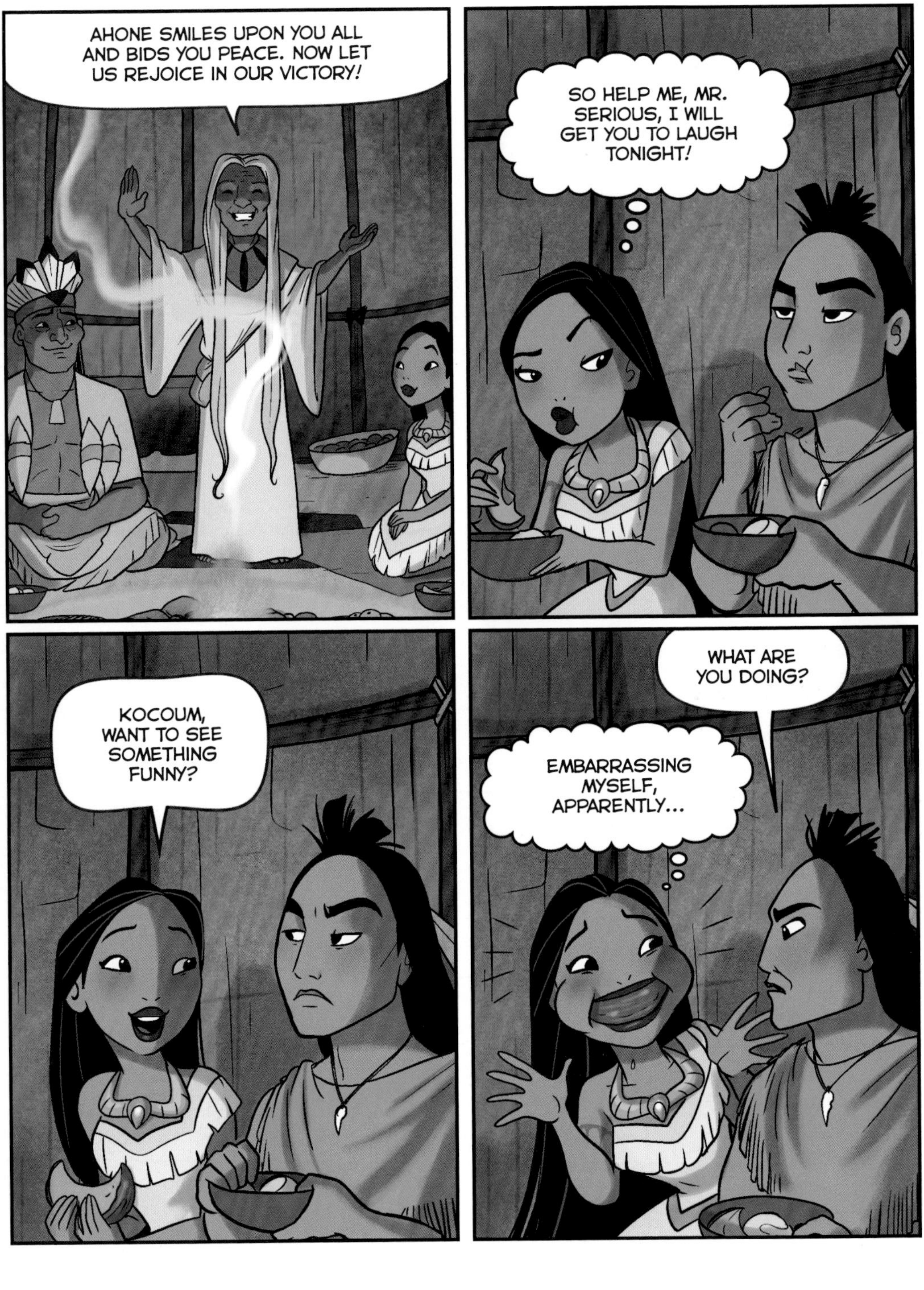
AHONE SMILES UPON YOU ALL AND BIDS YOU PEACE. NOW LET US REJOICE IN OUR VICTORY!
SO HELP ME, MR. SERIOUS, I WILL GET YOU TO LAUGH TONIGHT!
KOCOUM, WANT TO SEE SOMETHING FUNNY?
WHAT ARE YOU DOING?
EMBARRASSING MYSELF, APPARENTLY...

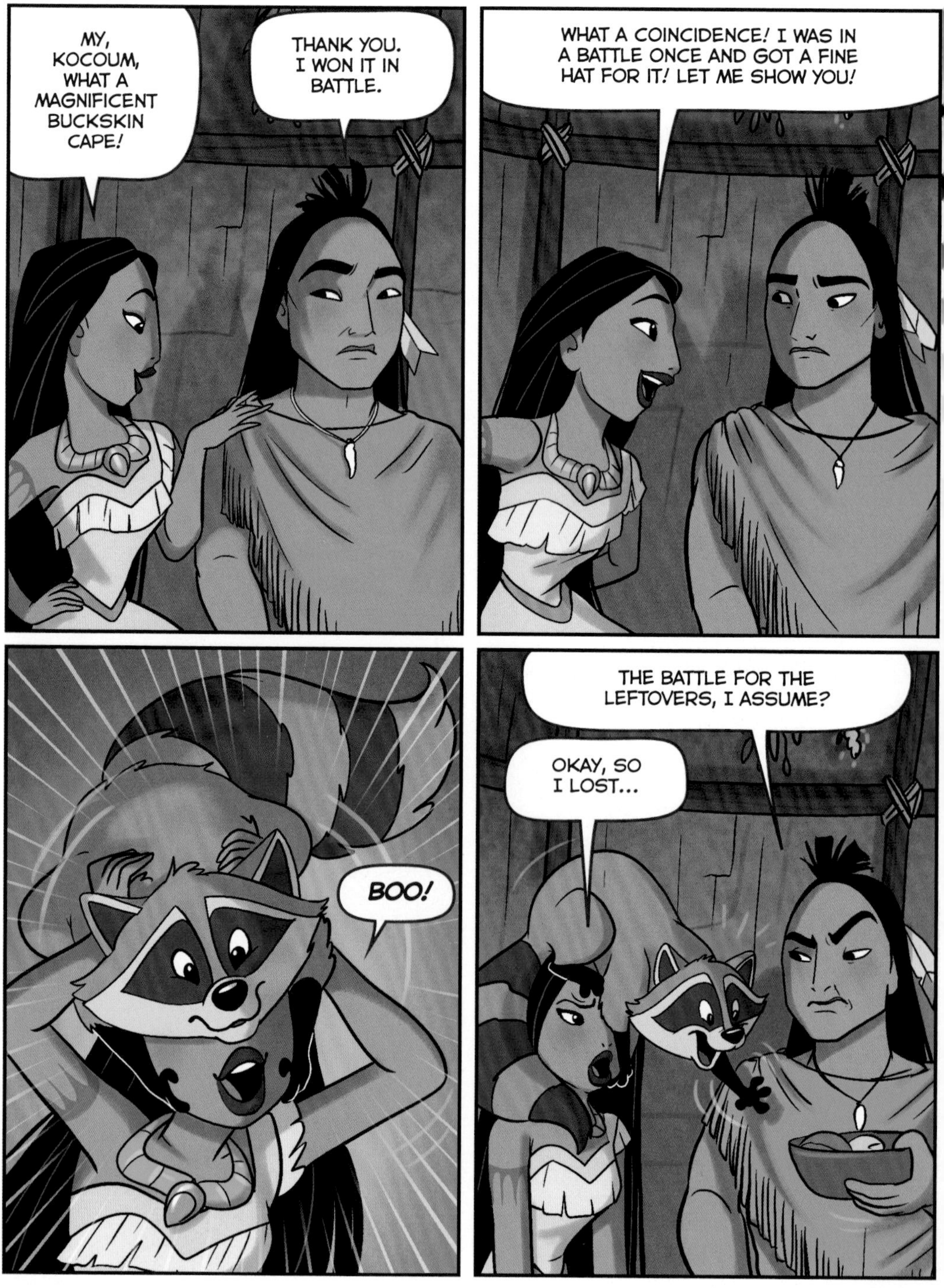
MY, KOCOUM, WHAT A MAGNIFICENT BUCKSKIN CAPE!
THANK YOU. I WON IT IN BATTLE.
WHAT A COINCIDENCE! I WAS IN A BATTLE ONCE AND GOT A FINE HAT FOR IT! LET ME SHOW YOU!
BOO!
THE BATTLE FOR THE LEFTOVERS, I ASSUME?
OKAY, SO I LOST...

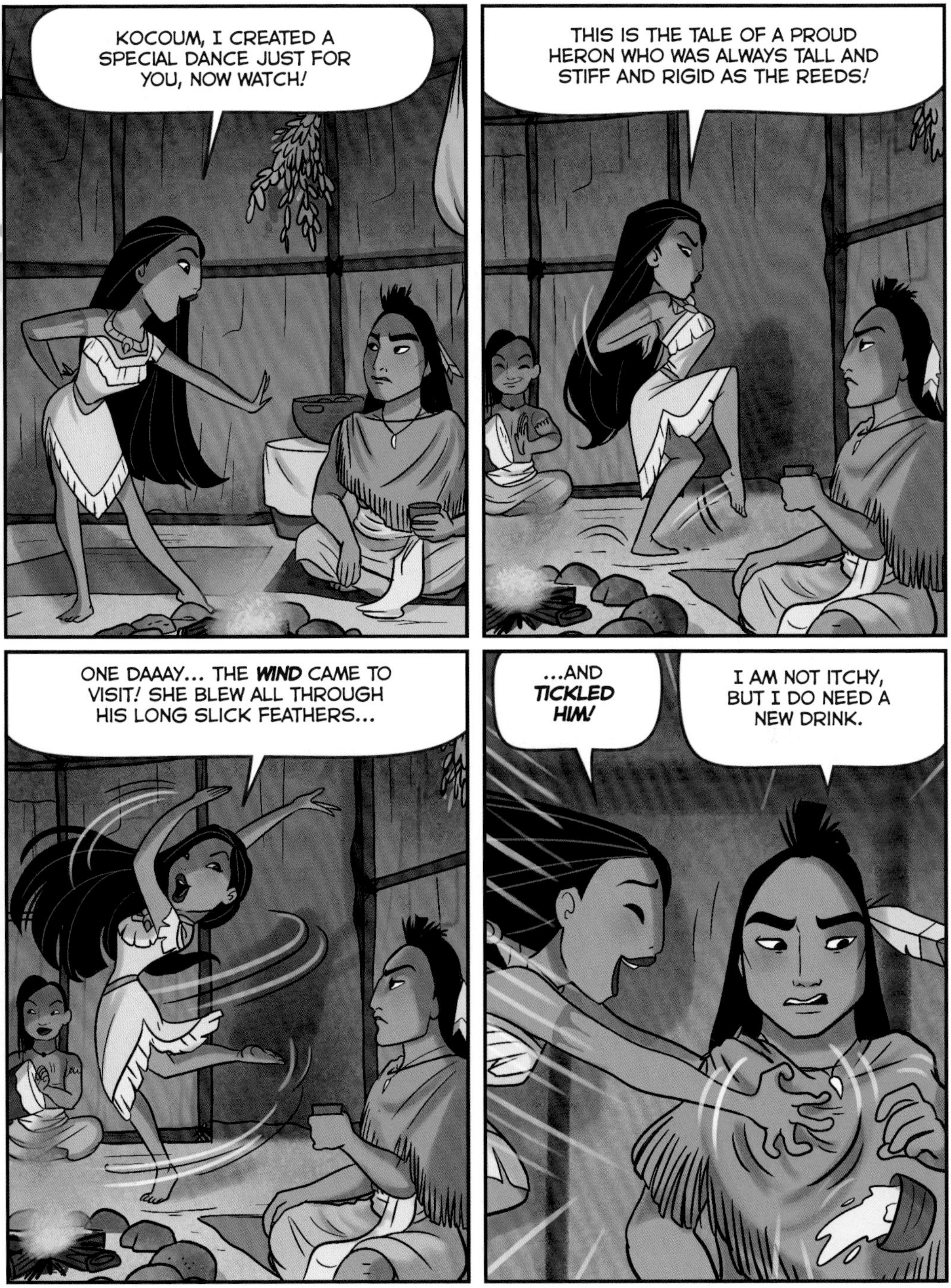
KOCOUM, I CREATED A SPECIAL DANCE JUST FOR YOU, NOW WATCH!
THIS IS THE TALE OF A PROUD HERON WHO WAS ALWAYS TALL AND STIFF AND RIGID AS THE REEDS!
ONE DAAAY... THE **WIND** CAME TO VISIT! SHE BLEW ALL THROUGH HIS LONG SLICK FEATHERS...
...AND **TICKLED HIM!**
I AM NOT ITCHY, BUT I DO NEED A NEW DRINK.

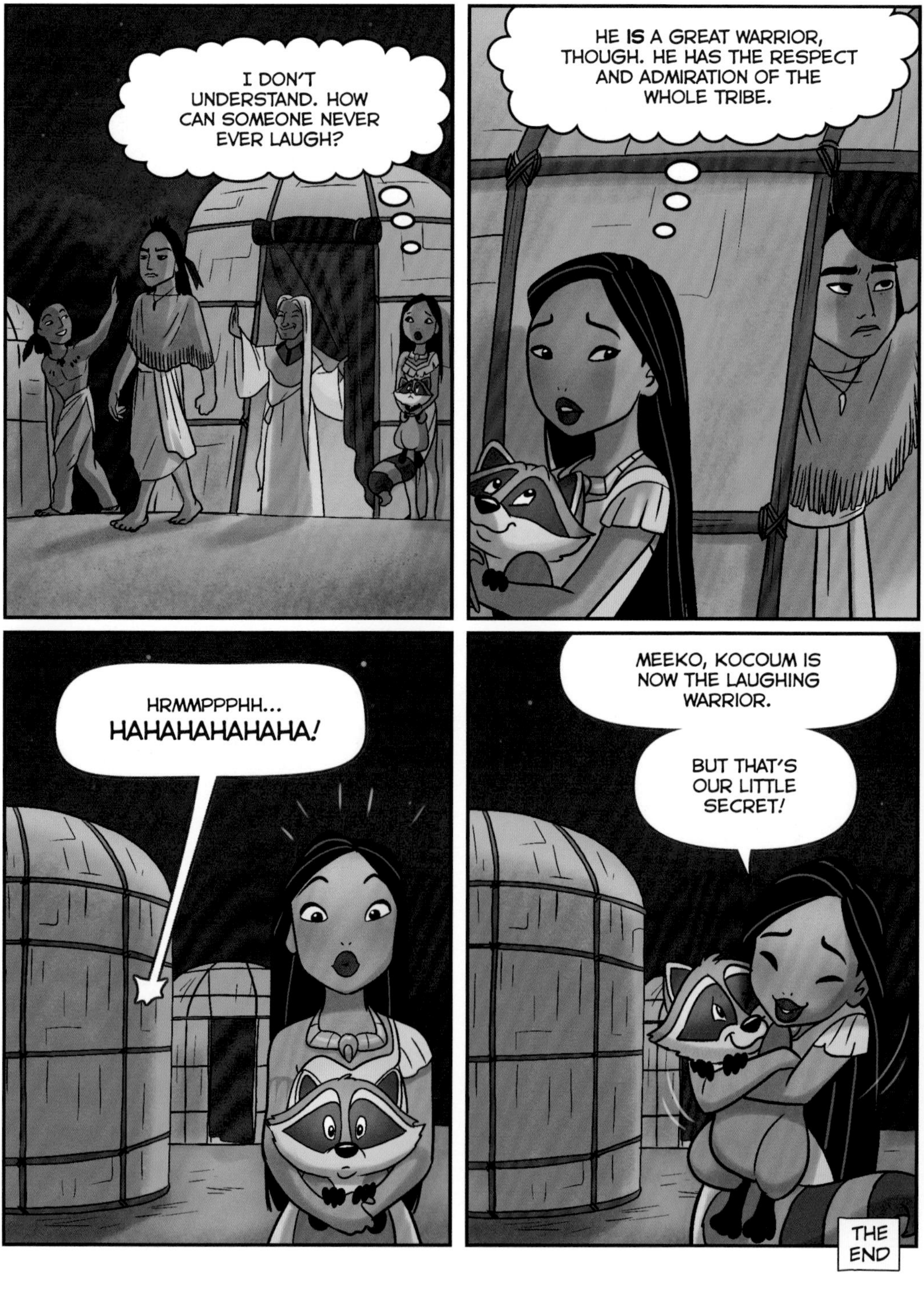
I DON'T UNDERSTAND. HOW CAN SOMEONE NEVER EVER LAUGH?
HE IS A GREAT WARRIOR, THOUGH. HE HAS THE RESPECT AND ADMIRATION OF THE WHOLE TRIBE.
HRMMPPPHH... HAHAHAHAHAHA!
MEEKO, KOCOUM IS NOW THE LAUGHING WARRIOR.
BUT THAT'S OUR LITTLE SECRET!
THE END

# "RAINY DAY"

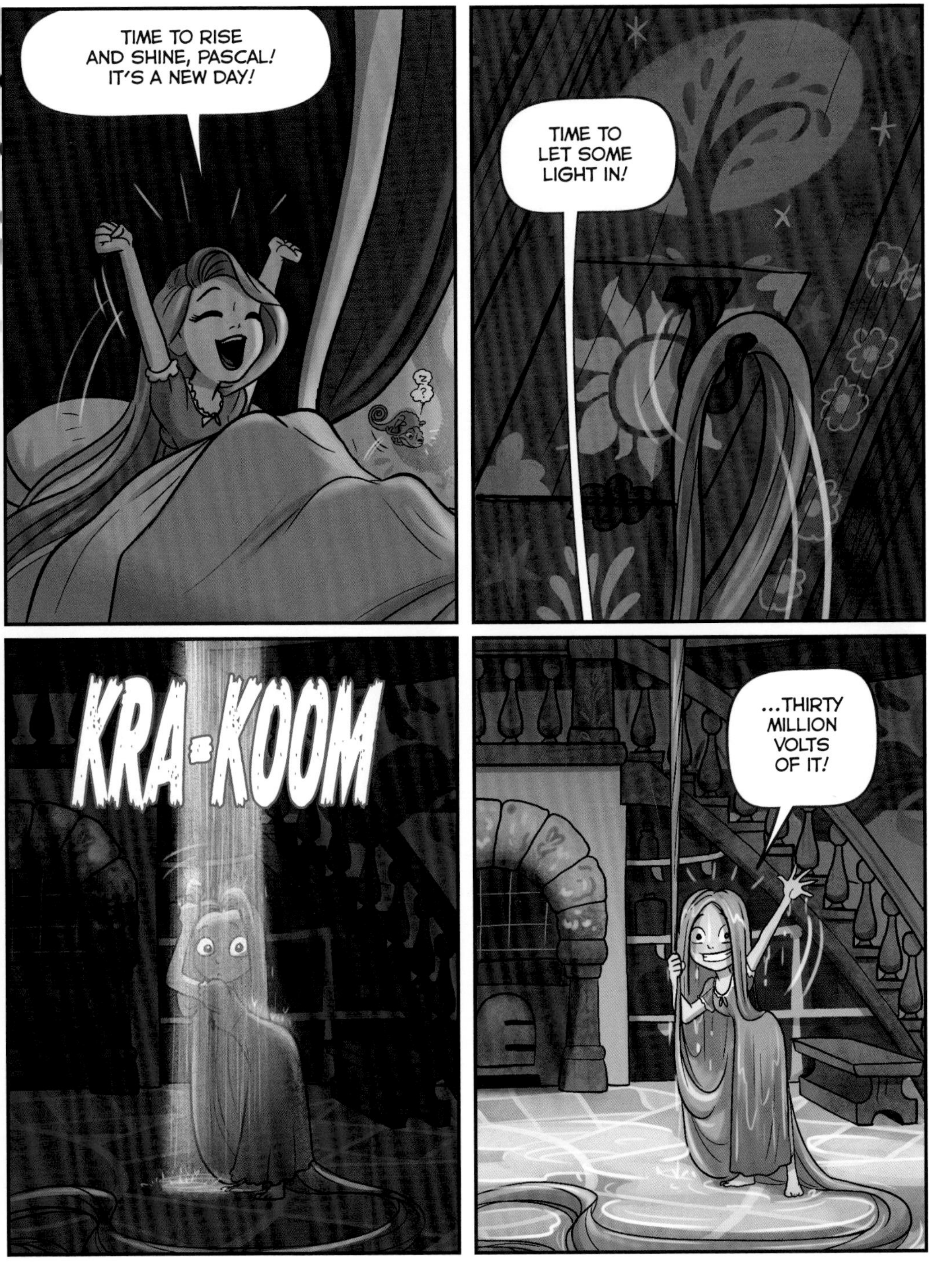

TIME TO RISE AND SHINE, PASCAL! IT'S A NEW DAY!
Z ?
TIME TO LET SOME LIGHT IN!
KRA-KOOM
...THIRTY MILLION VOLTS OF IT!

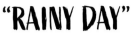

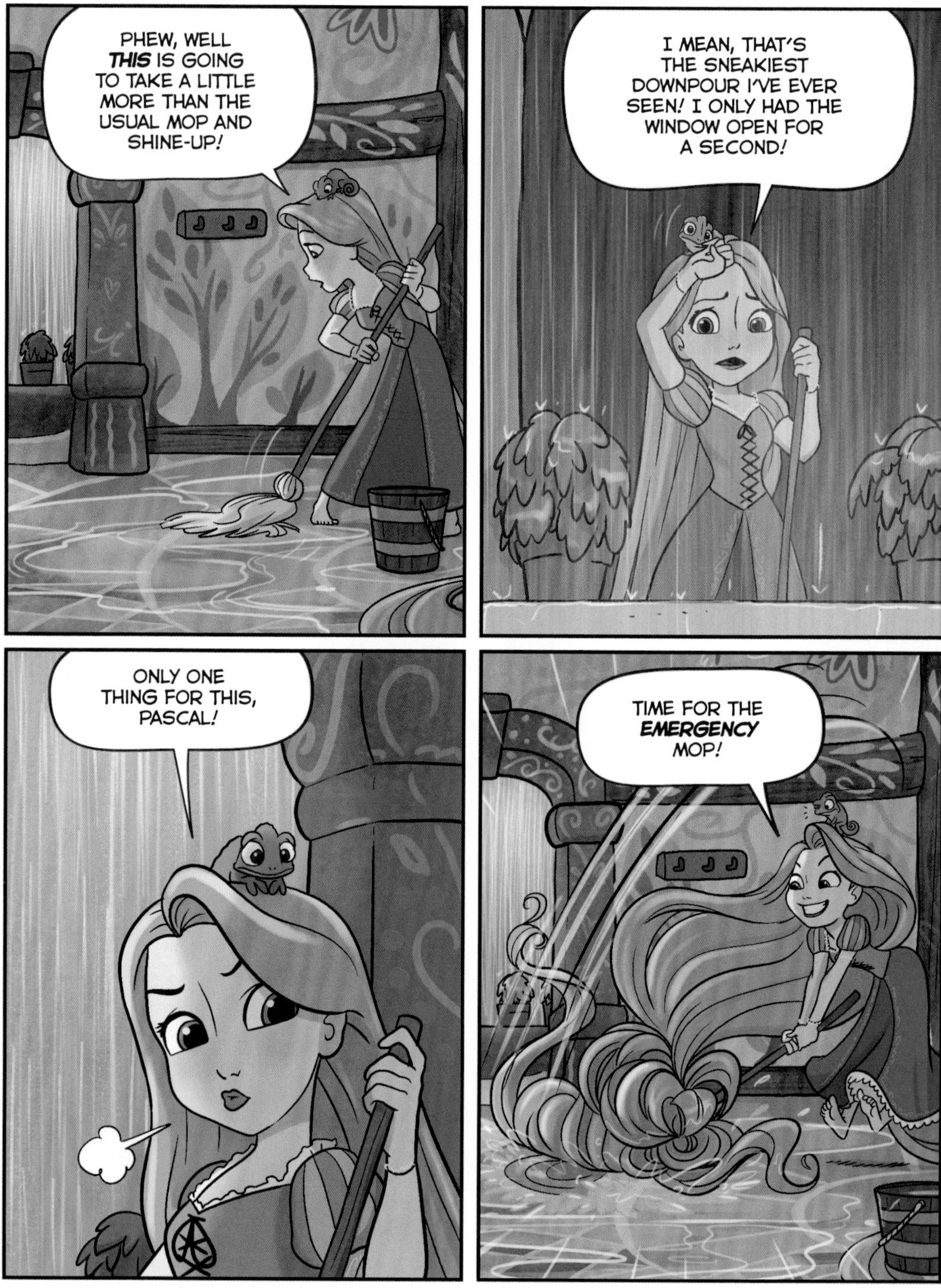
PHEW, WELL **THIS** IS GOING TO TAKE A LITTLE MORE THAN THE USUAL MOP AND SHINE-UP!
I MEAN, THAT'S THE SNEAKIEST DOWNPOUR I'VE EVER SEEN! I ONLY HAD THE WINDOW OPEN FOR A SECOND!
ONLY ONE THING FOR THIS, PASCAL!
TIME FOR THE **EMERGENCY** MOP!

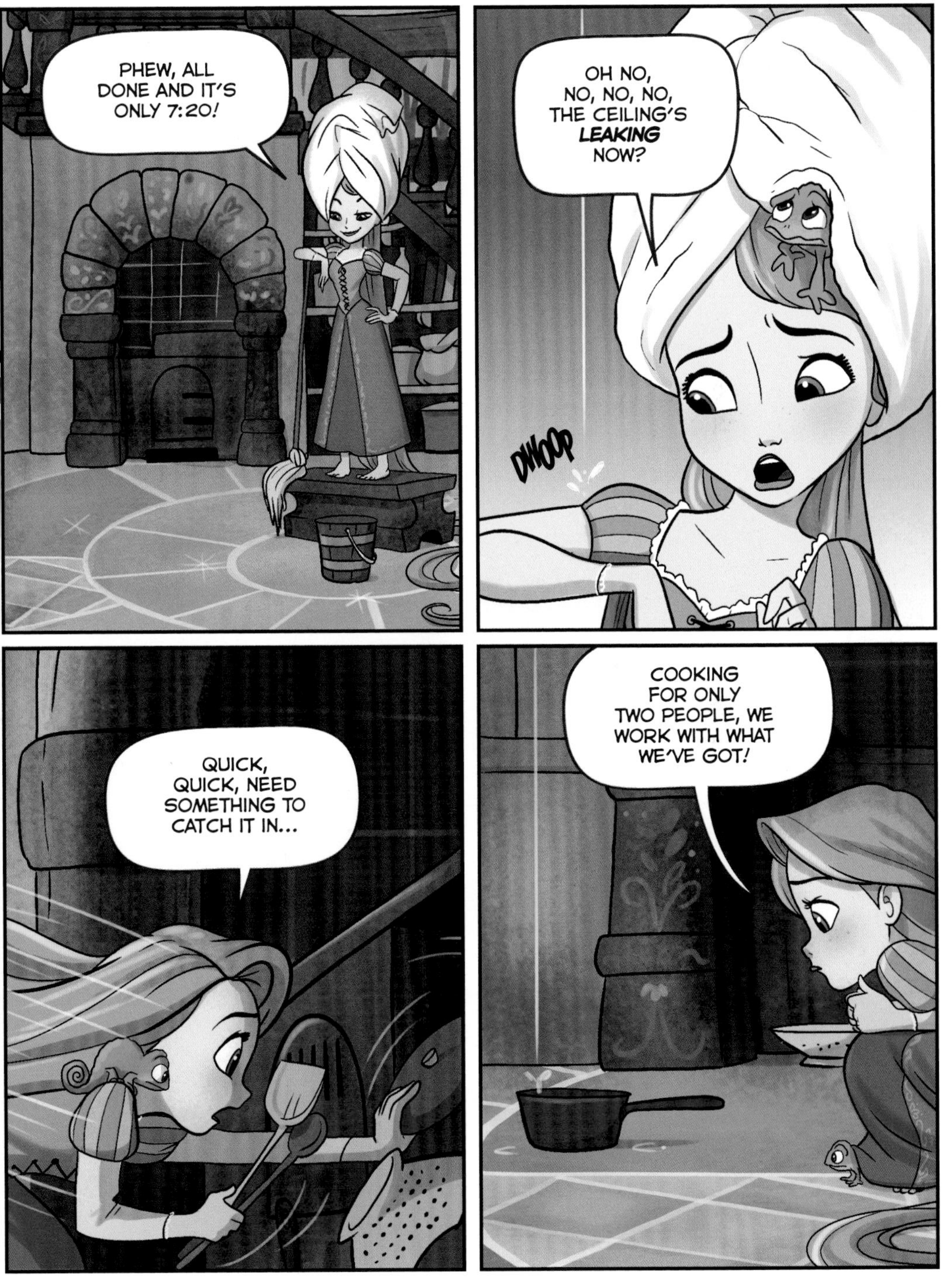
PHEW, ALL DONE AND IT'S ONLY 7:20!
OH NO, NO, NO, NO, THE CEILING'S LEAKING NOW?
DHOOP
QUICK, QUICK, NEED SOMETHING TO CATCH IT IN...
COOKING FOR ONLY TWO PEOPLE, WE WORK WITH WHAT WE'VE GOT!

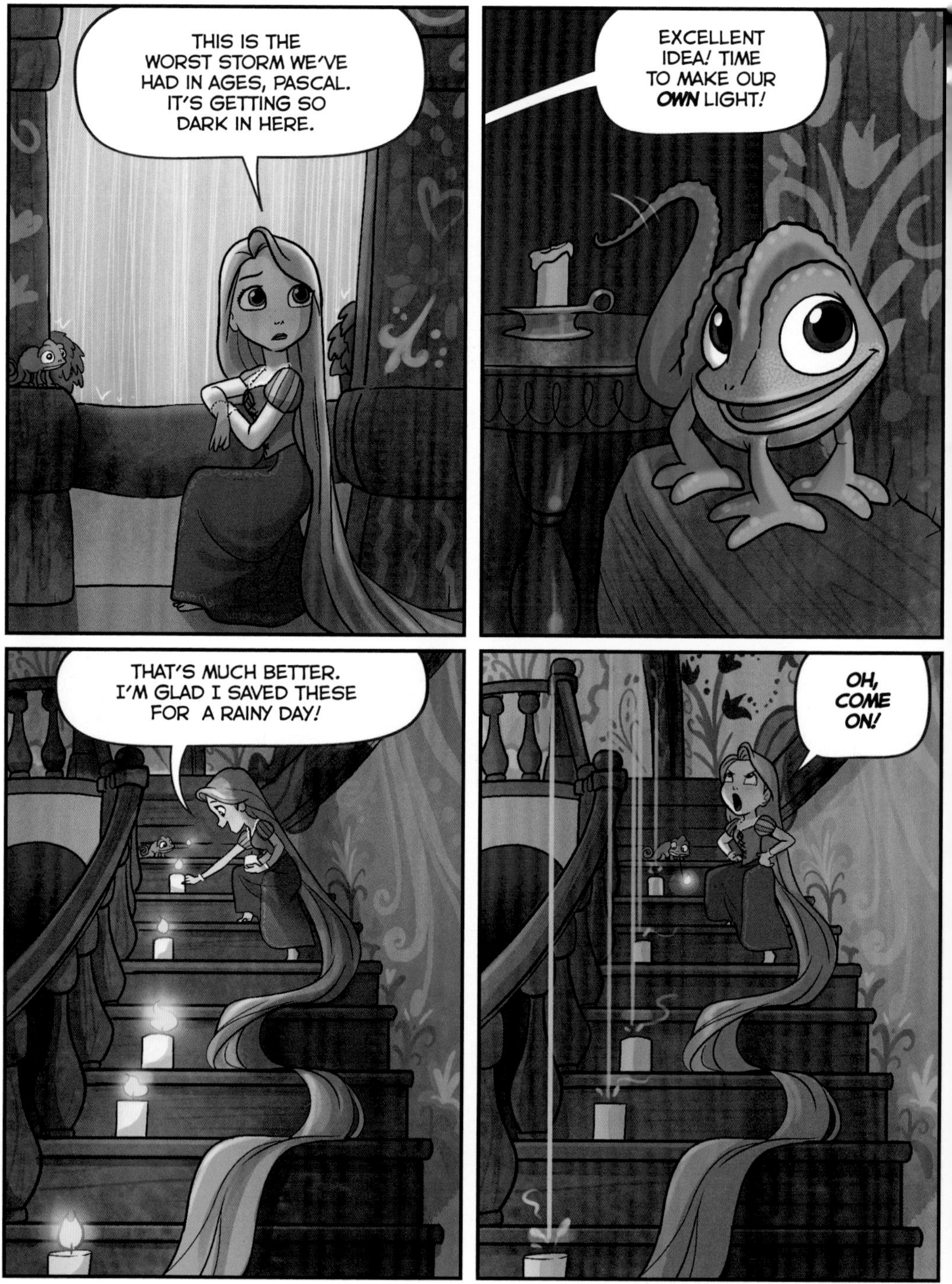
THIS IS THE WORST STORM WE'VE HAD IN AGES, PASCAL. IT'S GETTING SO DARK IN HERE.
EXCELLENT IDEA! TIME TO MAKE OUR *OWN* LIGHT!
THAT'S MUCH BETTER. I'M GLAD I SAVED THESE FOR A RAINY DAY!
OH, COME ON!

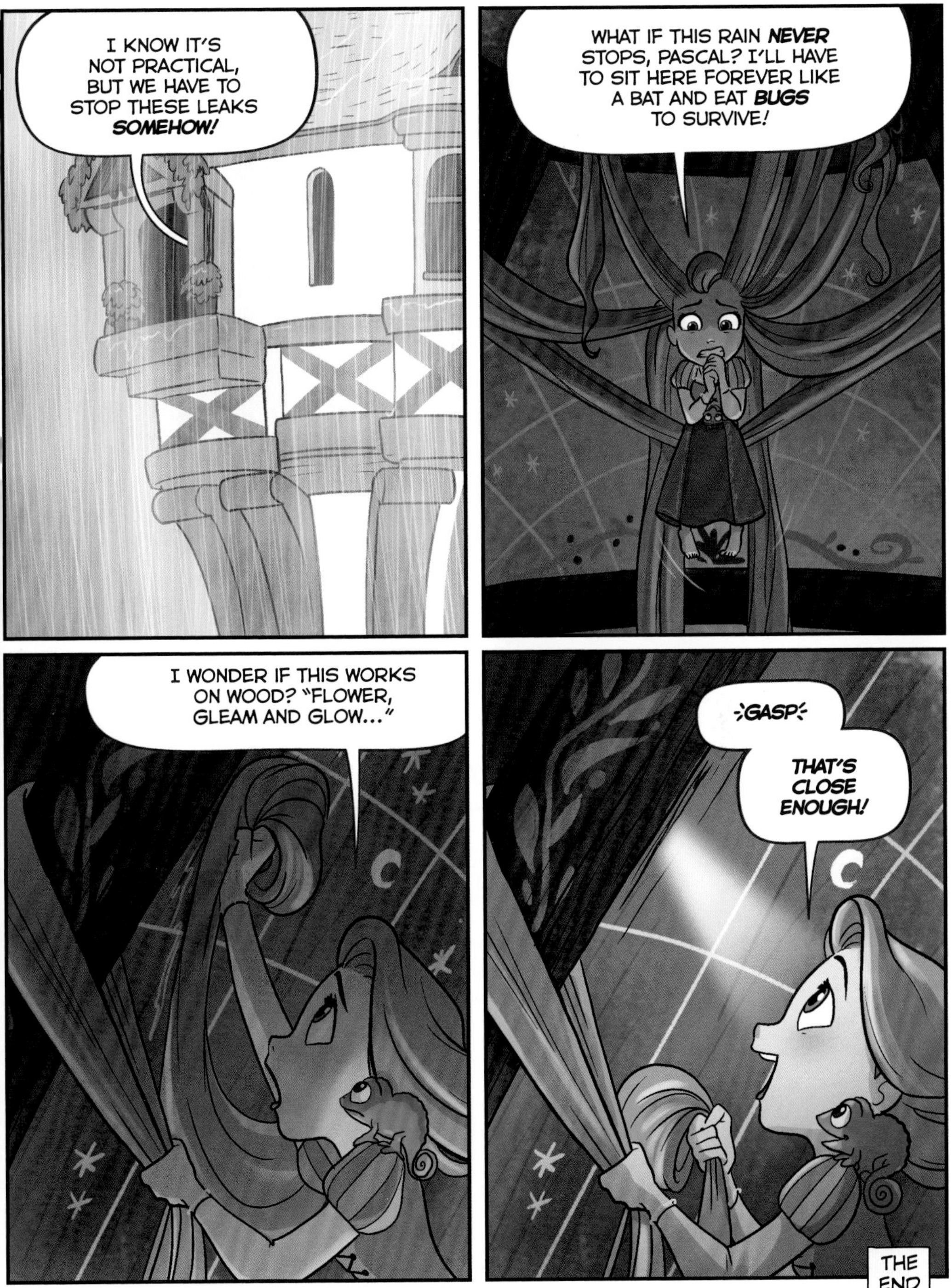
I KNOW IT'S NOT PRACTICAL, BUT WE HAVE TO STOP THESE LEAKS ***SOMEHOW!***
WHAT IF THIS RAIN ***NEVER*** STOPS, PASCAL? I'LL HAVE TO SIT HERE FOREVER LIKE A BAT AND EAT ***BUGS*** TO SURVIVE!
I WONDER IF THIS WORKS ON WOOD? "FLOWER, GLEAM AND GLOW..."
*GASP*
***THAT'S CLOSE ENOUGH!***
THE END

# "MATCHMAKER"

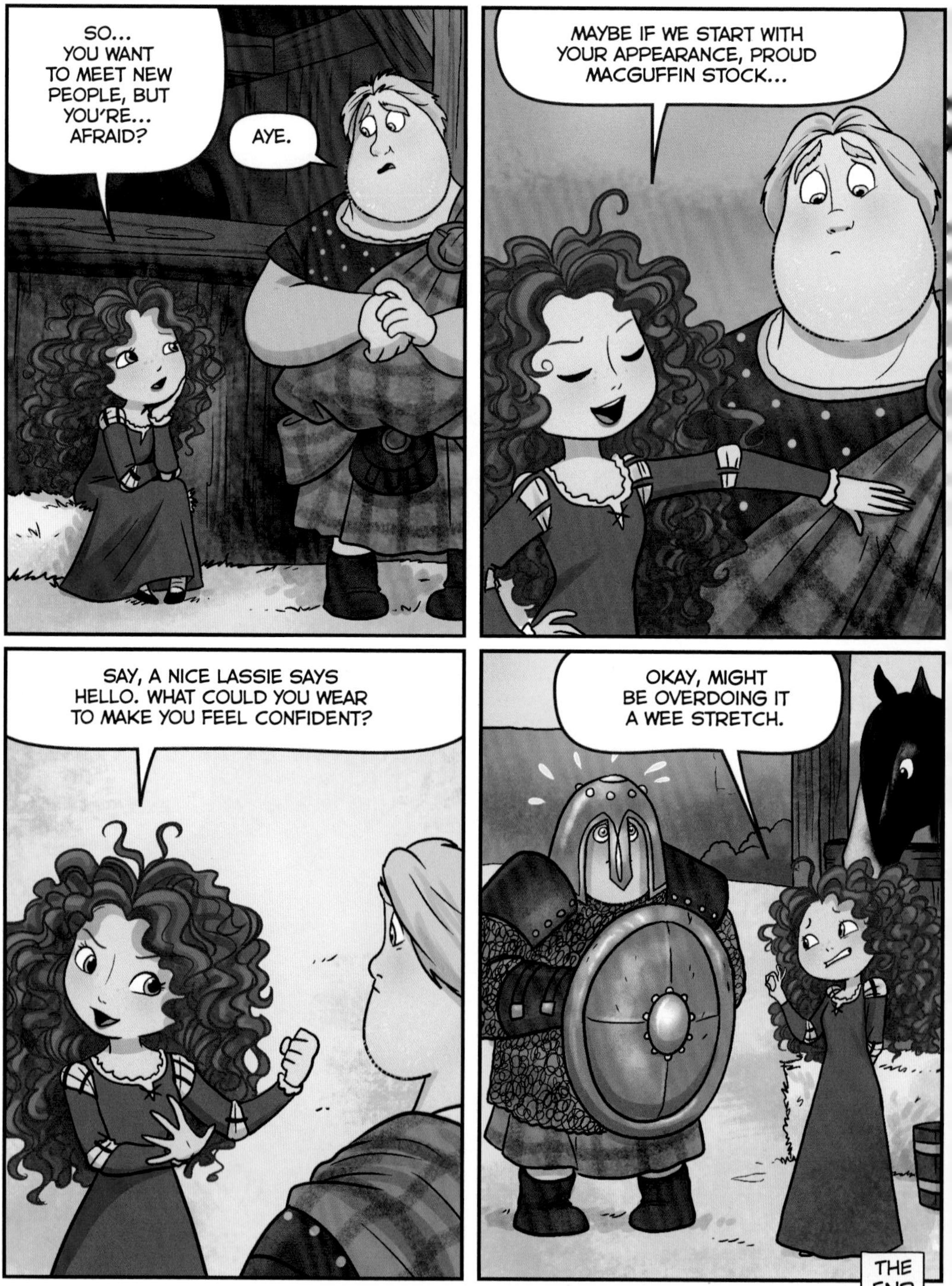
SO... YOU WANT TO MEET NEW PEOPLE, BUT YOU'RE... AFRAID?
AYE.
MAYBE IF WE START WITH YOUR APPEARANCE, PROUD MACGUFFIN STOCK...
SAY, A NICE LASSIE SAYS HELLO. WHAT COULD YOU WEAR TO MAKE YOU FEEL CONFIDENT?
OKAY, MIGHT BE OVERDOING IT A WEE STRETCH.
THE END

# "NATURE WALK"

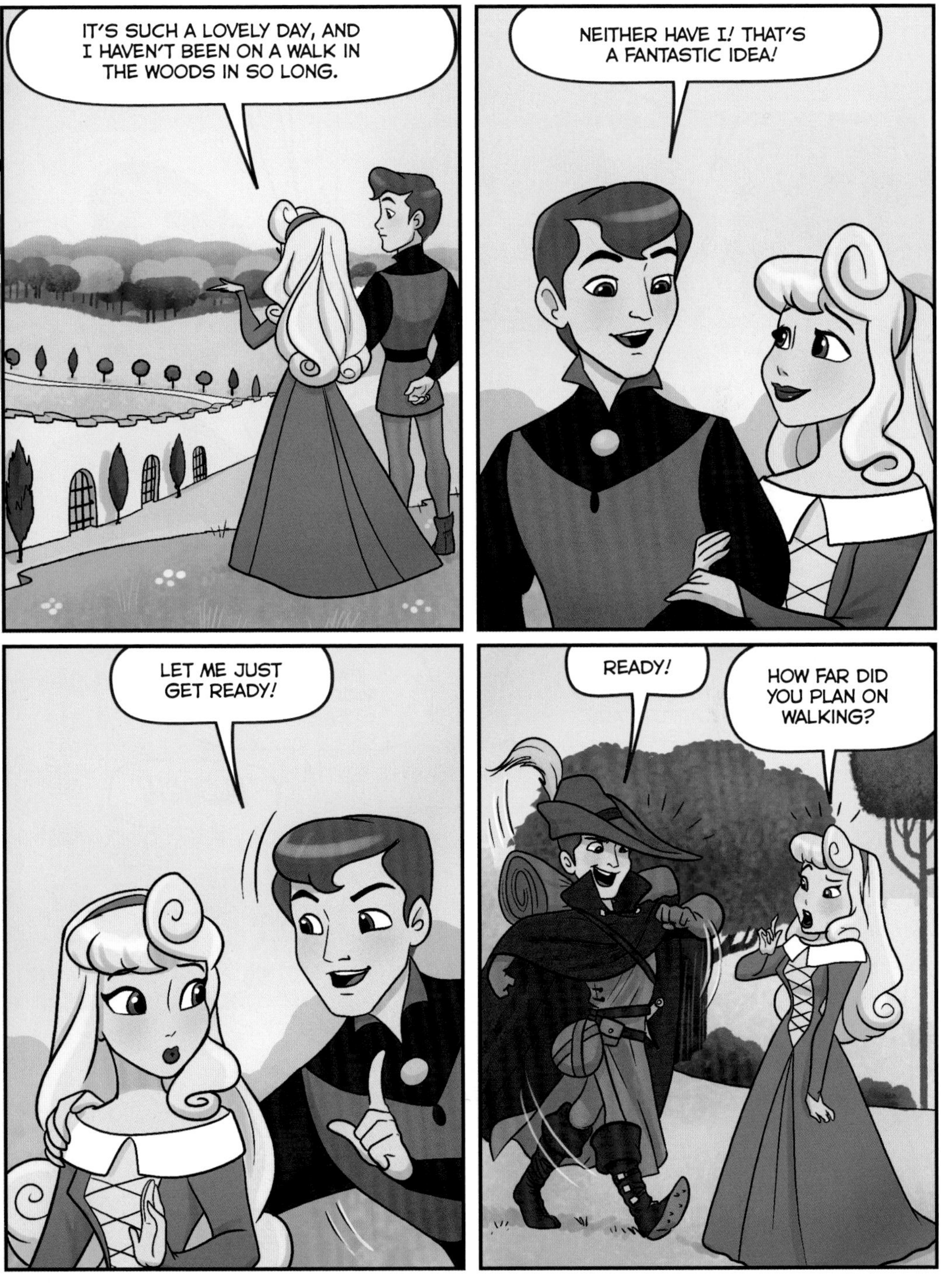
IT'S SUCH A LOVELY DAY, AND I HAVEN'T BEEN ON A WALK IN THE WOODS IN SO LONG.
NEITHER HAVE I! THAT'S A FANTASTIC IDEA!
LET ME JUST GET READY!
READY!
HOW FAR DID YOU PLAN ON WALKING?

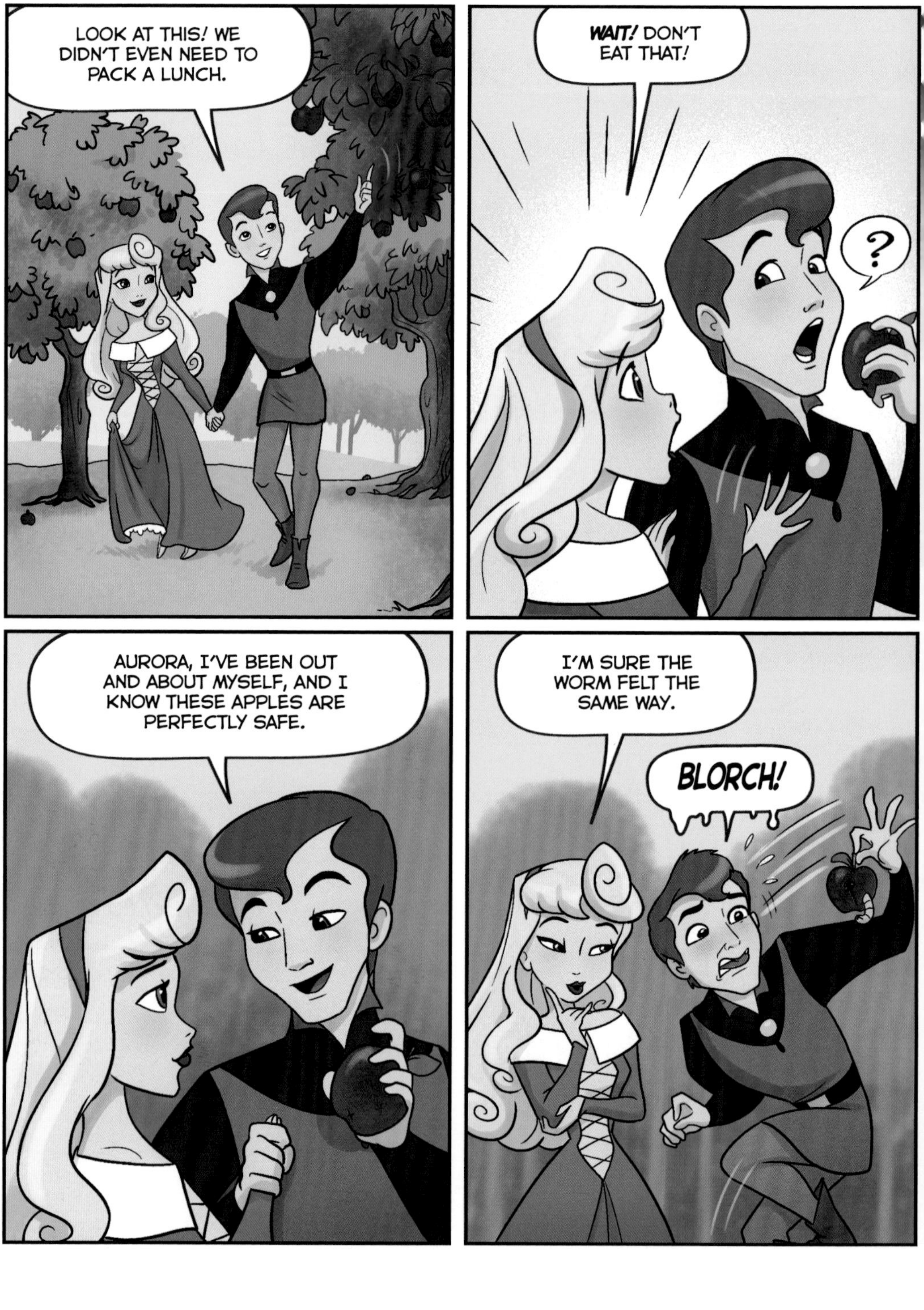

LOOK AT THIS! WE DIDN'T EVEN NEED TO PACK A LUNCH.
WAIT! DON'T EAT THAT!
?
AURORA, I'VE BEEN OUT AND ABOUT MYSELF, AND I KNOW THESE APPLES ARE PERFECTLY SAFE.
I'M SURE THE WORM FELT THE SAME WAY.
BLORCH!

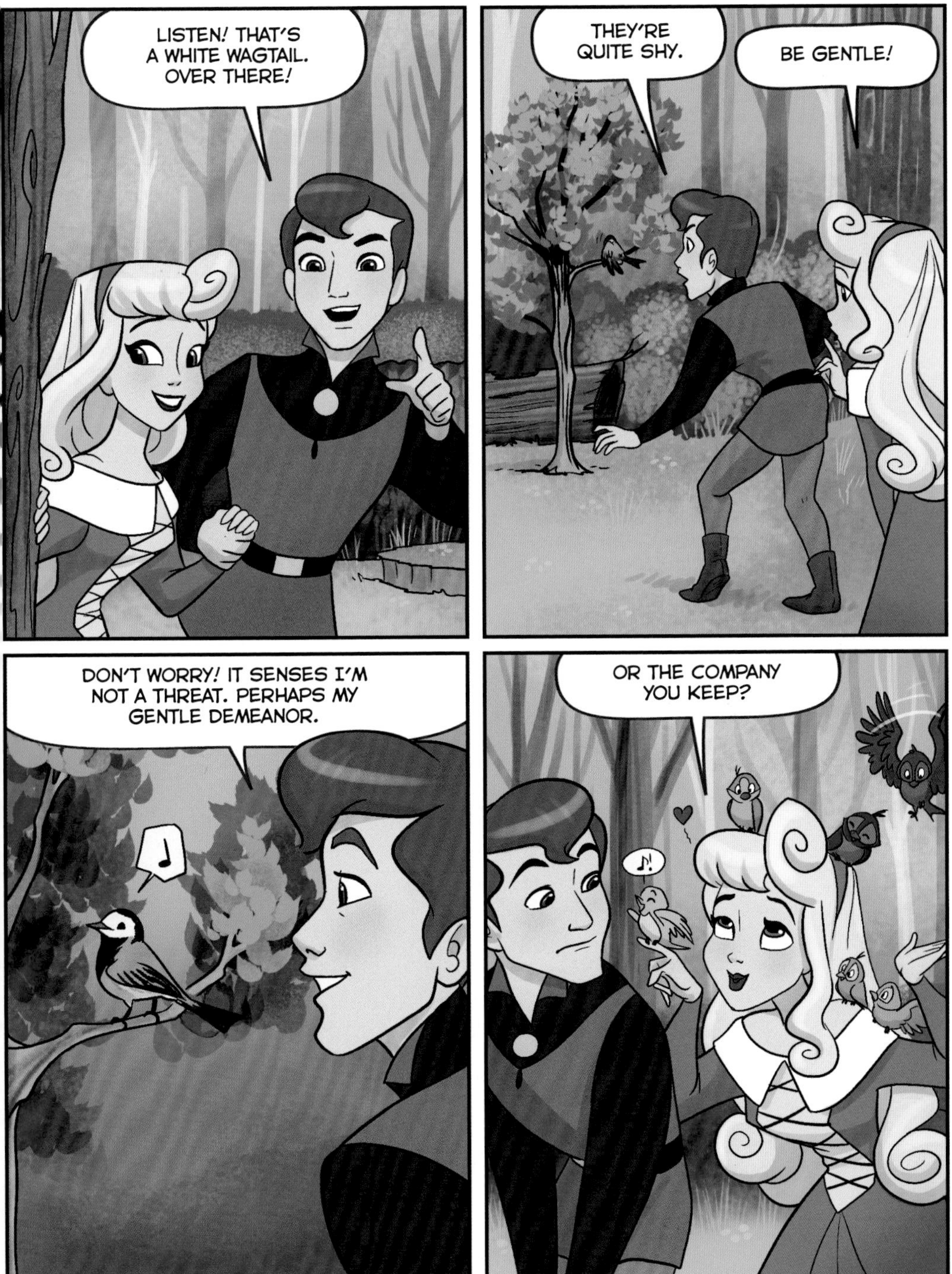
LISTEN! THAT'S A WHITE WAGTAIL. OVER THERE!
THEY'RE QUITE SHY.
BE GENTLE!
DON'T WORRY! IT SENSES I'M NOT A THREAT. PERHAPS MY GENTLE DEMEANOR.
OR THE COMPANY YOU KEEP?

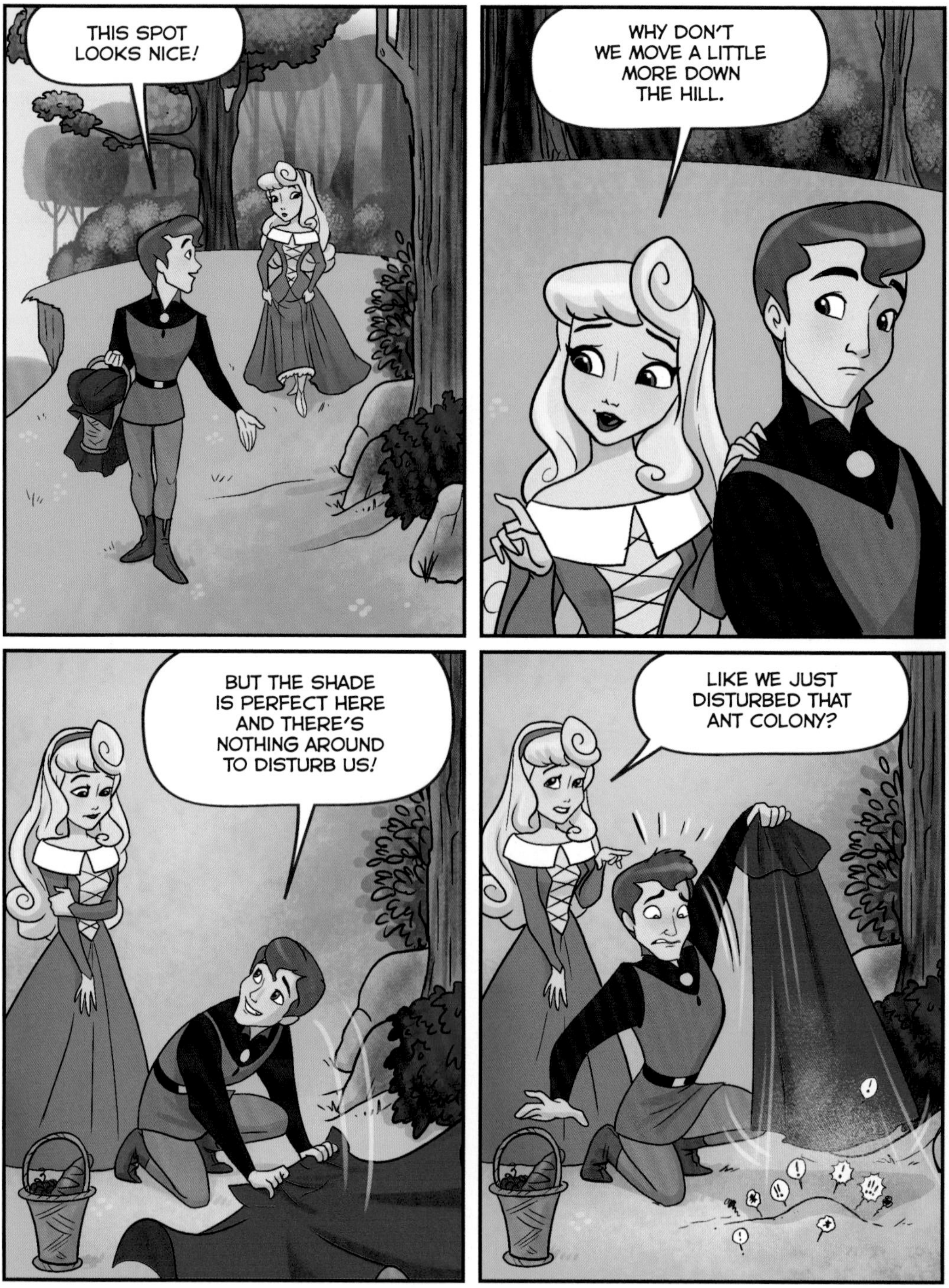
THIS SPOT LOOKS NICE!
WHY DON'T WE MOVE A LITTLE MORE DOWN THE HILL.
BUT THE SHADE IS PERFECT HERE AND THERE'S NOTHING AROUND TO DISTURB US!
LIKE WE JUST DISTURBED THAT ANT COLONY?

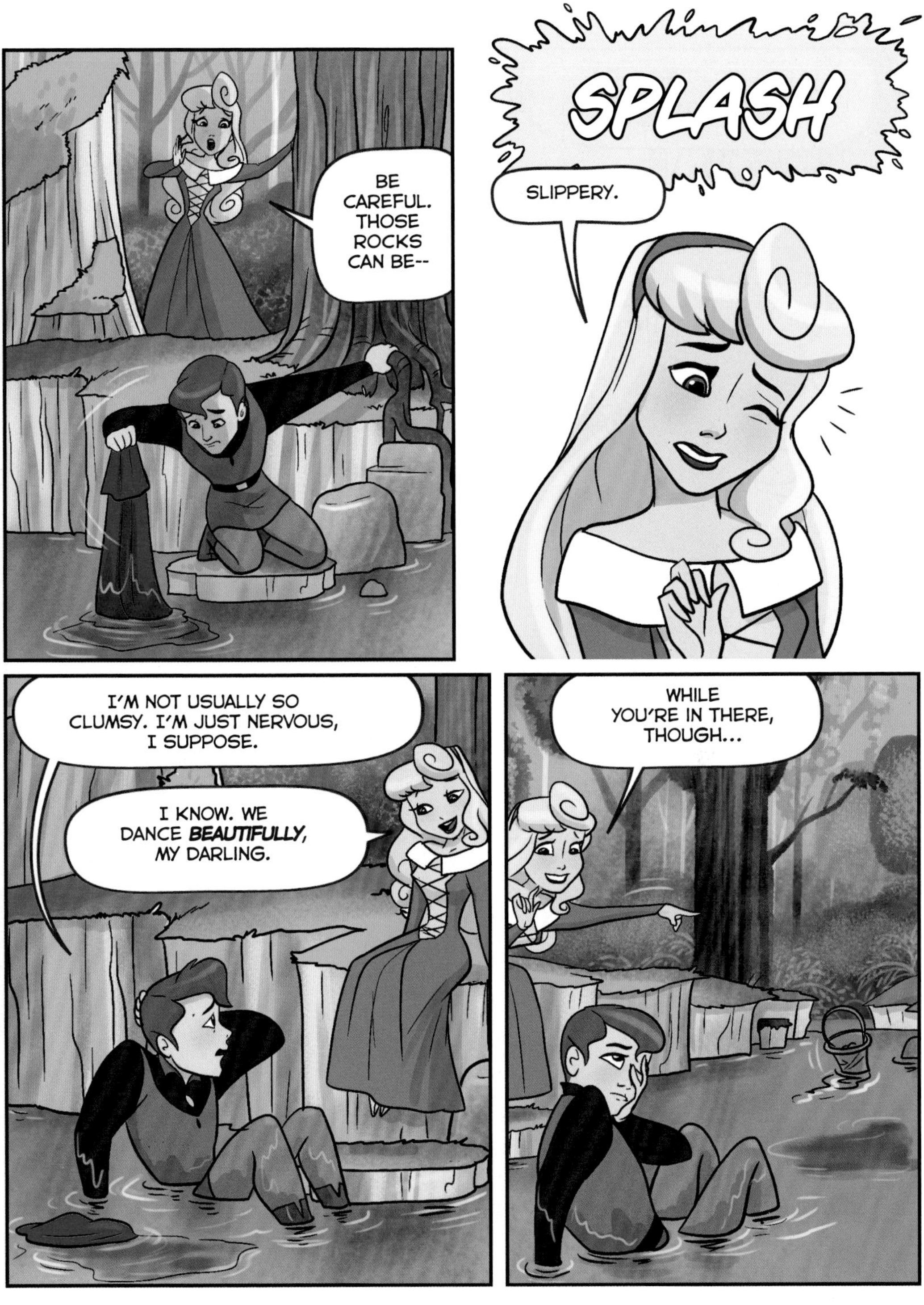
BE CAREFUL. THOSE ROCKS CAN BE--
SPLASH
SLIPPERY.
I'M NOT USUALLY SO CLUMSY. I'M JUST NERVOUS, I SUPPOSE.
I KNOW. WE DANCE **BEAUTIFULLY**, MY DARLING.
WHILE YOU'RE IN THERE, THOUGH...

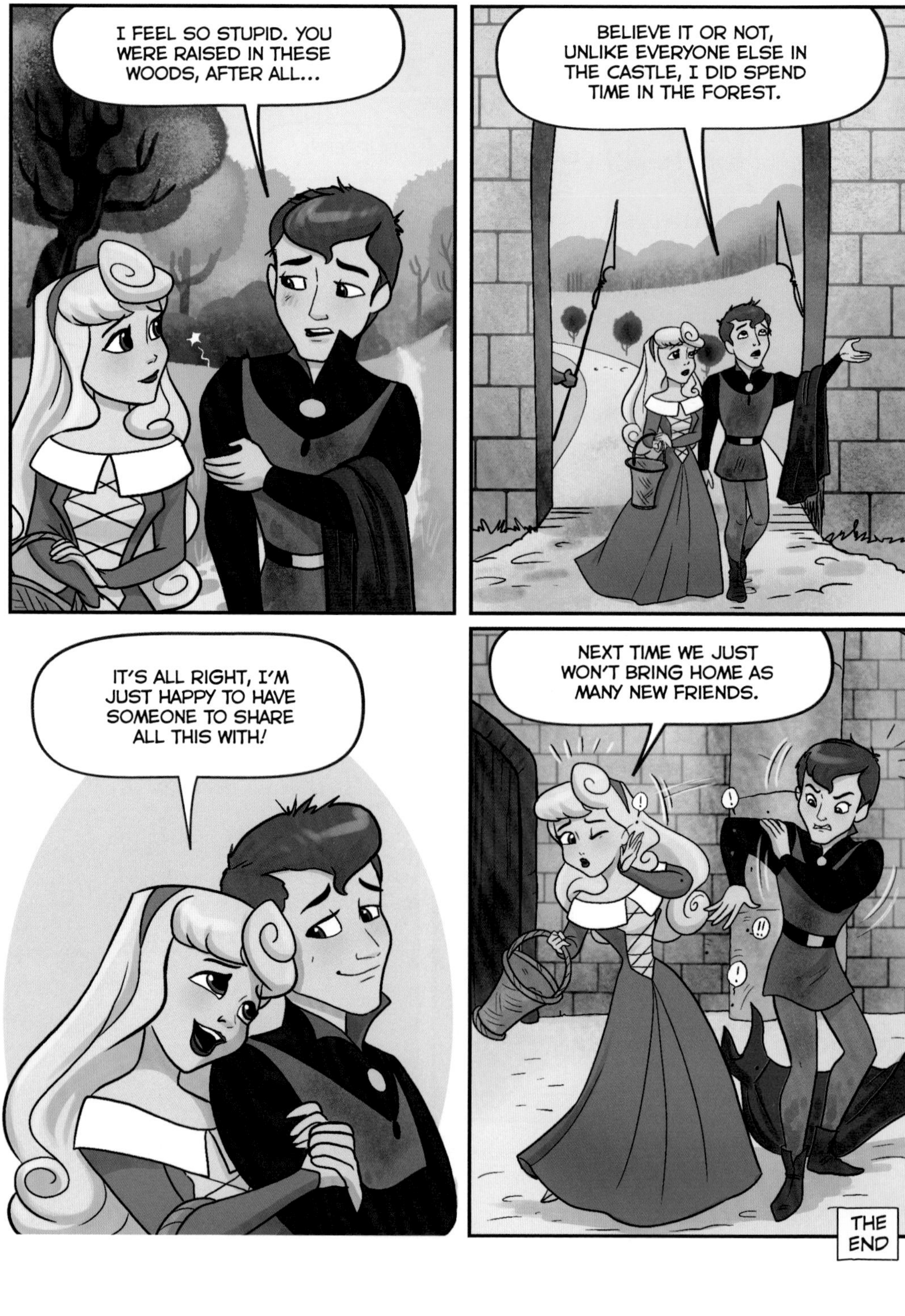
I FEEL SO STUPID. YOU WERE RAISED IN THESE WOODS, AFTER ALL...
BELIEVE IT OR NOT, UNLIKE EVERYONE ELSE IN THE CASTLE, I DID SPEND TIME IN THE FOREST.
IT'S ALL RIGHT, I'M JUST HAPPY TO HAVE SOMEONE TO SHARE ALL THIS WITH!
NEXT TIME WE JUST WON'T BRING HOME AS MANY NEW FRIENDS.
!
!
!!
!
THE END

# "BELLE'S DILEMMA"

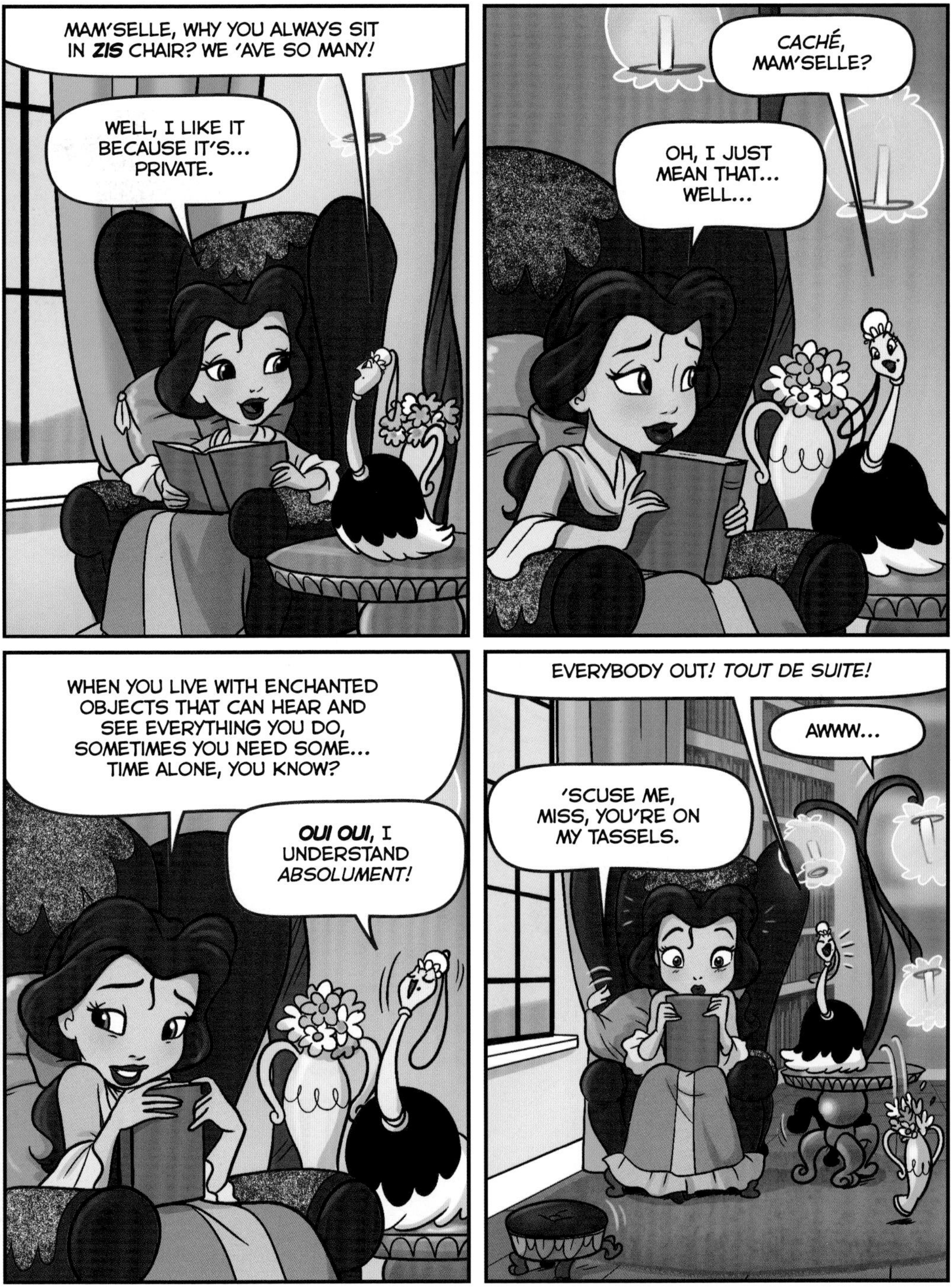
MAM'SELLE, WHY YOU ALWAYS SIT IN ZIS CHAIR? WE 'AVE SO MANY!
WELL, I LIKE IT BECAUSE IT'S... PRIVATE.
CACHÉ, MAM'SELLE?
OH, I JUST MEAN THAT... WELL...
WHEN YOU LIVE WITH ENCHANTED OBJECTS THAT CAN HEAR AND SEE EVERYTHING YOU DO, SOMETIMES YOU NEED SOME... TIME ALONE, YOU KNOW?
OUI OUI, I UNDERSTAND ABSOLUMENT!
EVERYBODY OUT! TOUT DE SUITE!
AWWW...
'SCUSE ME, MISS, YOU'RE ON MY TASSELS.

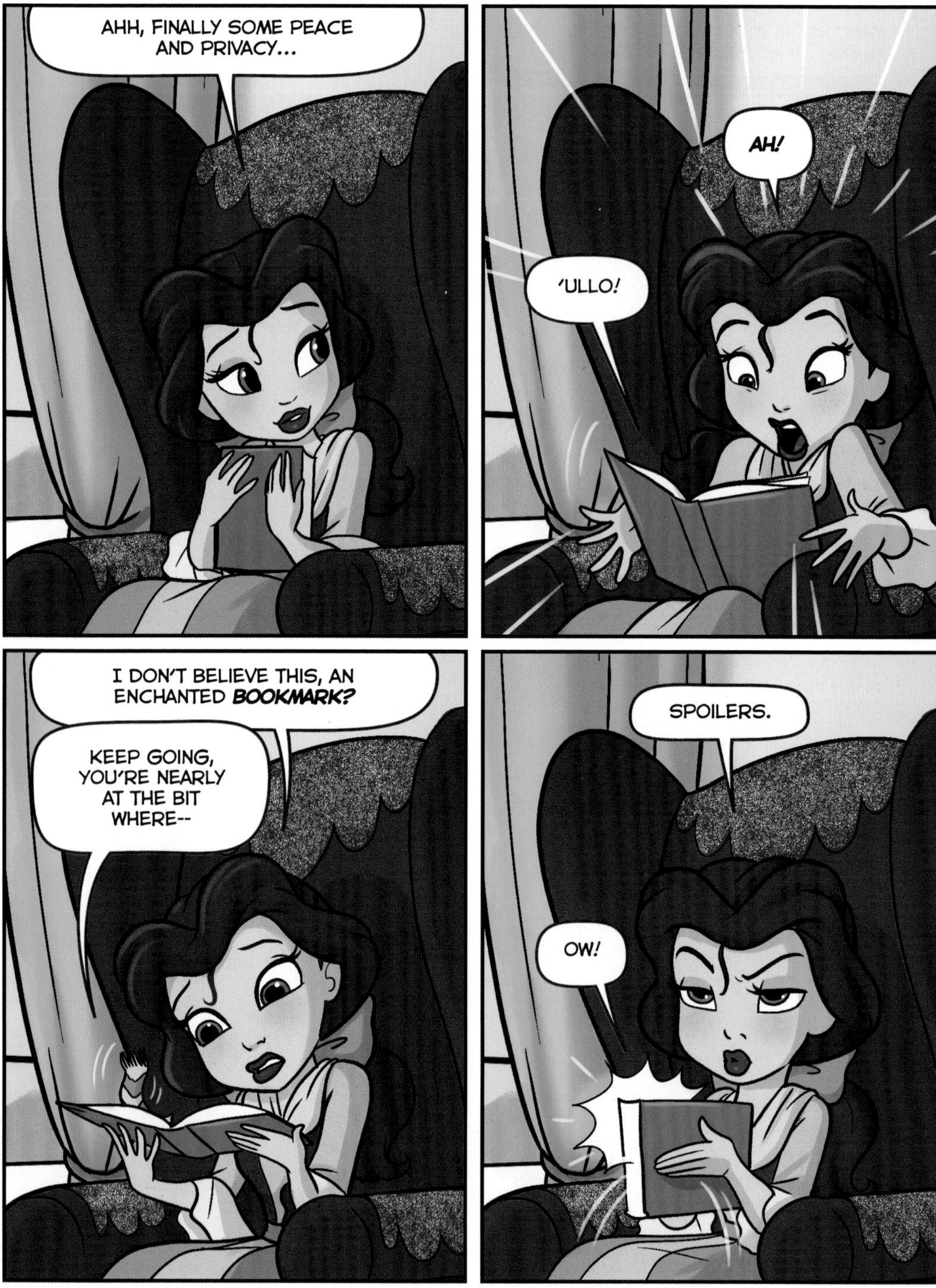
AHH, FINALLY SOME PEACE AND PRIVACY...
AH!
'ULLO!
I DON'T BELIEVE THIS, AN ENCHANTED BOOKMARK?
KEEP GOING, YOU'RE NEARLY AT THE BIT WHERE--
SPOILERS.
OW!

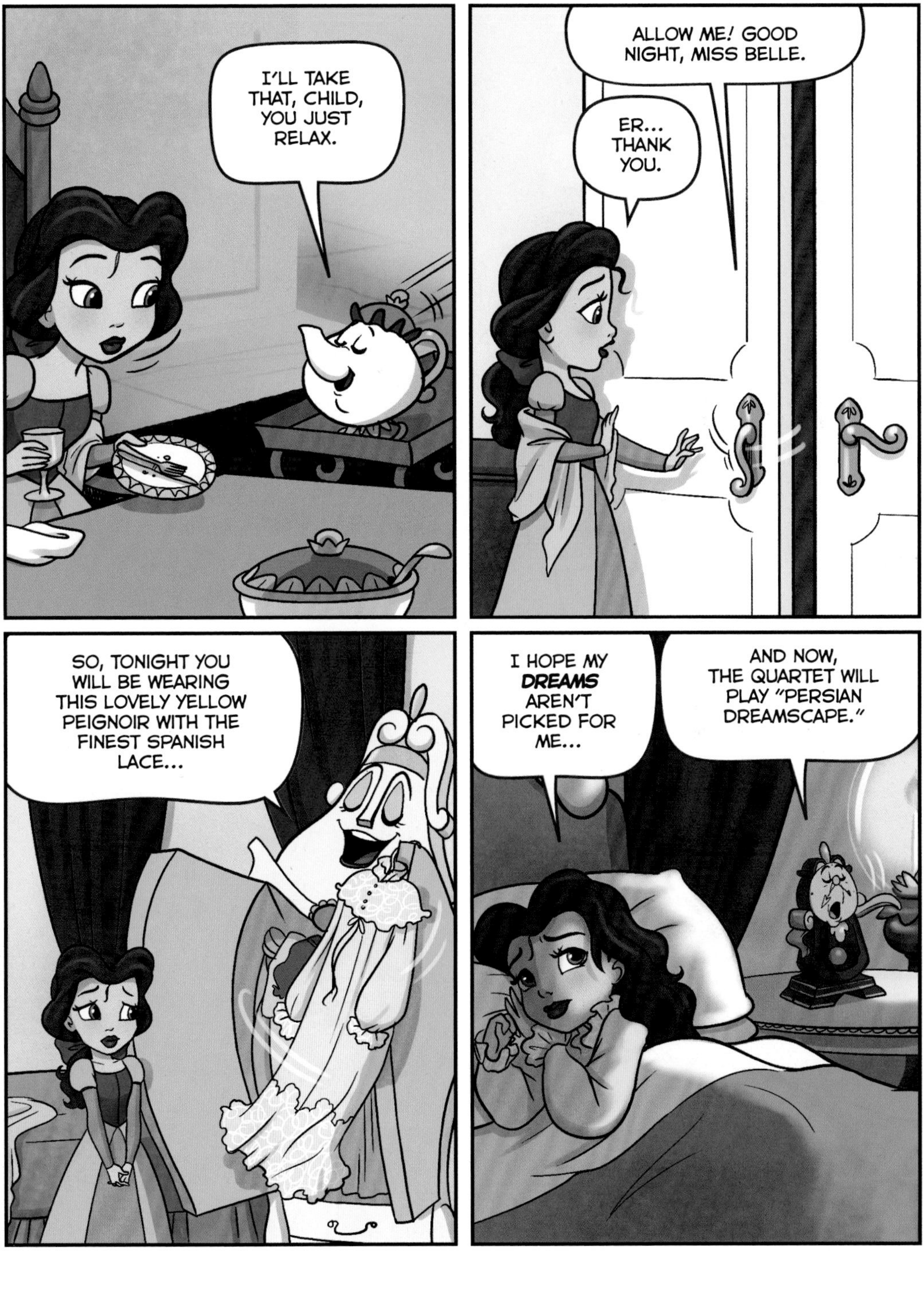
I'LL TAKE THAT, CHILD, YOU JUST RELAX.
ALLOW ME! GOOD NIGHT, MISS BELLE.
ER... THANK YOU.
SO, TONIGHT YOU WILL BE WEARING THIS LOVELY YELLOW PEIGNOIR WITH THE FINEST SPANISH LACE...
I HOPE MY **DREAMS** AREN'T PICKED FOR ME...
AND NOW, THE QUARTET WILL PLAY "PERSIAN DREAMSCAPE."

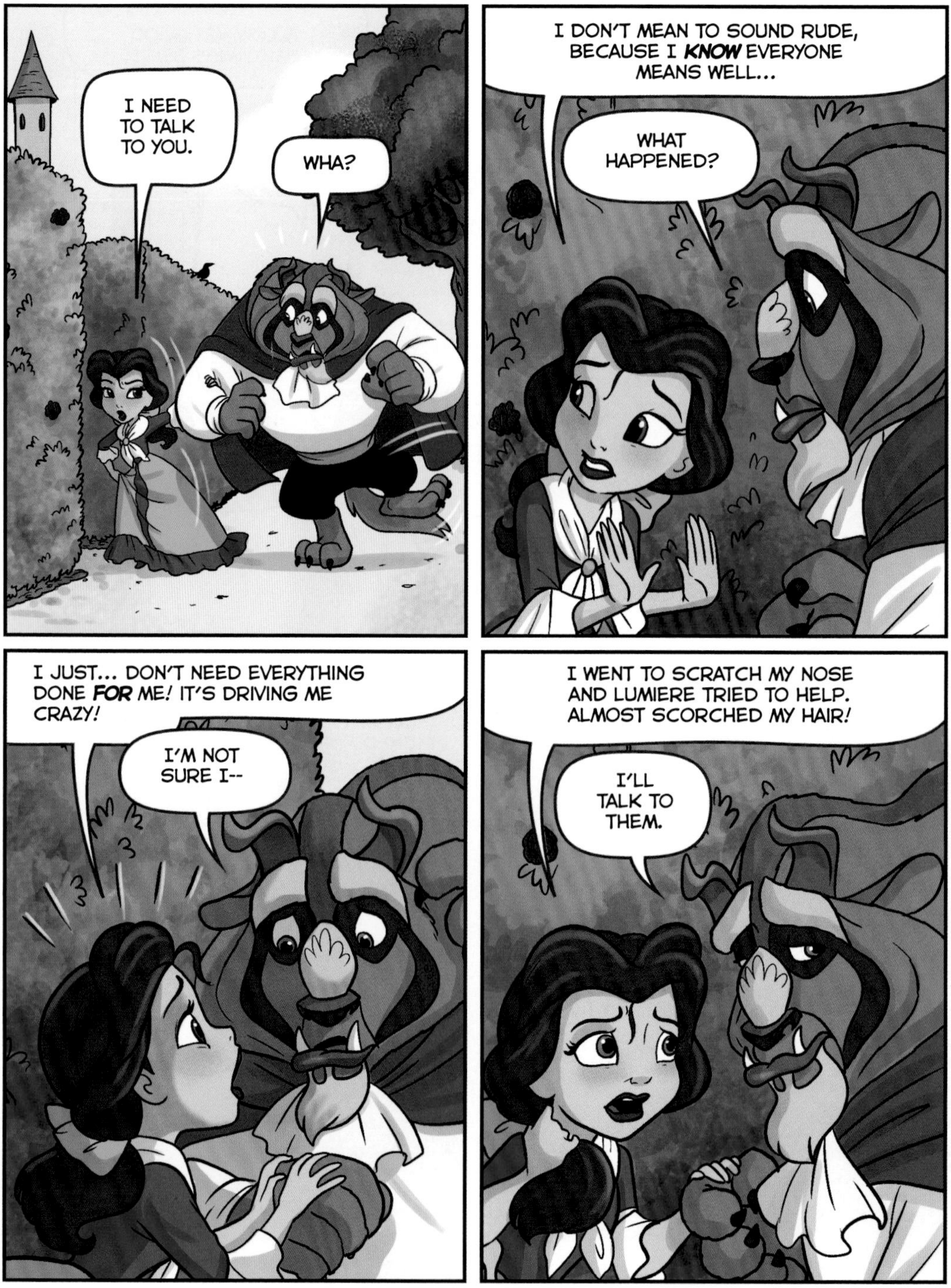
I NEED TO TALK TO YOU.
WHA?
I DON'T MEAN TO SOUND RUDE, BECAUSE I **KNOW** EVERYONE MEANS WELL...
WHAT HAPPENED?
I JUST... DON'T NEED EVERYTHING DONE **FOR** ME! IT'S DRIVING ME CRAZY!
I'M NOT SURE I--
I WENT TO SCRATCH MY NOSE AND LUMIERE TRIED TO HELP. ALMOST SCORCHED MY HAIR!
I'LL TALK TO THEM.

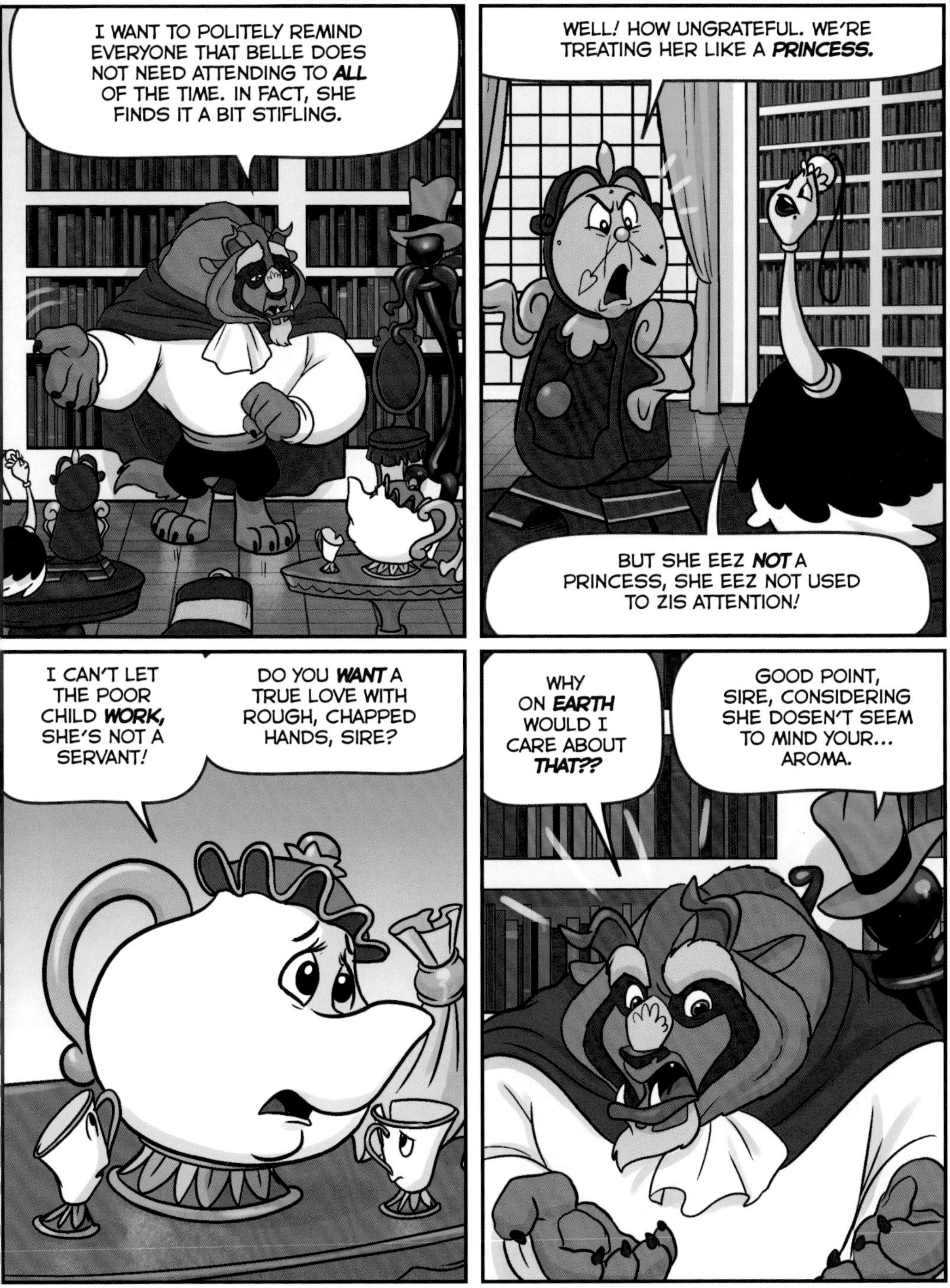
I WANT TO POLITELY REMIND EVERYONE THAT BELLE DOES NOT NEED ATTENDING TO ALL OF THE TIME. IN FACT, SHE FINDS IT A BIT STIFLING.
WELL! HOW UNGRATEFUL. WE'RE TREATING HER LIKE A PRINCESS.
BUT SHE EEZ NOT A PRINCESS, SHE EEZ NOT USED TO ZIS ATTENTION!
I CAN'T LET THE POOR CHILD WORK, SHE'S NOT A SERVANT!
DO YOU WANT A TRUE LOVE WITH ROUGH, CHAPPED HANDS, SIRE?
WHY ON EARTH WOULD I CARE ABOUT THAT??
GOOD POINT, SIRE, CONSIDERING SHE DOSEN'T SEEM TO MIND YOUR... AROMA.

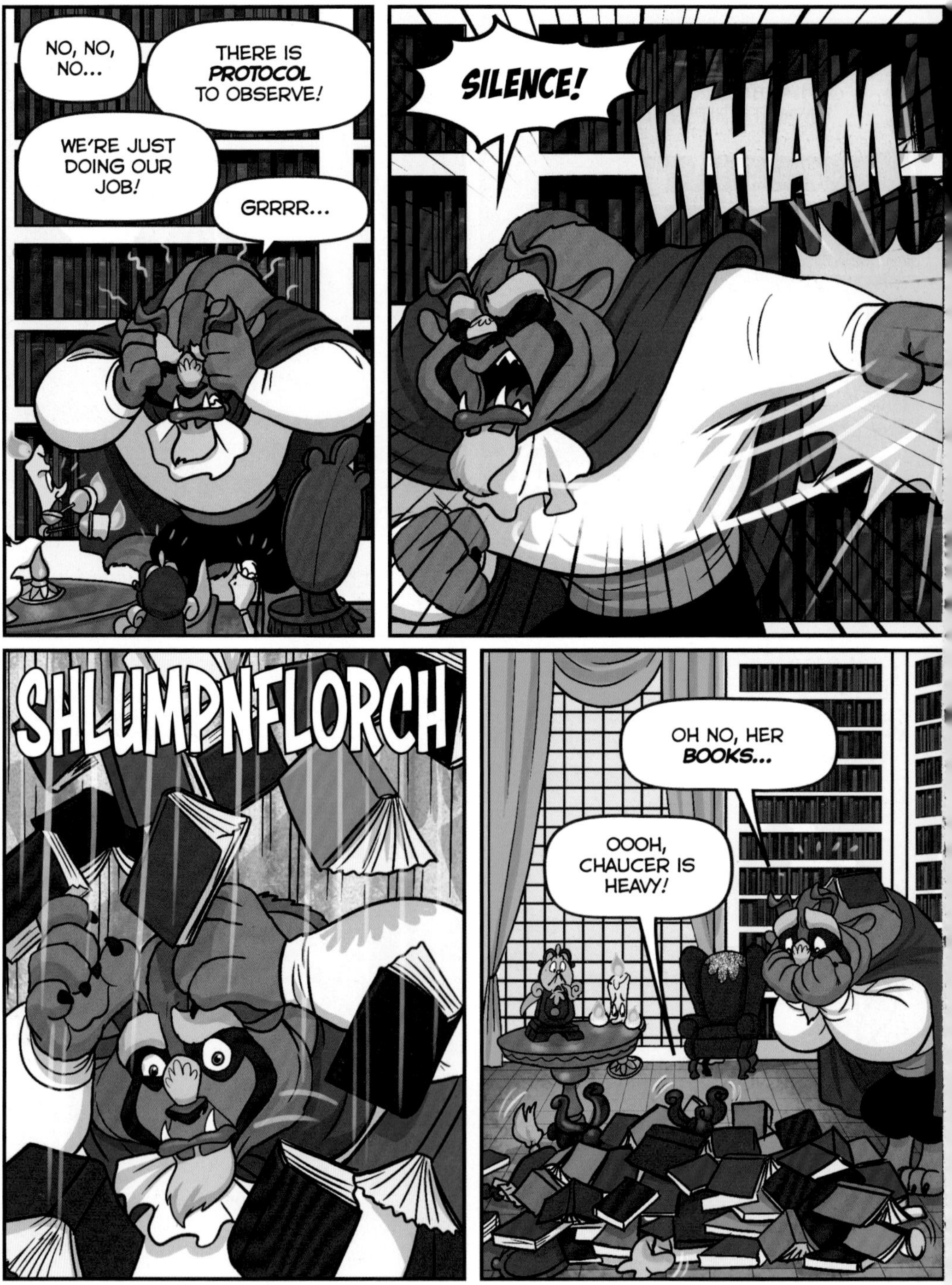
NO, NO, NO...
THERE IS PROTOCOL TO OBSERVE!
WE'RE JUST DOING OUR JOB!
GRRRR...
SILENCE!
WHAM
SHLUMPNFLORCH
OH NO, HER BOOKS...
OOOH, CHAUCER IS HEAVY!

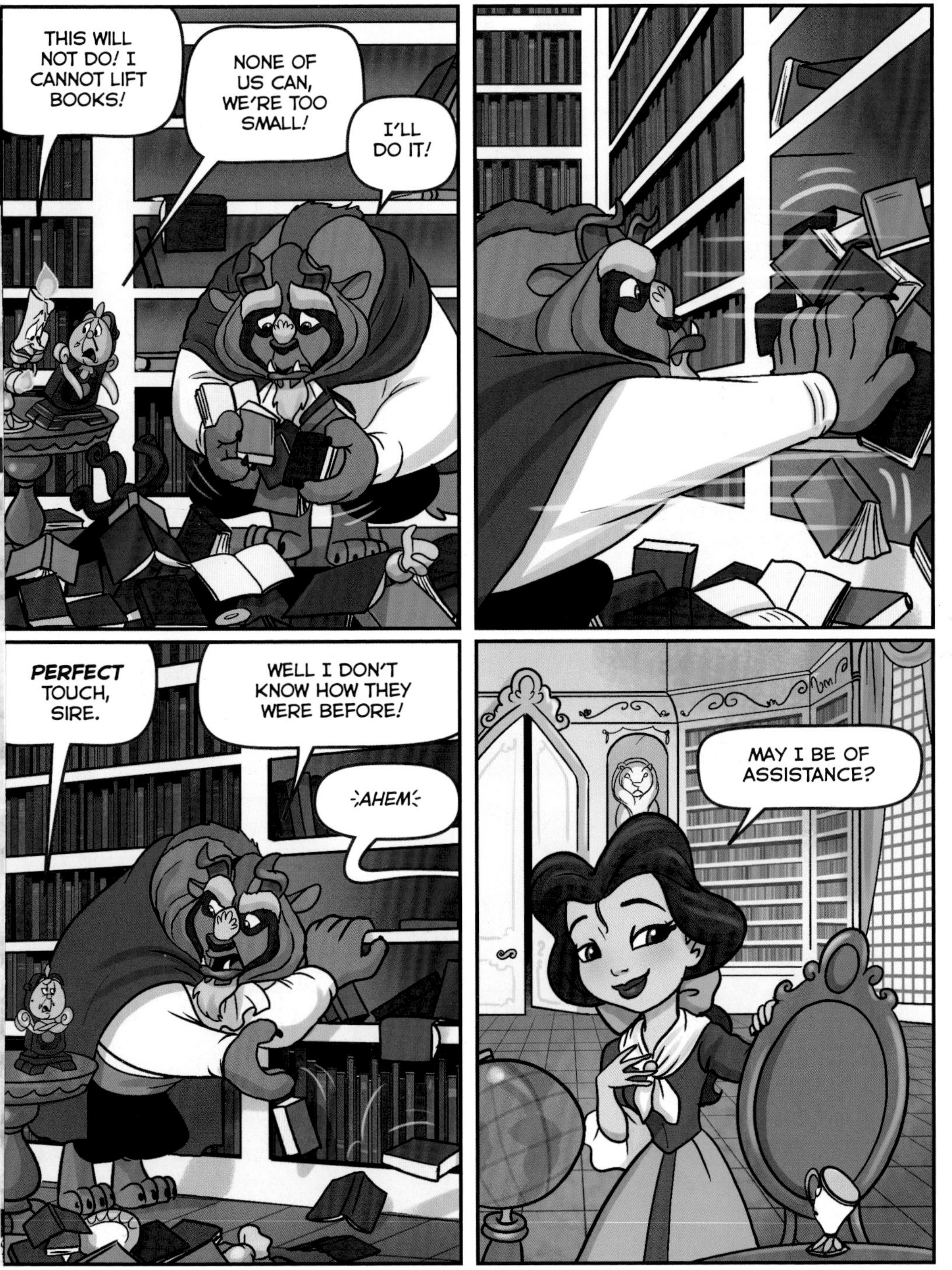
THIS WILL NOT DO! I CANNOT LIFT BOOKS!
NONE OF US CAN, WE'RE TOO SMALL!
I'LL DO IT!
PERFECT TOUCH, SIRE.
WELL I DON'T KNOW HOW THEY WERE BEFORE!
AHEM
MAY I BE OF ASSISTANCE?

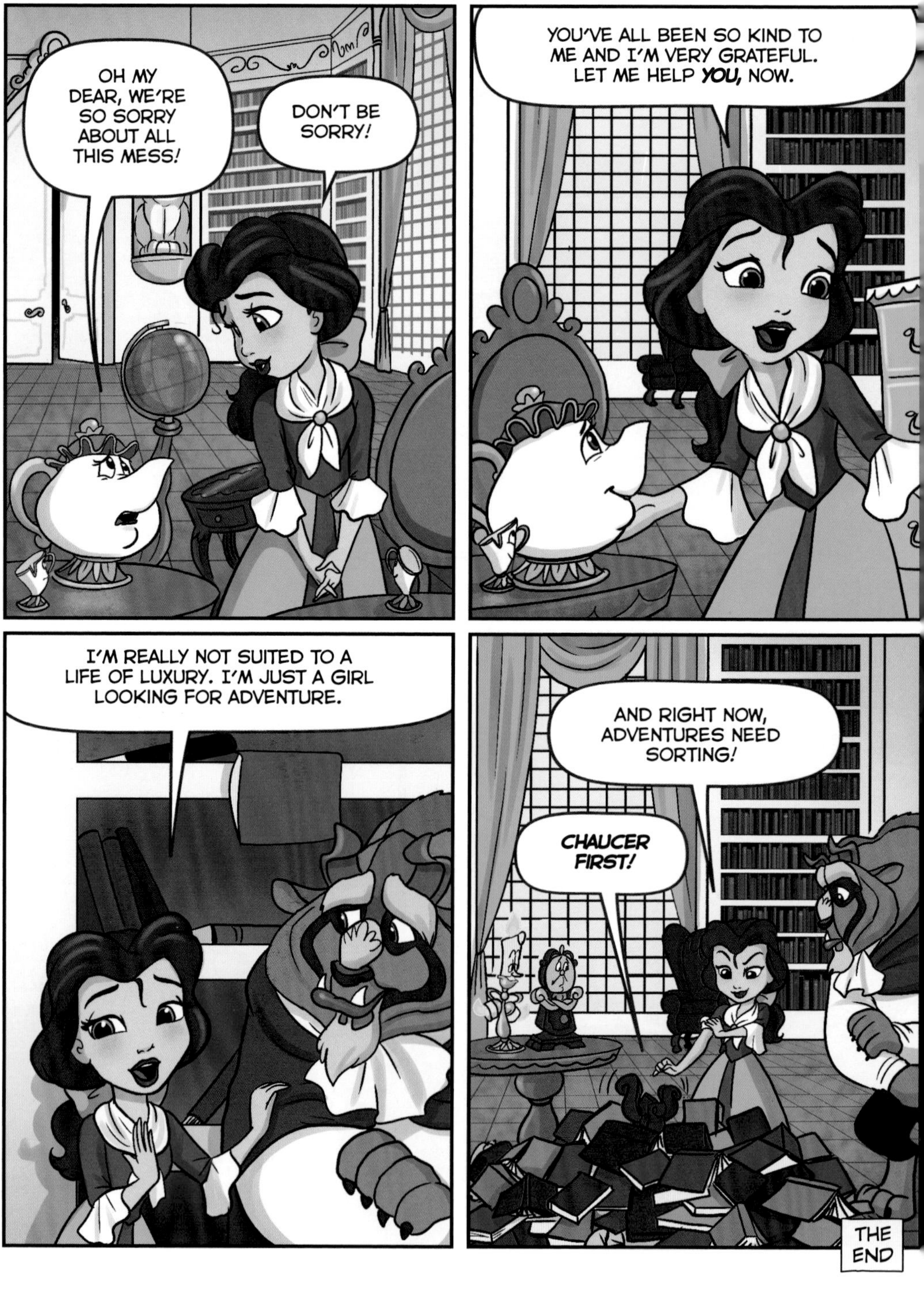
OH MY DEAR, WE'RE SO SORRY ABOUT ALL THIS MESS!
DON'T BE SORRY!
YOU'VE ALL BEEN SO KIND TO ME AND I'M VERY GRATEFUL. LET ME HELP ***YOU,*** NOW.
I'M REALLY NOT SUITED TO A LIFE OF LUXURY. I'M JUST A GIRL LOOKING FOR ADVENTURE.
AND RIGHT NOW, ADVENTURES NEED SORTING!
***CHAUCER FIRST!***
THE END

# "MEDITATION TRAINING"

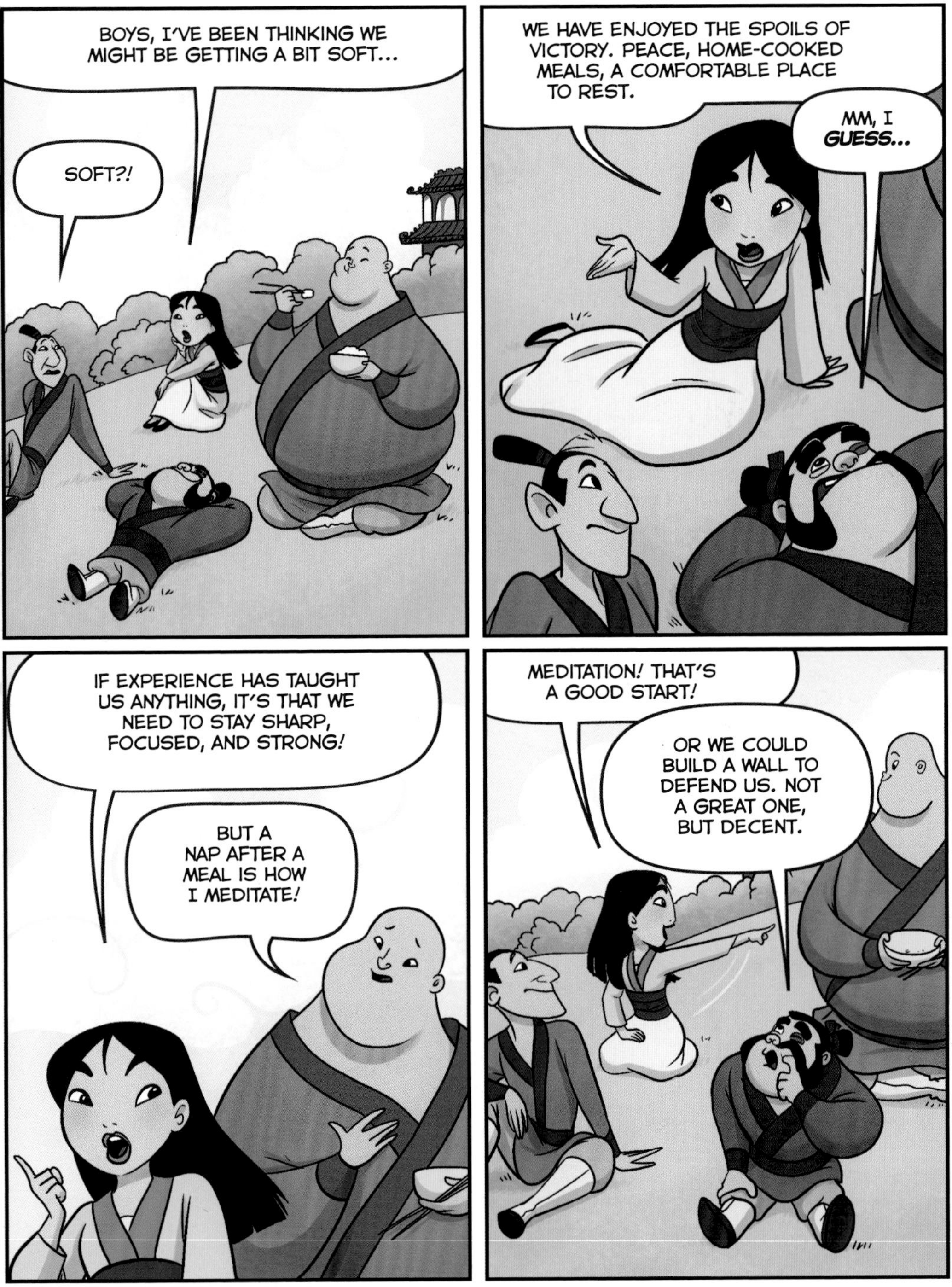
BOYS, I'VE BEEN THINKING WE MIGHT BE GETTING A BIT SOFT...
SOFT?!
WE HAVE ENJOYED THE SPOILS OF VICTORY. PEACE, HOME-COOKED MEALS, A COMFORTABLE PLACE TO REST.
MM, I **GUESS...**
IF EXPERIENCE HAS TAUGHT US ANYTHING, IT'S THAT WE NEED TO STAY SHARP, FOCUSED, AND STRONG!
BUT A NAP AFTER A MEAL IS HOW I MEDITATE!
MEDITATION! THAT'S A GOOD START!
OR WE COULD BUILD A WALL TO DEFEND US. NOT A GREAT ONE, BUT DECENT.

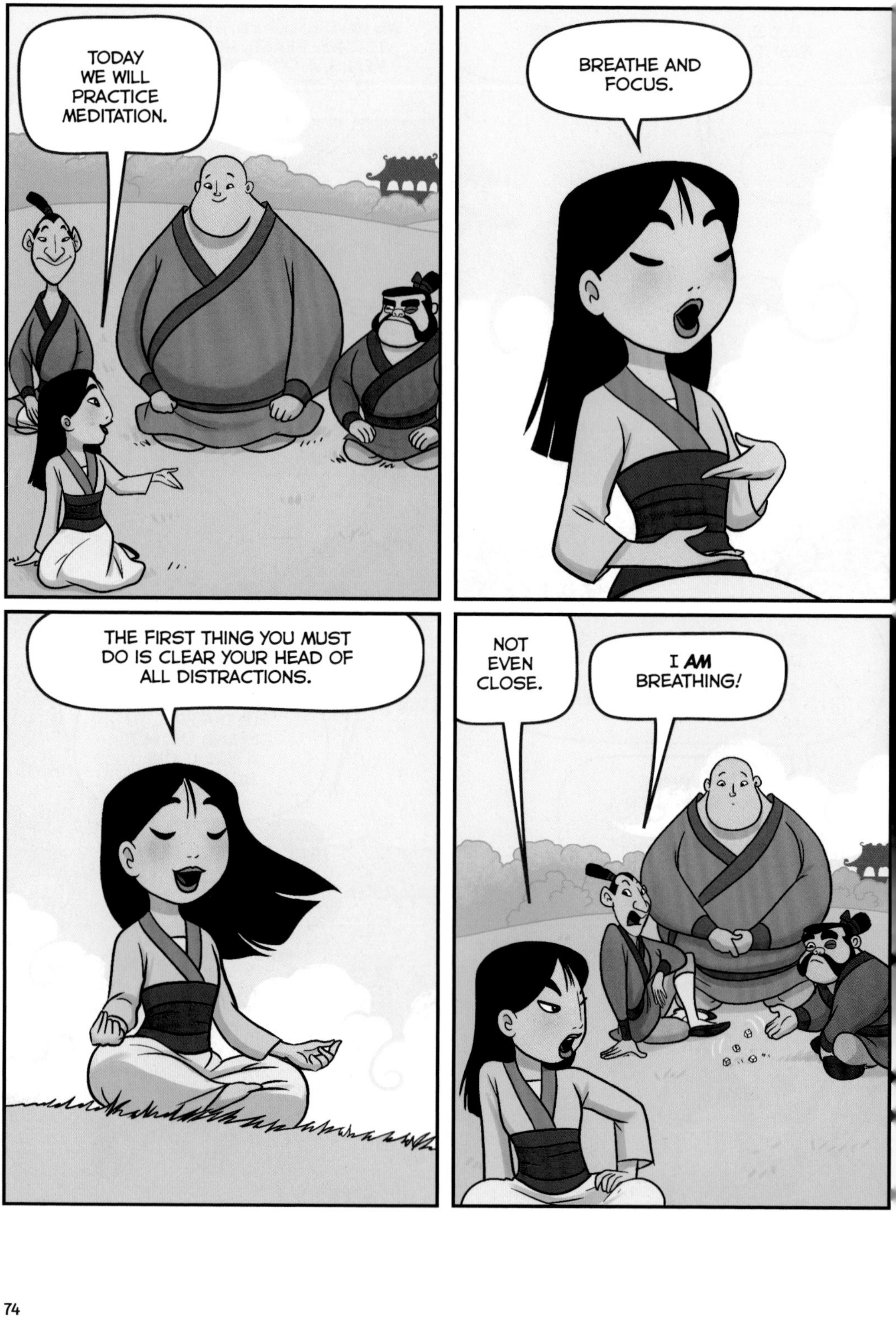
TODAY WE WILL PRACTICE MEDITATION.
BREATHE AND FOCUS.
THE FIRST THING YOU MUST DO IS CLEAR YOUR HEAD OF ALL DISTRACTIONS.
NOT EVEN CLOSE.
I AM BREATHING!

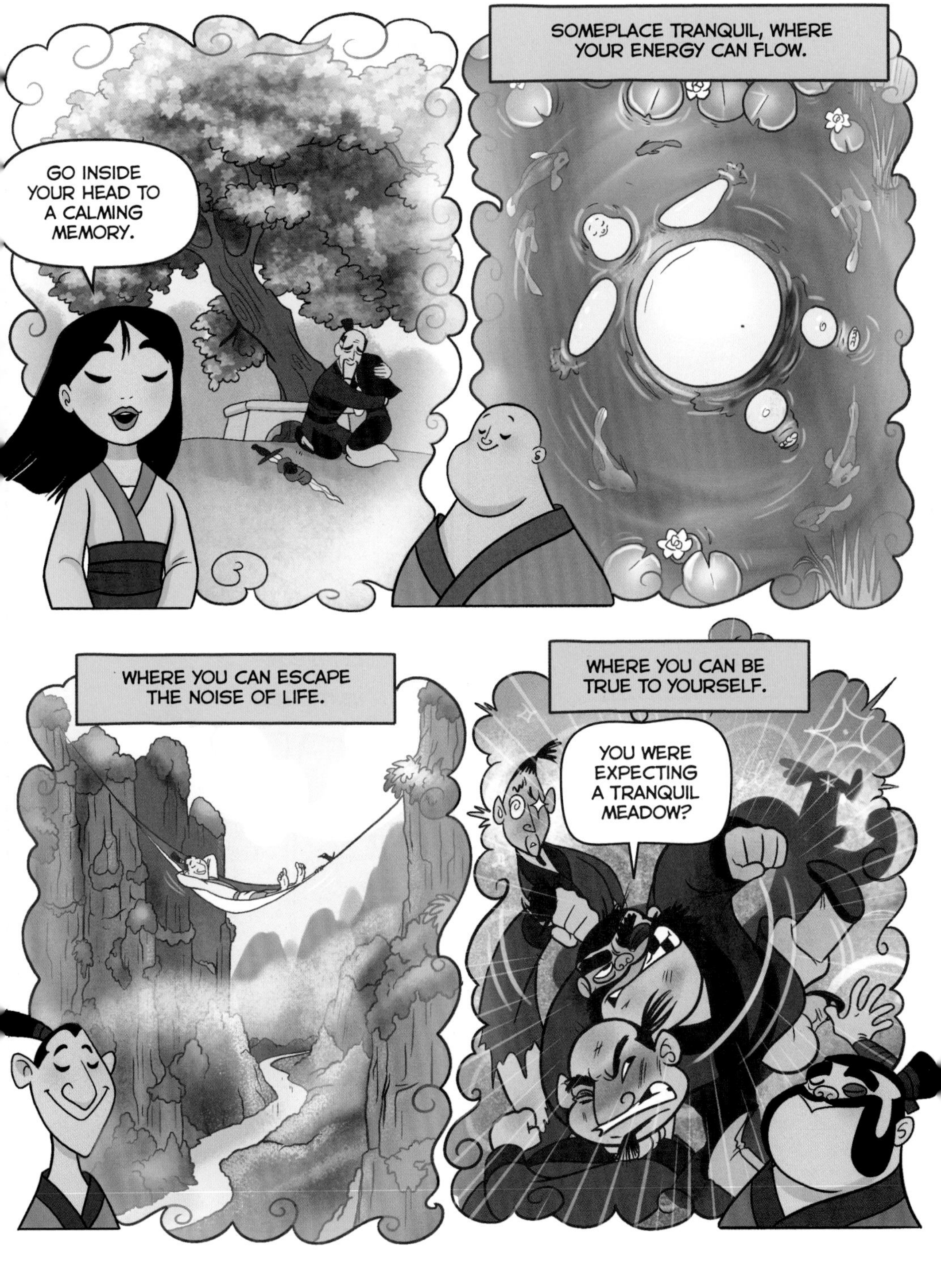
GO INSIDE YOUR HEAD TO A CALMING MEMORY.
SOMEPLACE TRANQUIL, WHERE YOUR ENERGY CAN FLOW.
WHERE YOU CAN ESCAPE THE NOISE OF LIFE.
WHERE YOU CAN BE TRUE TO YOURSELF.
YOU WERE EXPECTING A TRANQUIL MEADOW?

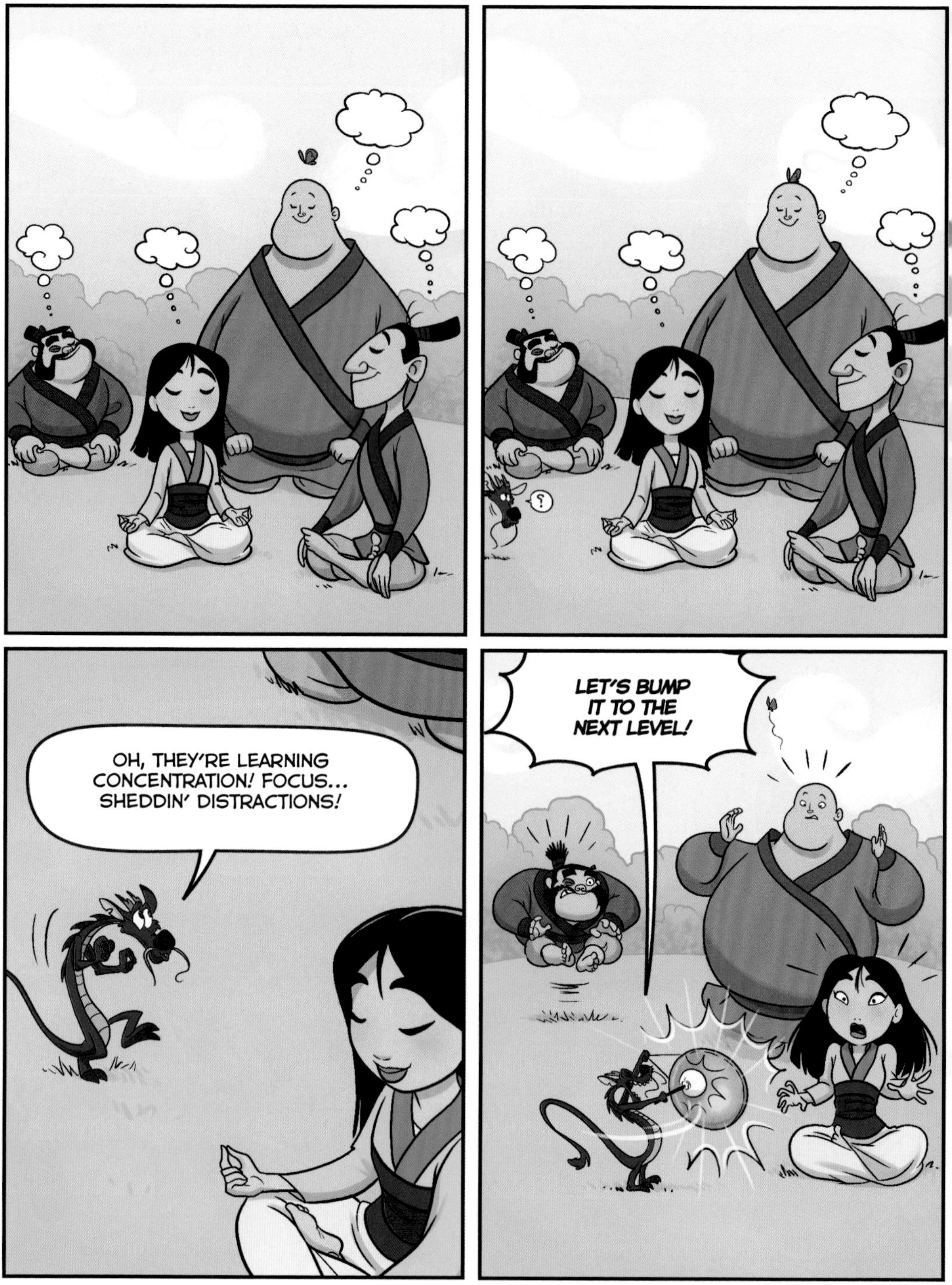
?
OH, THEY'RE LEARNING CONCENTRATION! FOCUS... SHEDDIN' DISTRACTIONS!
LET'S BUMP IT TO THE NEXT LEVEL!

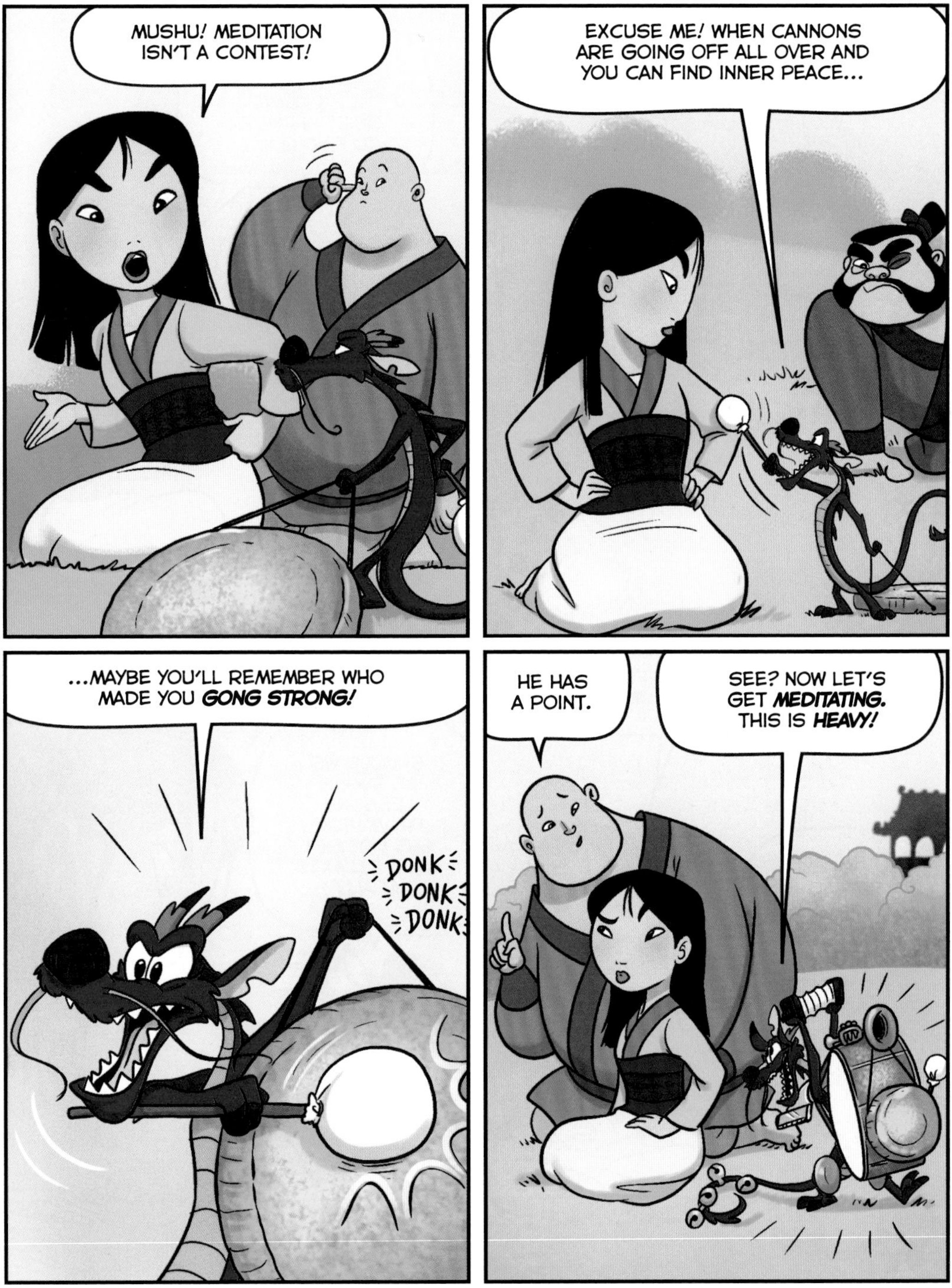
MUSHU! MEDITATION ISN'T A CONTEST!
EXCUSE ME! WHEN CANNONS ARE GOING OFF ALL OVER AND YOU CAN FIND INNER PEACE...
...MAYBE YOU'LL REMEMBER WHO MADE YOU **GONG STRONG!**
DONK DONK DONK
HE HAS A POINT.
SEE? NOW LET'S GET **MEDITATING.** THIS IS **HEAVY!**

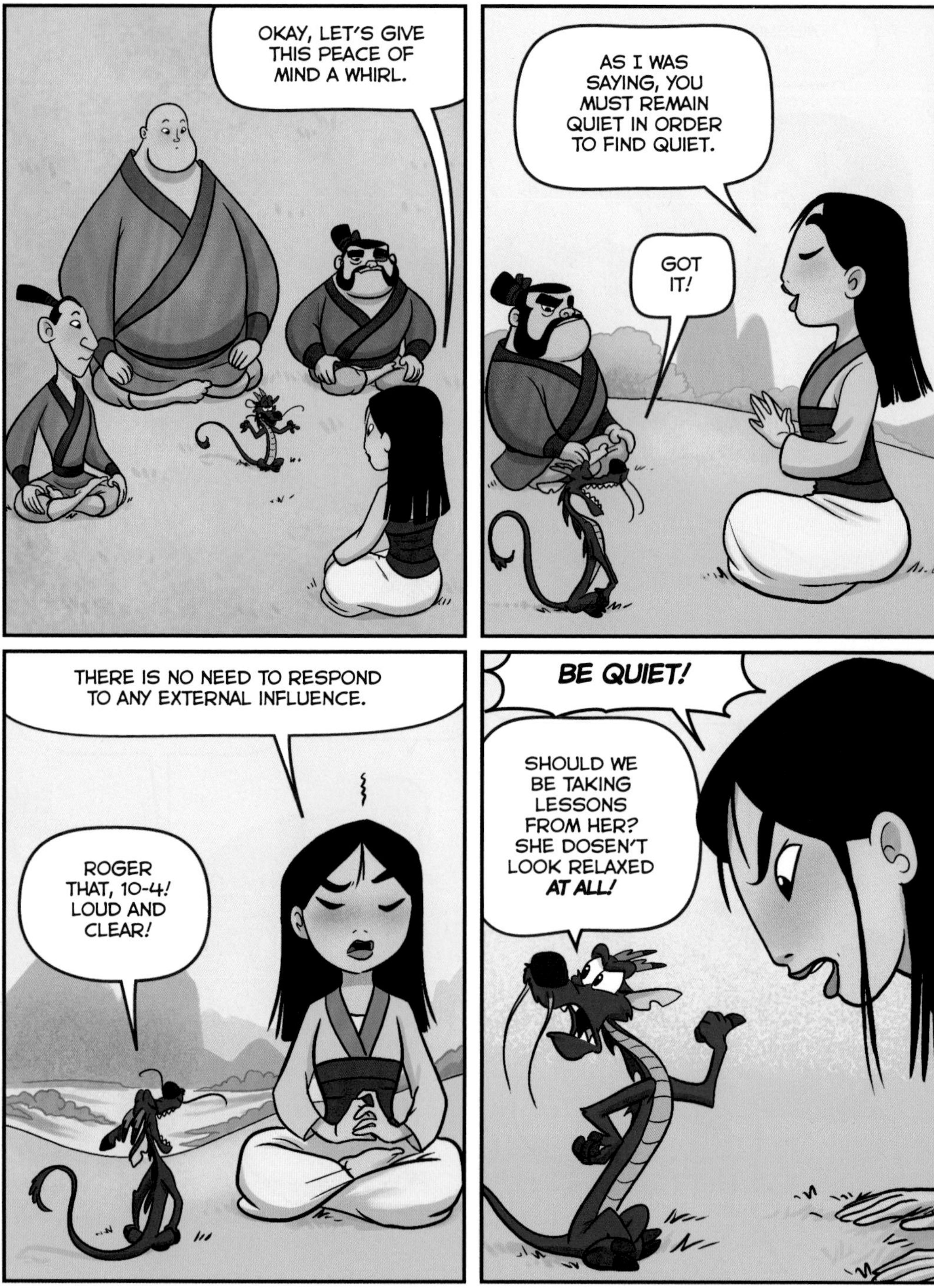
OKAY, LET'S GIVE THIS PEACE OF MIND A WHIRL.
AS I WAS SAYING, YOU MUST REMAIN QUIET IN ORDER TO FIND QUIET.
GOT IT!
THERE IS NO NEED TO RESPOND TO ANY EXTERNAL INFLUENCE.
ROGER THAT, 10-4! LOUD AND CLEAR!
BE QUIET!
SHOULD WE BE TAKING LESSONS FROM HER? SHE DOSEN'T LOOK RELAXED *AT ALL!*

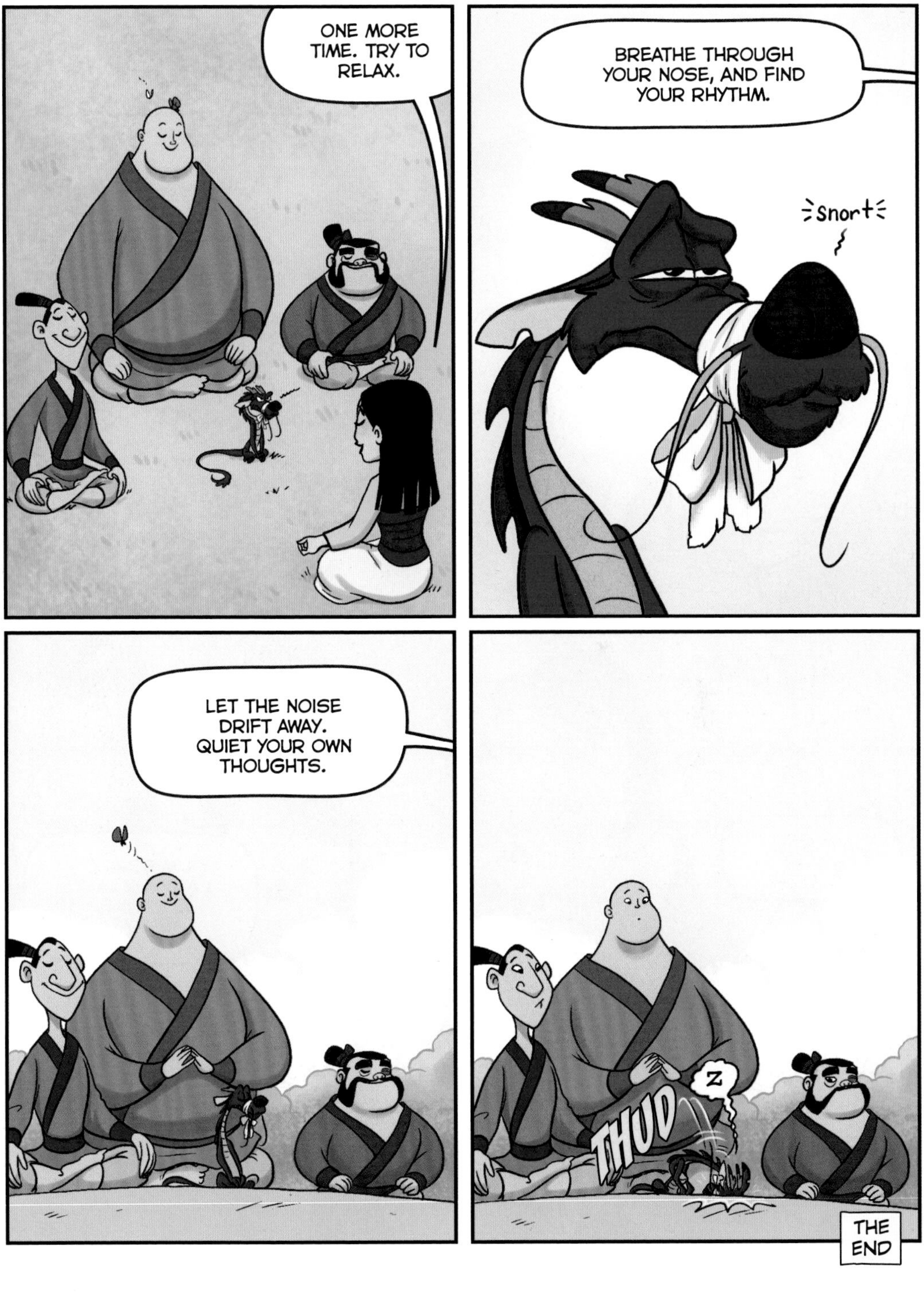
ONE MORE TIME. TRY TO RELAX.
BREATHE THROUGH YOUR NOSE, AND FIND YOUR RHYTHM.
Snort
LET THE NOISE DRIFT AWAY. QUIET YOUR OWN THOUGHTS.
Z
THUD
THE END

# "A DISH SERVED COLD"

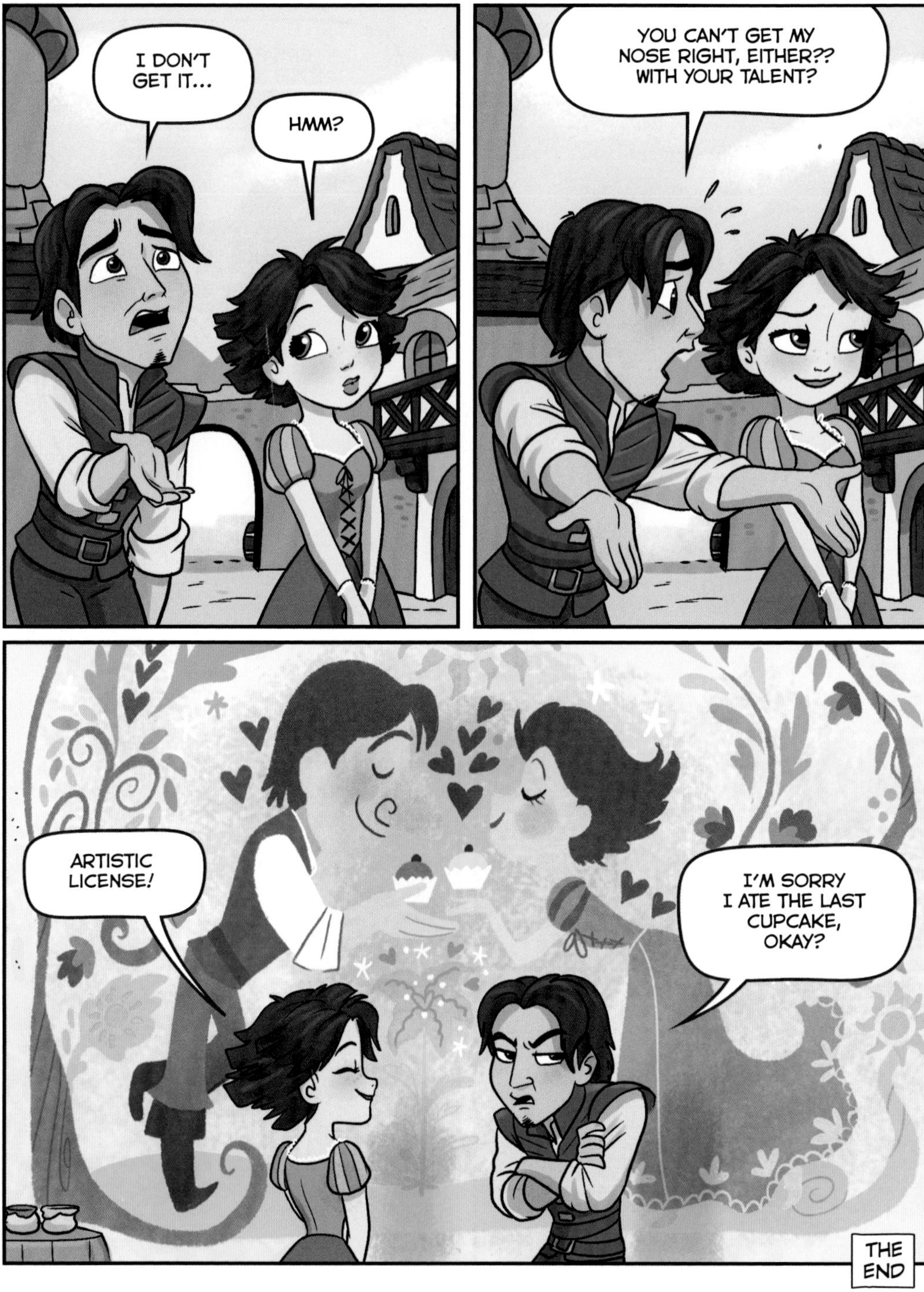
I DON'T GET IT...
HMM?
YOU CAN'T GET MY NOSE RIGHT, EITHER?? WITH YOUR TALENT?
ARTISTIC LICENSE!
I'M SORRY I ATE THE LAST CUPCAKE, OKAY?
THE END

# "TRYOUTS"

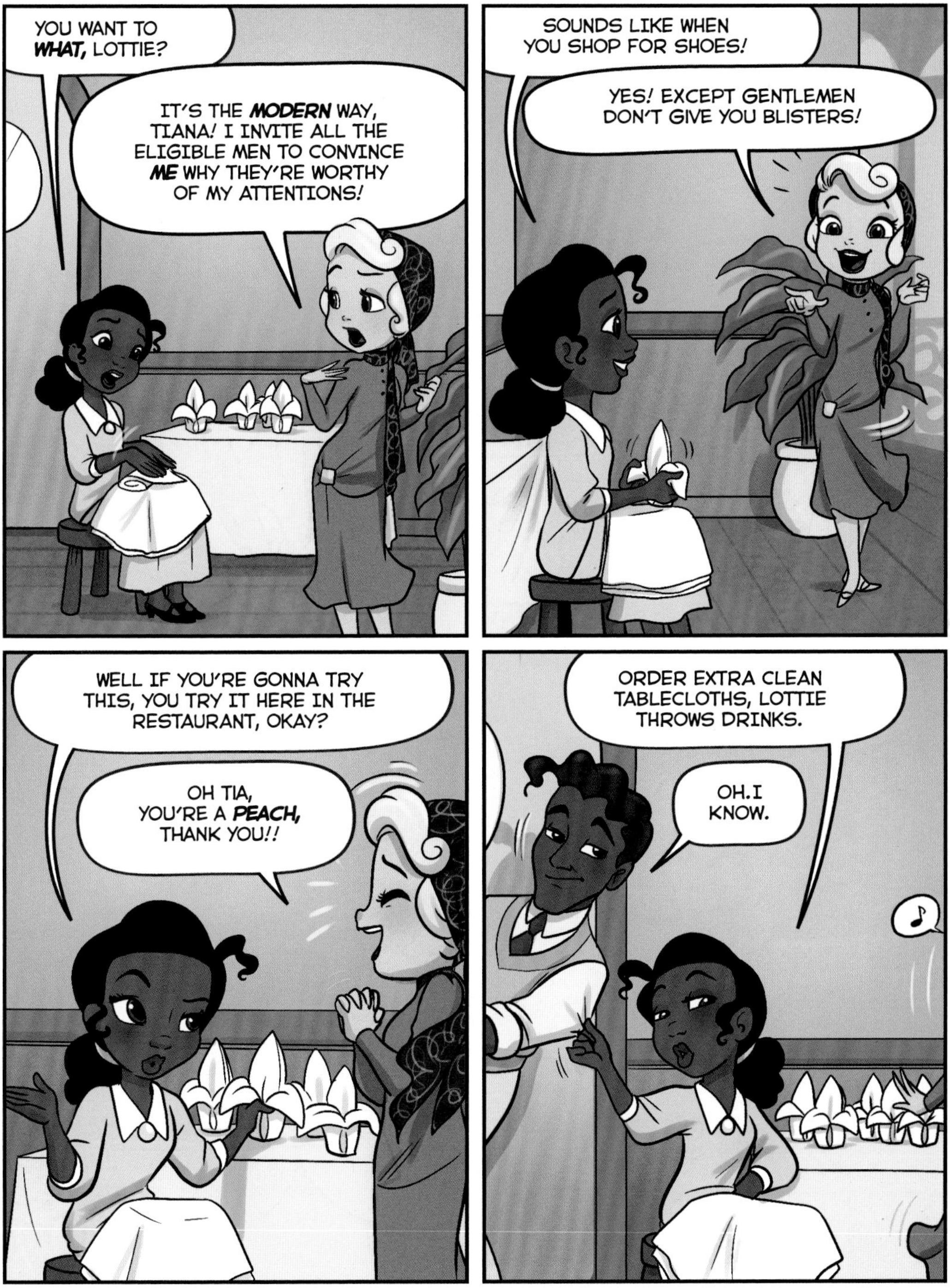

YOU WANT TO **WHAT,** LOTTIE?
IT'S THE **MODERN** WAY, TIANA! I INVITE ALL THE ELIGIBLE MEN TO CONVINCE **ME** WHY THEY'RE WORTHY OF MY ATTENTIONS!
SOUNDS LIKE WHEN YOU SHOP FOR SHOES!
YES! EXCEPT GENTLEMEN DON'T GIVE YOU BLISTERS!
WELL IF YOU'RE GONNA TRY THIS, YOU TRY IT HERE IN THE RESTAURANT, OKAY?
OH TIA, YOU'RE A **PEACH,** THANK YOU!!
ORDER EXTRA CLEAN TABLECLOTHS, LOTTIE THROWS DRINKS.
OH. I KNOW.

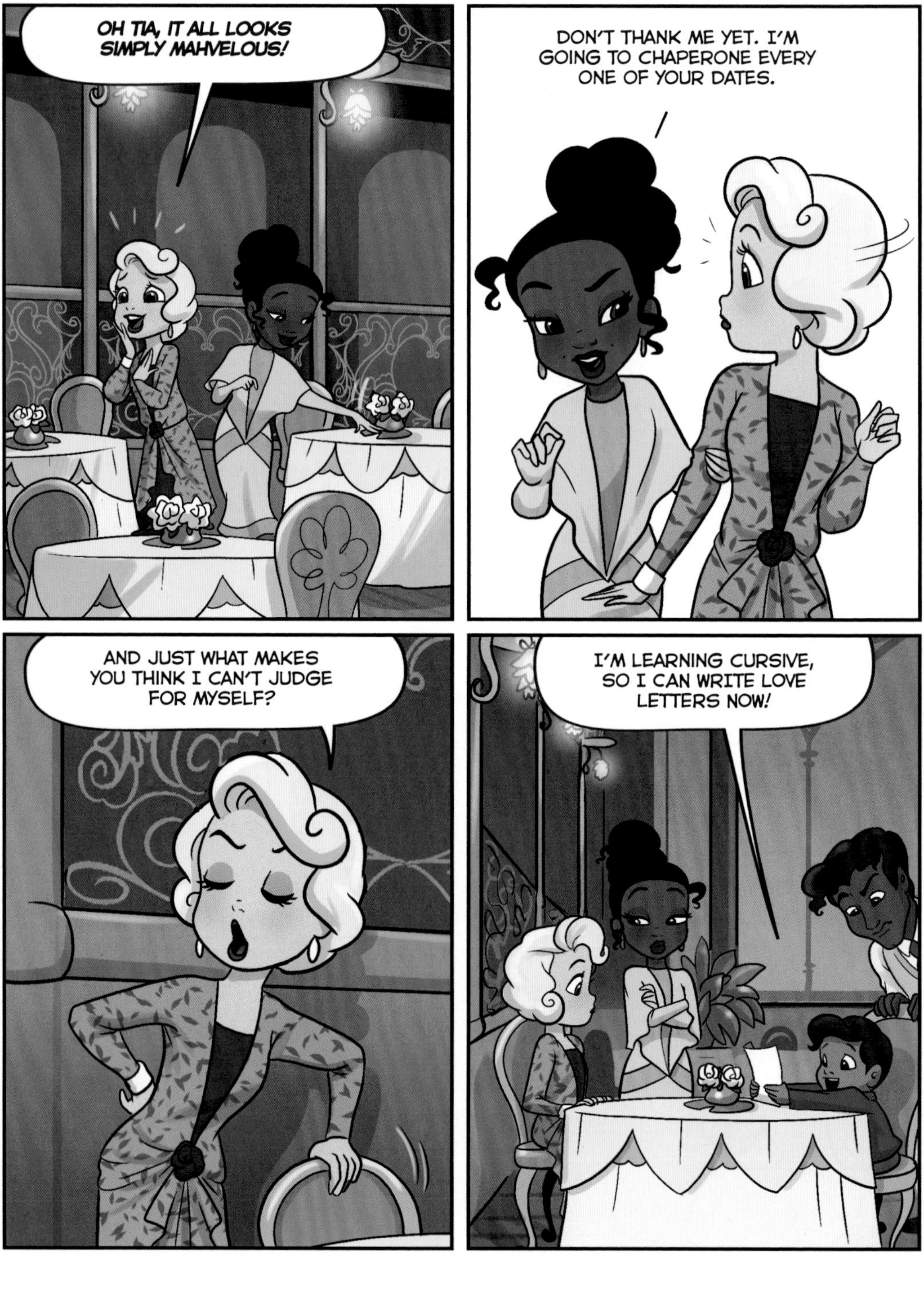
OH TIA, IT ALL LOOKS SIMPLY MAHVELOUS!
DON'T THANK ME YET. I'M GOING TO CHAPERONE EVERY ONE OF YOUR DATES.
AND JUST WHAT MAKES YOU THINK I CAN'T JUDGE FOR MYSELF?
I'M LEARNING CURSIVE, SO I CAN WRITE LOVE LETTERS NOW!

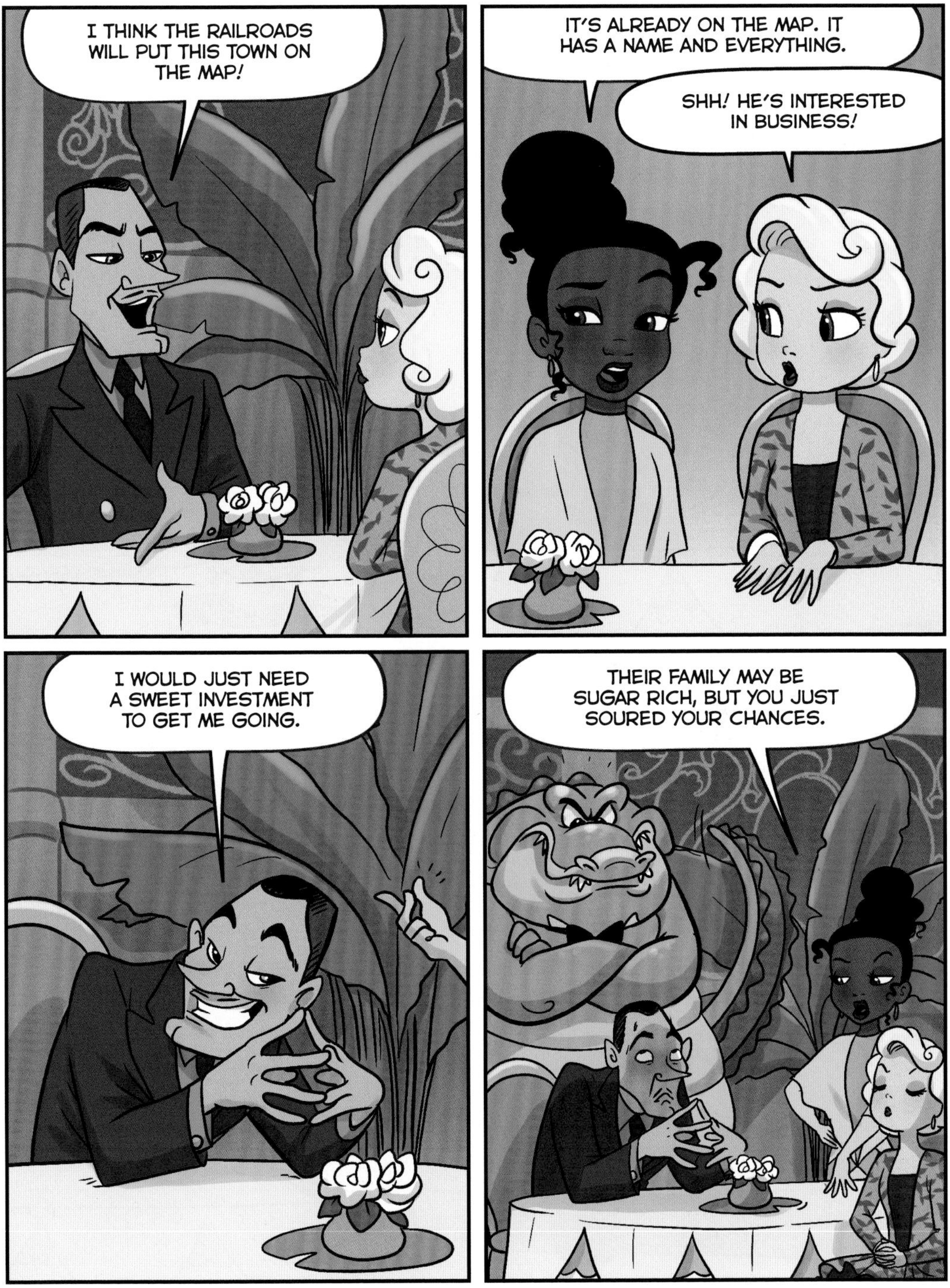
I THINK THE RAILROADS WILL PUT THIS TOWN ON THE MAP!
IT'S ALREADY ON THE MAP. IT HAS A NAME AND EVERYTHING.
SHH! HE'S INTERESTED IN BUSINESS!
I WOULD JUST NEED A SWEET INVESTMENT TO GET ME GOING.
THEIR FAMILY MAY BE SUGAR RICH, BUT YOU JUST SOURED YOUR CHANCES.

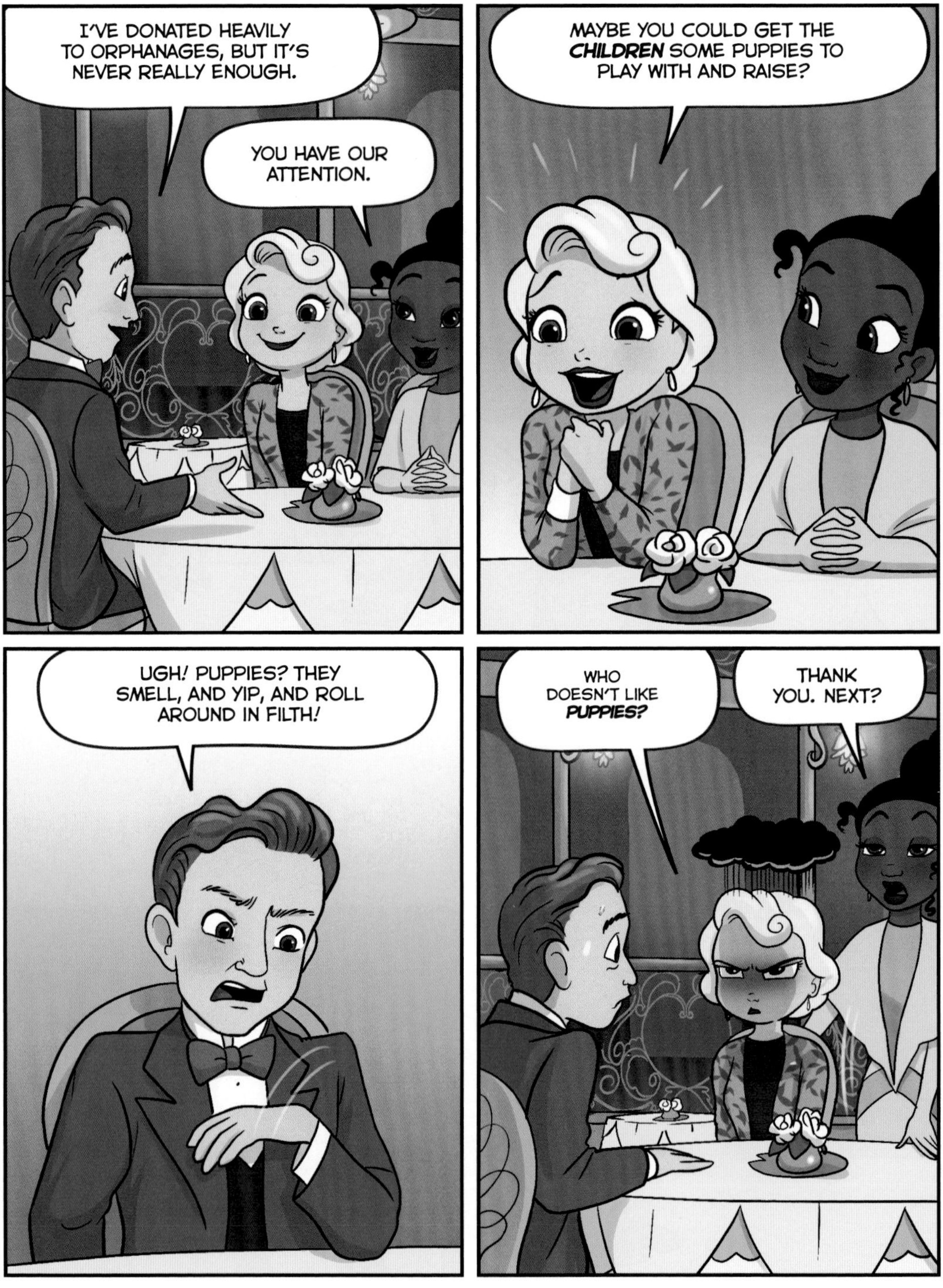
I'VE DONATED HEAVILY TO ORPHANAGES, BUT IT'S NEVER REALLY ENOUGH.
YOU HAVE OUR ATTENTION.
MAYBE YOU COULD GET THE ***CHILDREN*** SOME PUPPIES TO PLAY WITH AND RAISE?
UGH! PUPPIES? THEY SMELL, AND YIP, AND ROLL AROUND IN FILTH!
WHO DOESN'T LIKE ***PUPPIES?***
THANK YOU. NEXT?

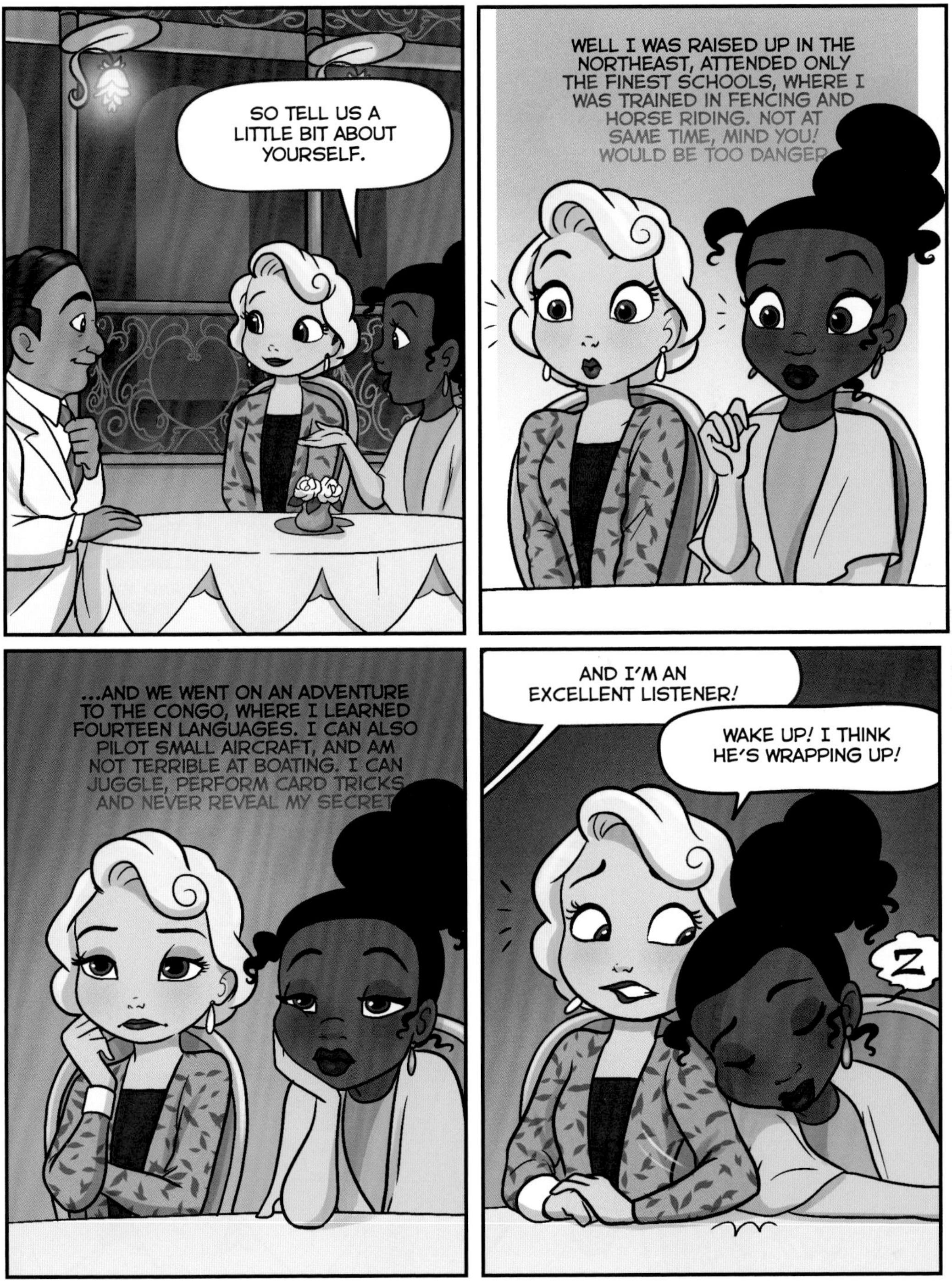
SO TELL US A LITTLE BIT ABOUT YOURSELF.
WELL I WAS RAISED UP IN THE NORTHEAST, ATTENDED ONLY THE FINEST SCHOOLS, WHERE I WAS TRAINED IN FENCING AND HORSE RIDING. NOT AT SAME TIME, MIND YOU! WOULD BE TOO DANGER
...AND WE WENT ON AN ADVENTURE TO THE CONGO, WHERE I LEARNED FOURTEEN LANGUAGES. I CAN ALSO PILOT SMALL AIRCRAFT, AND AM NOT TERRIBLE AT BOATING. I CAN JUGGLE, PERFORM CARD TRICKS AND NEVER REVEAL MY SECRET
AND I'M AN EXCELLENT LISTENER!
WAKE UP! I THINK HE'S WRAPPING UP!
Z

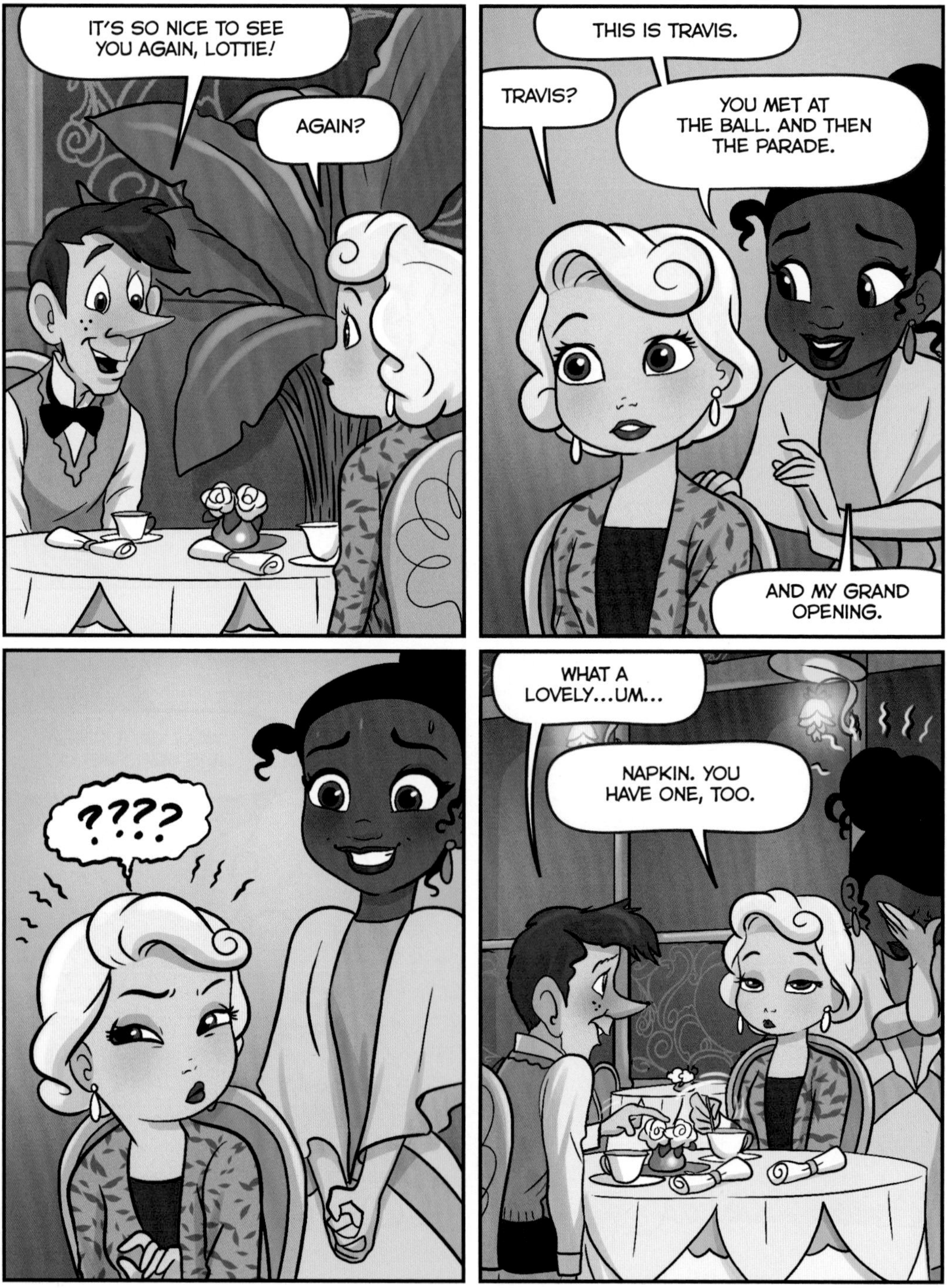
IT'S SO NICE TO SEE YOU AGAIN, LOTTIE!
AGAIN?
THIS IS TRAVIS.
TRAVIS?
YOU MET AT THE BALL. AND THEN THE PARADE.
AND MY GRAND OPENING.
????
WHAT A LOVELY...UM...
NAPKIN. YOU HAVE ONE, TOO.

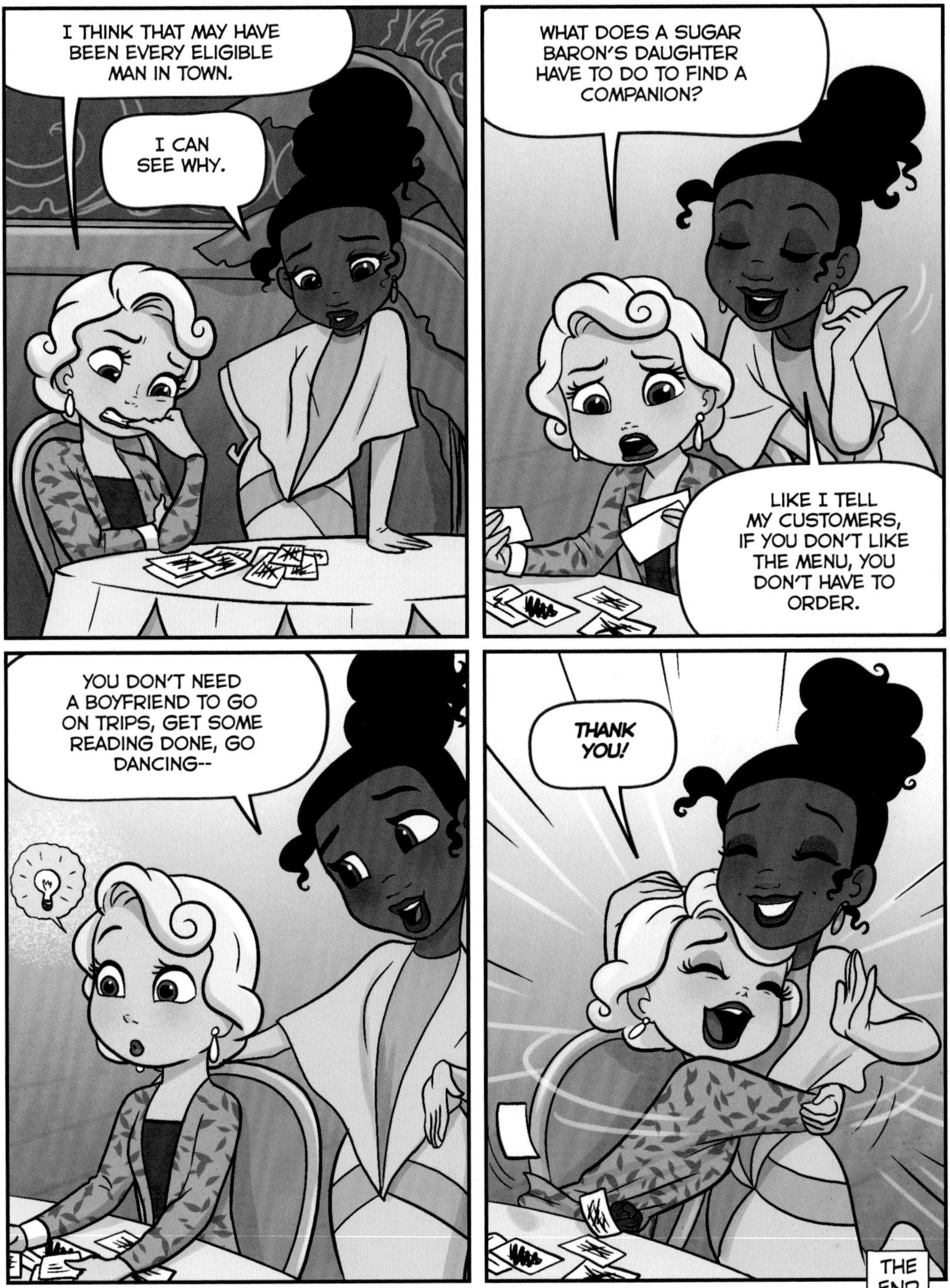
I THINK THAT MAY HAVE BEEN EVERY ELIGIBLE MAN IN TOWN.
I CAN SEE WHY.
WHAT DOES A SUGAR BARON'S DAUGHTER HAVE TO DO TO FIND A COMPANION?
LIKE I TELL MY CUSTOMERS, IF YOU DON'T LIKE THE MENU, YOU DON'T HAVE TO ORDER.
YOU DON'T NEED A BOYFRIEND TO GO ON TRIPS, GET SOME READING DONE, GO DANCING--
THANK YOU!
THE END

# "CARPET SALE"

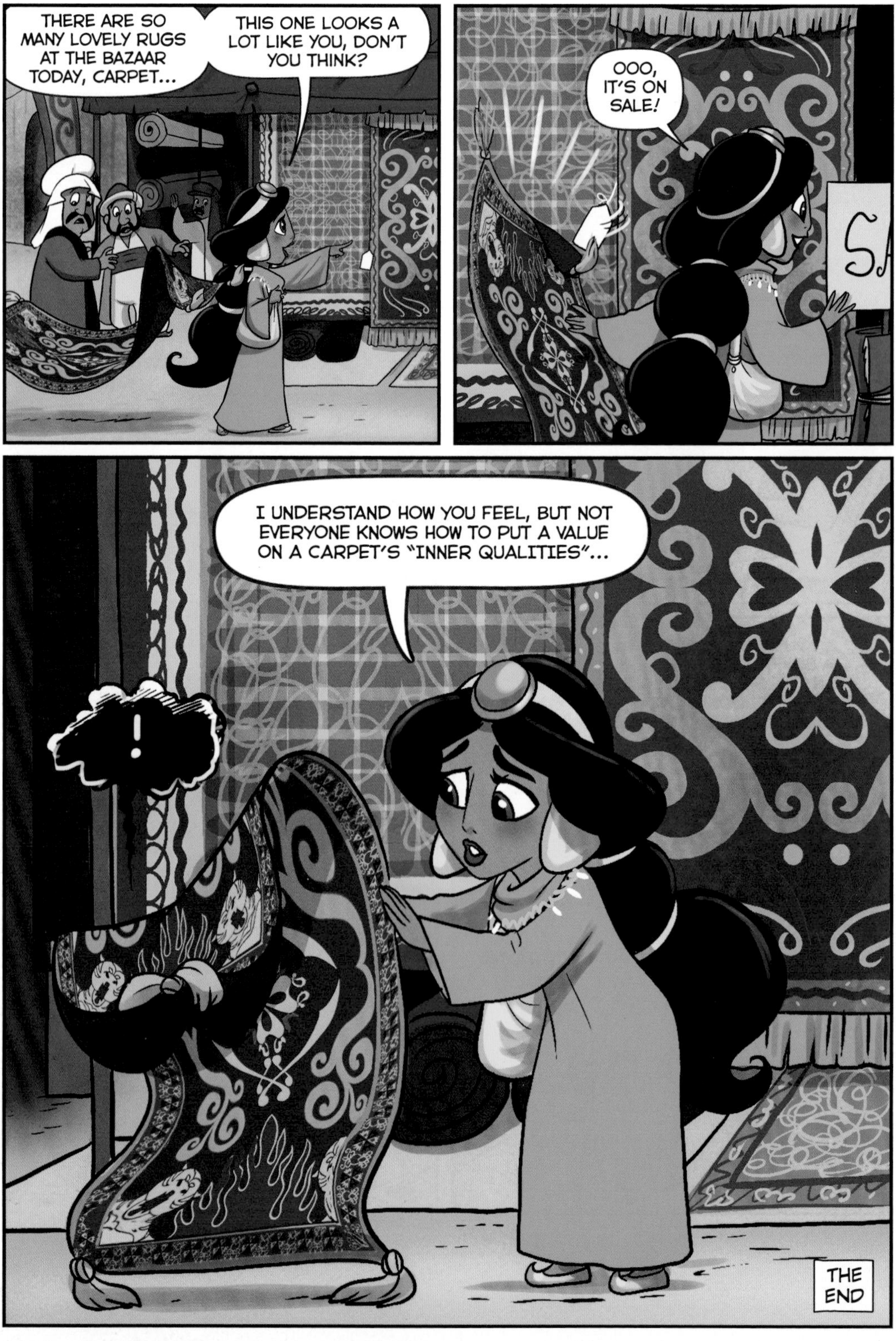
THERE ARE SO MANY LOVELY RUGS AT THE BAZAAR TODAY, CARPET...
THIS ONE LOOKS A LOT LIKE YOU, DON'T YOU THINK?
OOO, IT'S ON SALE!
SA
I UNDERSTAND HOW YOU FEEL, BUT NOT EVERYONE KNOWS HOW TO PUT A VALUE ON A CARPET'S "INNER QUALITIES"...
!
THE END

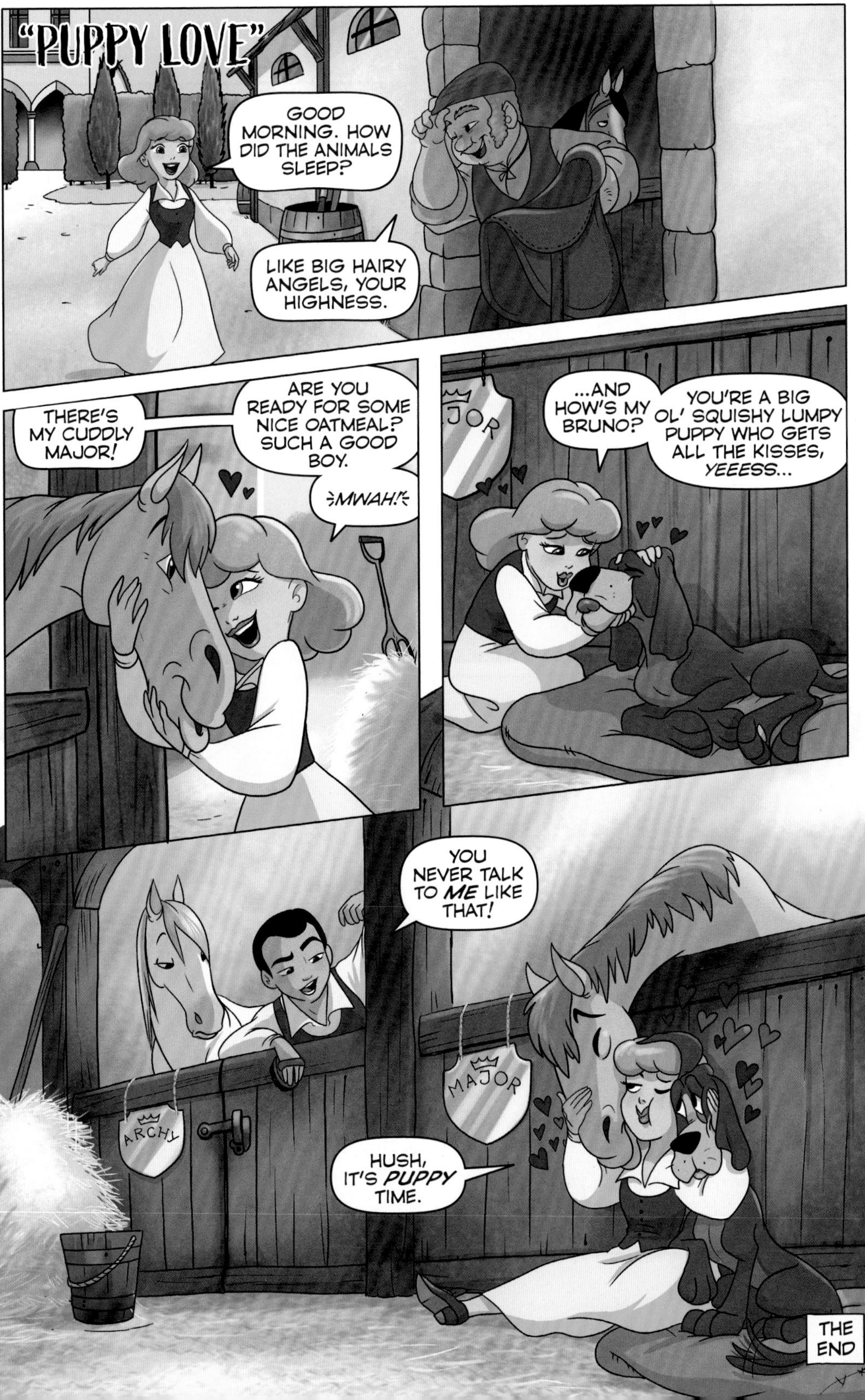
"PUPPY LOVE"
GOOD MORNING. HOW DID THE ANIMALS SLEEP?
LIKE BIG HAIRY ANGELS, YOUR HIGHNESS.
THERE'S MY CUDDLY MAJOR!
ARE YOU READY FOR SOME NICE OATMEAL? SUCH A GOOD BOY.
MWAH!
MAJOR
...AND HOW'S MY BRUNO?
YOU'RE A BIG OL' SQUISHY LUMPY PUPPY WHO GETS ALL THE KISSES, *YEEESS...*
YOU NEVER TALK TO *ME* LIKE THAT!
ARCHY
MAJOR
HUSH, IT'S *PUPPY* TIME.
THE END

# "SNEAKING"

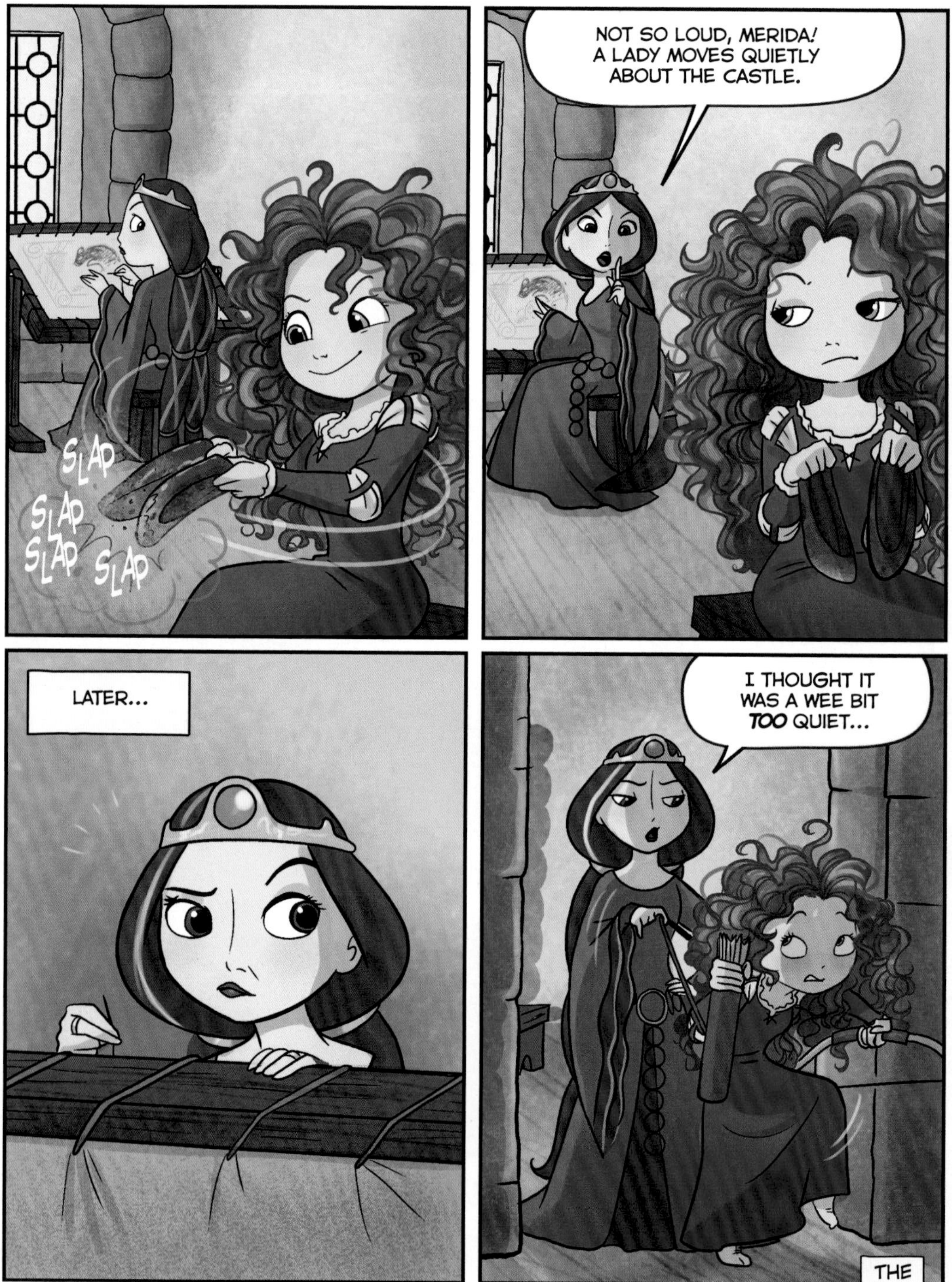
SLAP
SLAP
SLAP
SLAP
NOT SO LOUD, MERIDA! A LADY MOVES QUIETLY ABOUT THE CASTLE.
LATER...
I THOUGHT IT WAS A WEE BIT ***TOO*** QUIET...
THE END

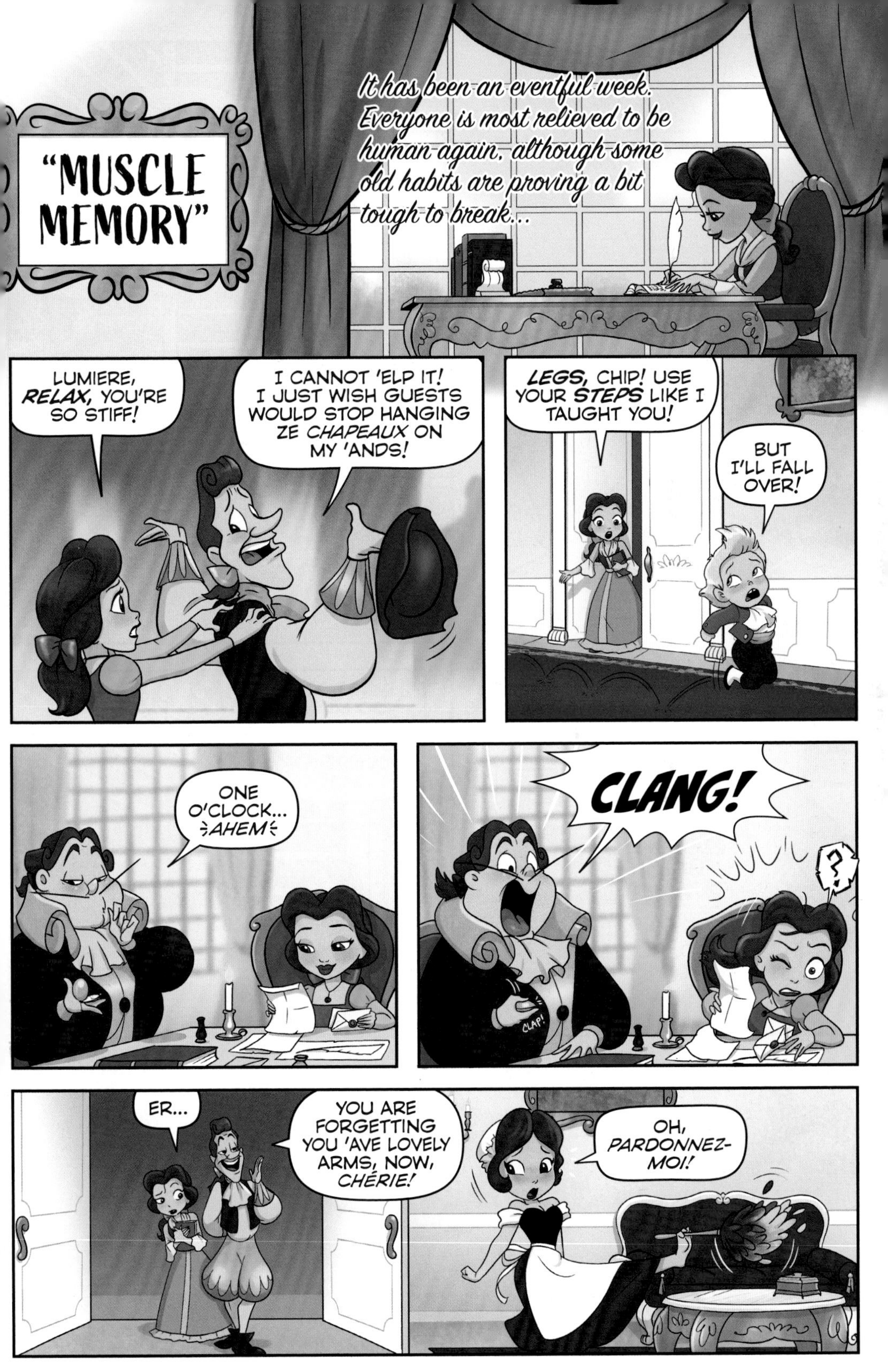
"MUSCLE MEMORY"
It has been an eventful week. Everyone is most relieved to be human again, although some old habits are proving a bit tough to break...
LUMIERE, RELAX, YOU'RE SO STIFF!
I CANNOT 'ELP IT! I JUST WISH GUESTS WOULD STOP HANGING ZE CHAPEAUX ON MY 'ANDS!
LEGS, CHIP! USE YOUR STEPS LIKE I TAUGHT YOU!
BUT I'LL FALL OVER!
ONE O'CLOCK... AHEM
CLANG!
CLAP!
?
ER...
YOU ARE FORGETTING YOU 'AVE LOVELY ARMS, NOW, CHÉRIE!
OH, PARDONNEZ-MOI!

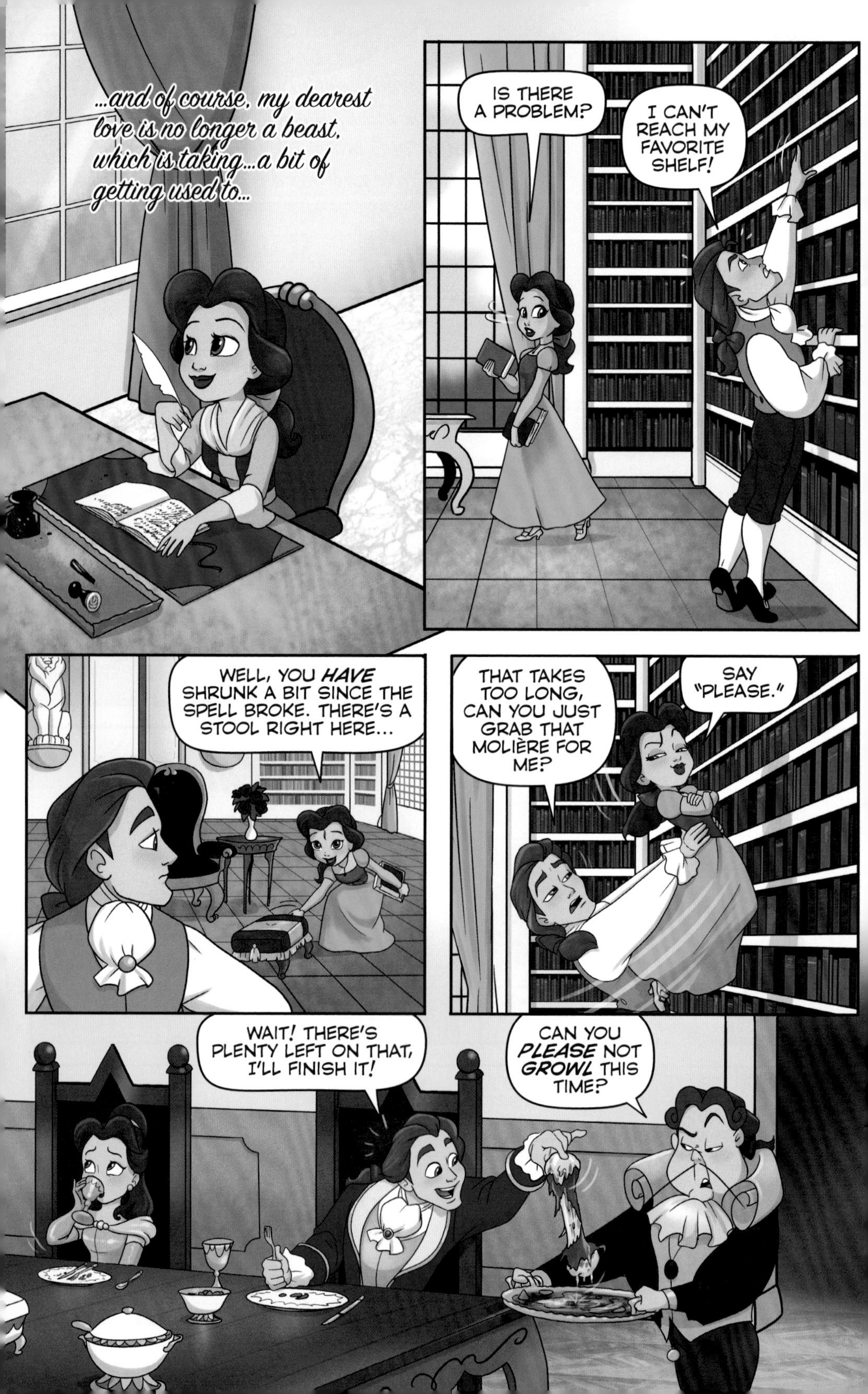
...and of course, my dearest love is no longer a beast, which is taking...a bit of getting used to...
IS THERE A PROBLEM?
I CAN'T REACH MY FAVORITE SHELF!
WELL, YOU *HAVE* SHRUNK A BIT SINCE THE SPELL BROKE. THERE'S A STOOL RIGHT HERE...
THAT TAKES TOO LONG, CAN YOU JUST GRAB THAT MOLIÈRE FOR ME?
SAY "PLEASE."
WAIT! THERE'S PLENTY LEFT ON THAT, I'LL FINISH IT!
CAN YOU *PLEASE* NOT *GROWL* THIS TIME?

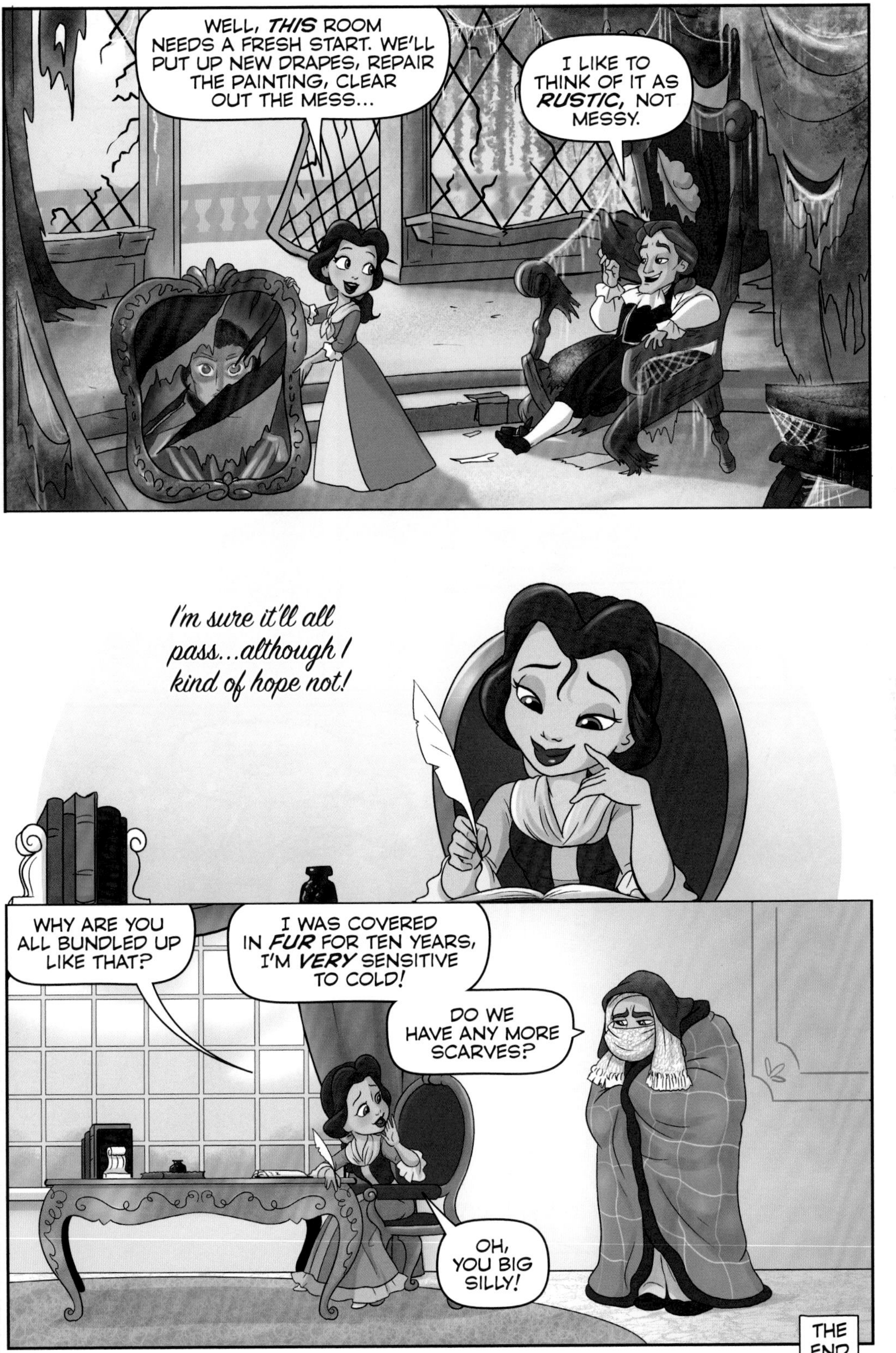
WELL, THIS ROOM NEEDS A FRESH START. WE'LL PUT UP NEW DRAPES, REPAIR THE PAINTING, CLEAR OUT THE MESS...
I LIKE TO THINK OF IT AS RUSTIC, NOT MESSY.
I'm sure it'll all pass...although I kind of hope not!
WHY ARE YOU ALL BUNDLED UP LIKE THAT?
I WAS COVERED IN FUR FOR TEN YEARS, I'M VERY SENSITIVE TO COLD!
DO WE HAVE ANY MORE SCARVES?
OH, YOU BIG SILLY!
THE END

# "WAKE UP CALL"

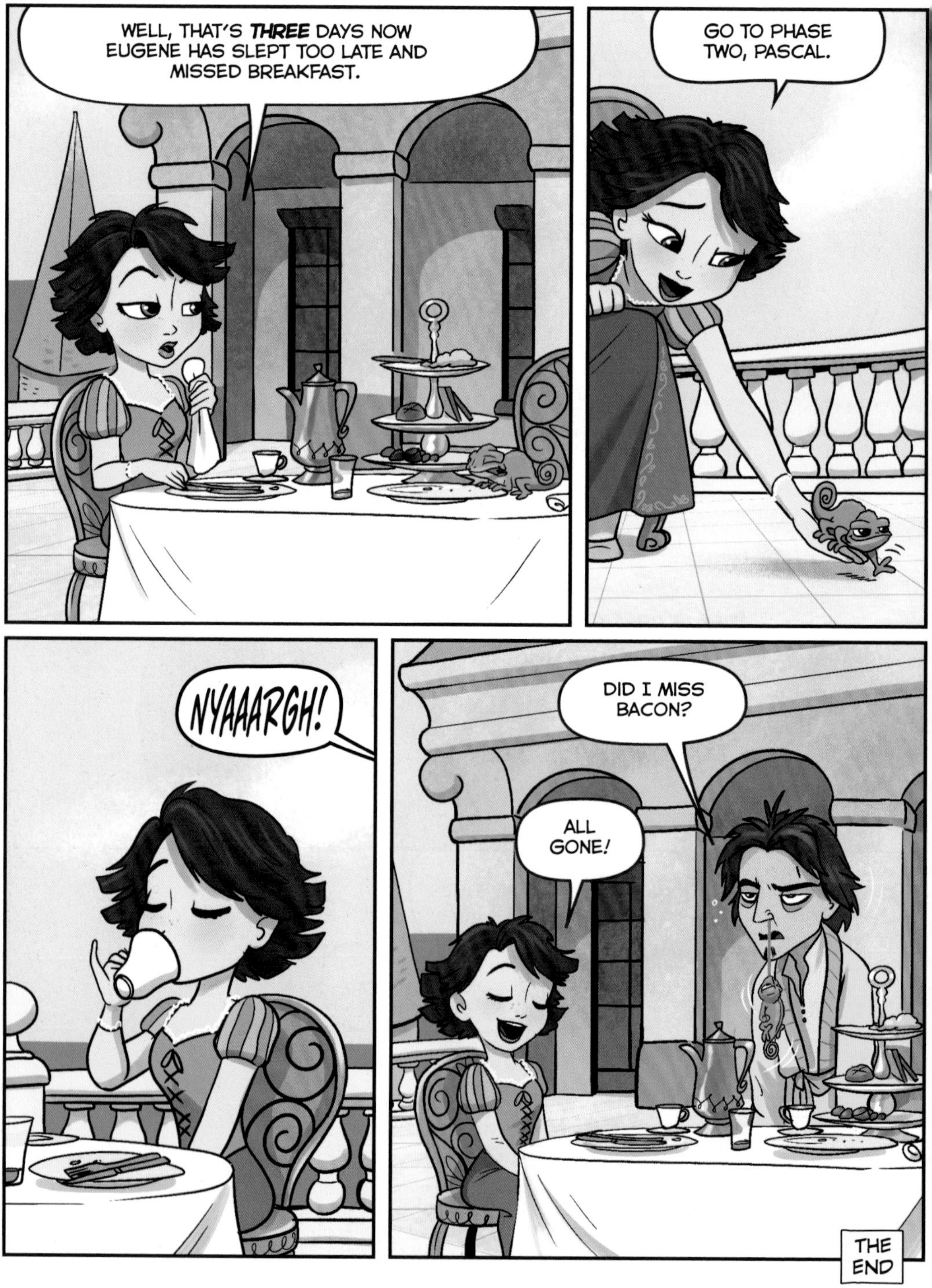

WELL, THAT'S THREE DAYS NOW EUGENE HAS SLEPT TOO LATE AND MISSED BREAKFAST.
GO TO PHASE TWO, PASCAL.
NYAAARGH!
DID I MISS BACON?
ALL GONE!
THE END

# "BIRD SONGS"

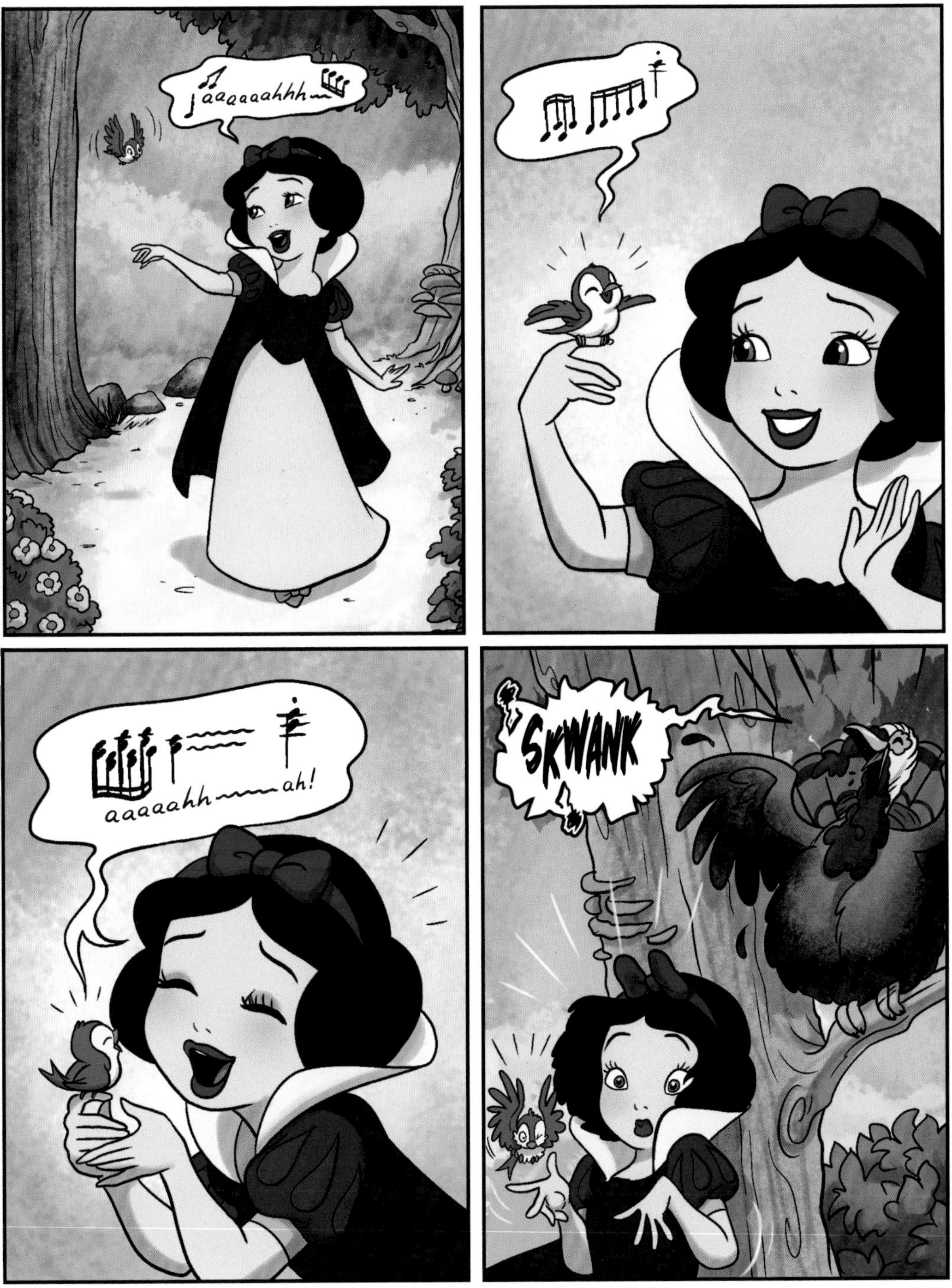
aaaaaaahhh
aaaaahh ah!
SKWANK

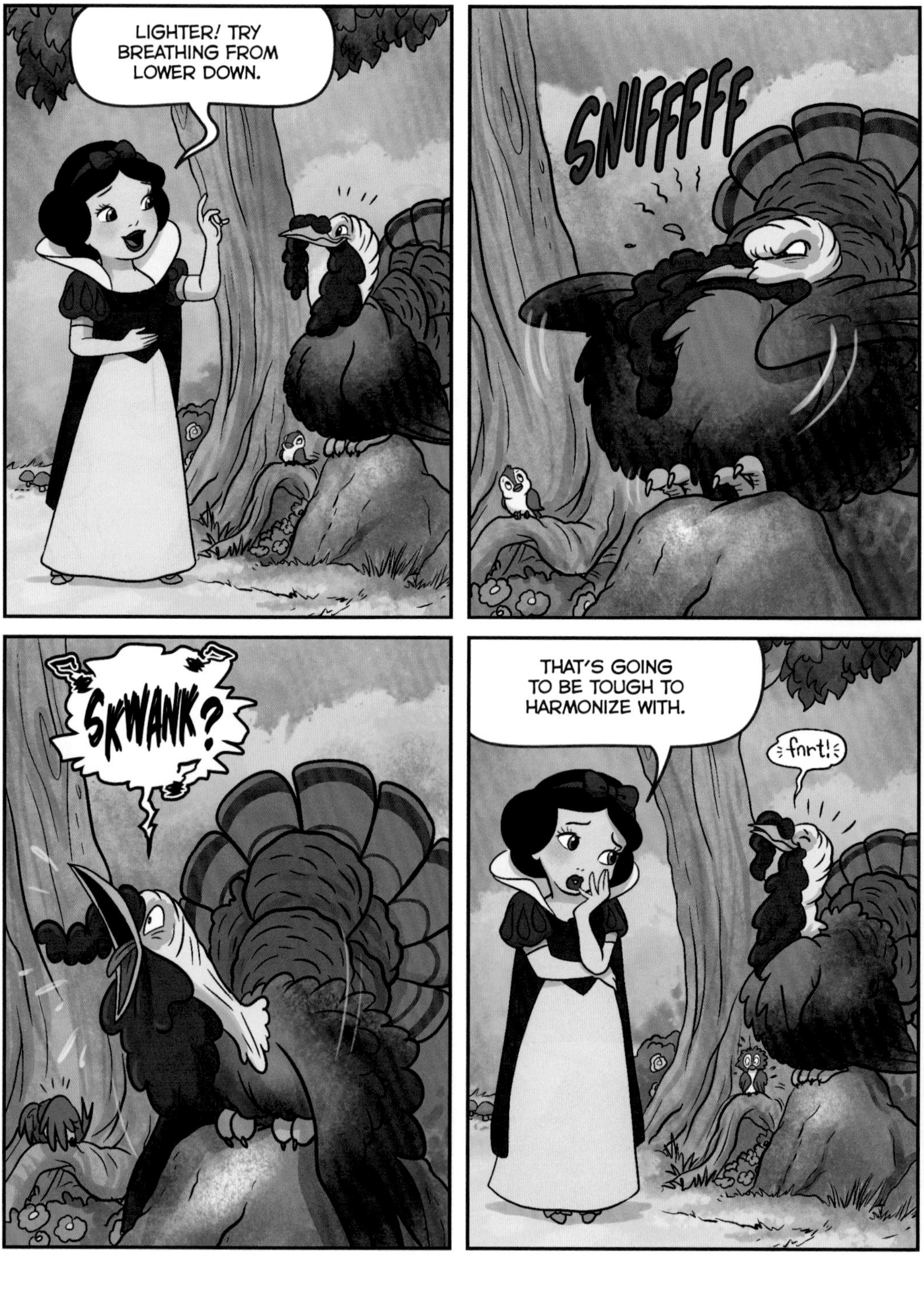
LIGHTER! TRY BREATHING FROM LOWER DOWN.
SNIFFFFF
SKWANK?
THAT'S GOING TO BE TOUGH TO HARMONIZE WITH.
fnrt!

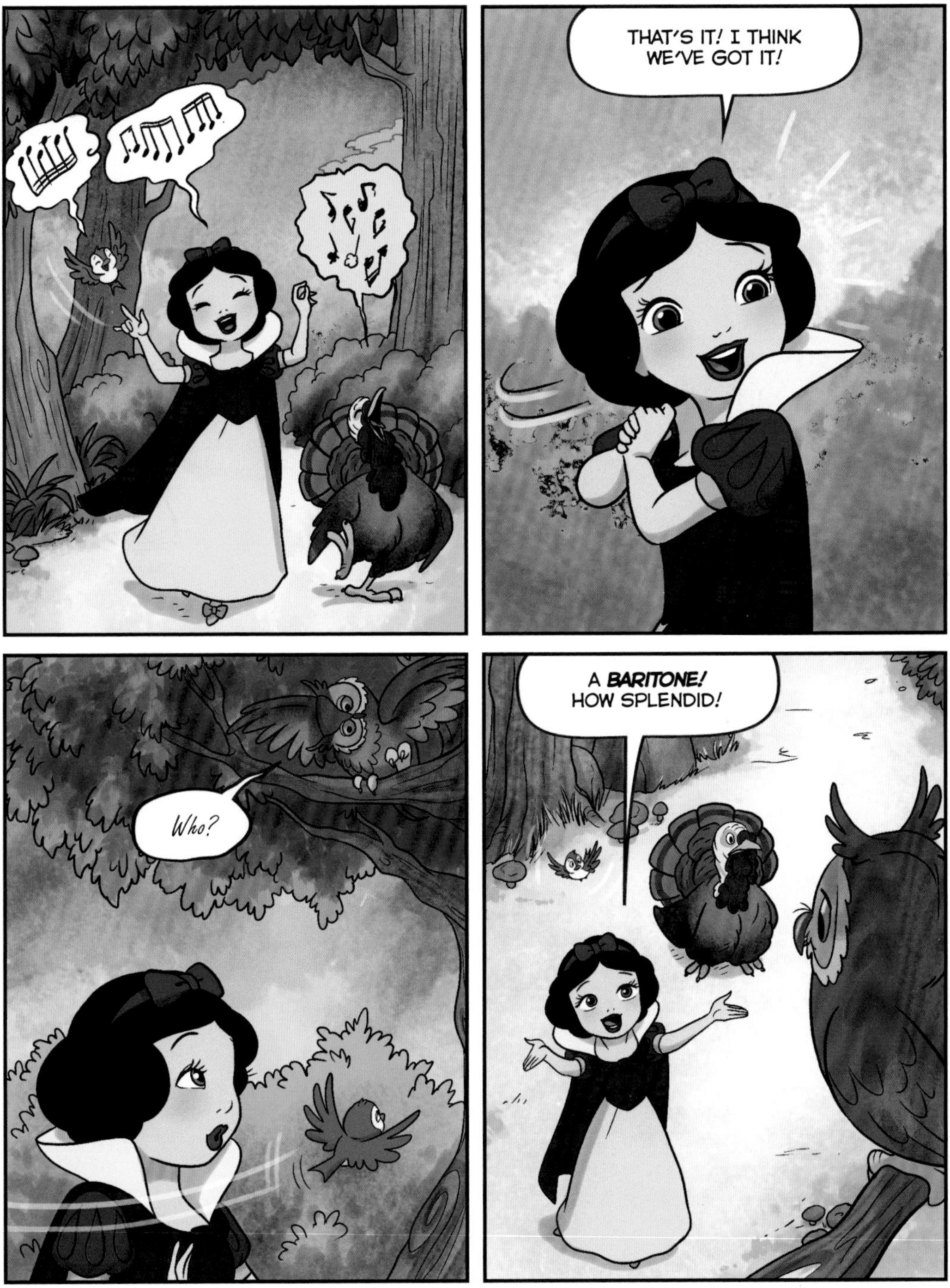
THAT'S IT! I THINK WE'VE GOT IT!
Who?
A **BARITONE!** HOW SPLENDID!

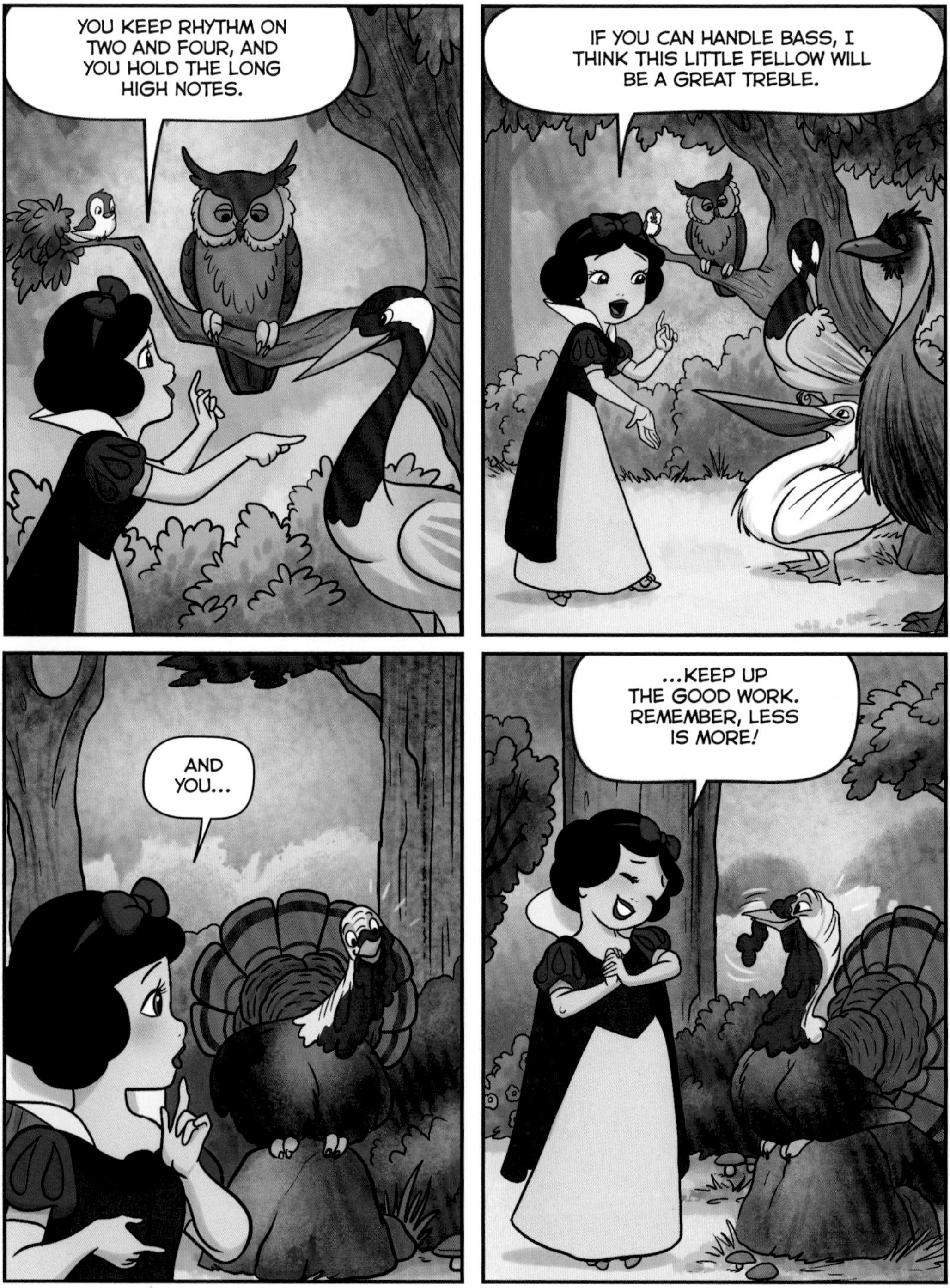
YOU KEEP RHYTHM ON TWO AND FOUR, AND YOU HOLD THE LONG HIGH NOTES.
IF YOU CAN HANDLE BASS, I THINK THIS LITTLE FELLOW WILL BE A GREAT TREBLE.
AND YOU...
...KEEP UP THE GOOD WORK. REMEMBER, LESS IS MORE!

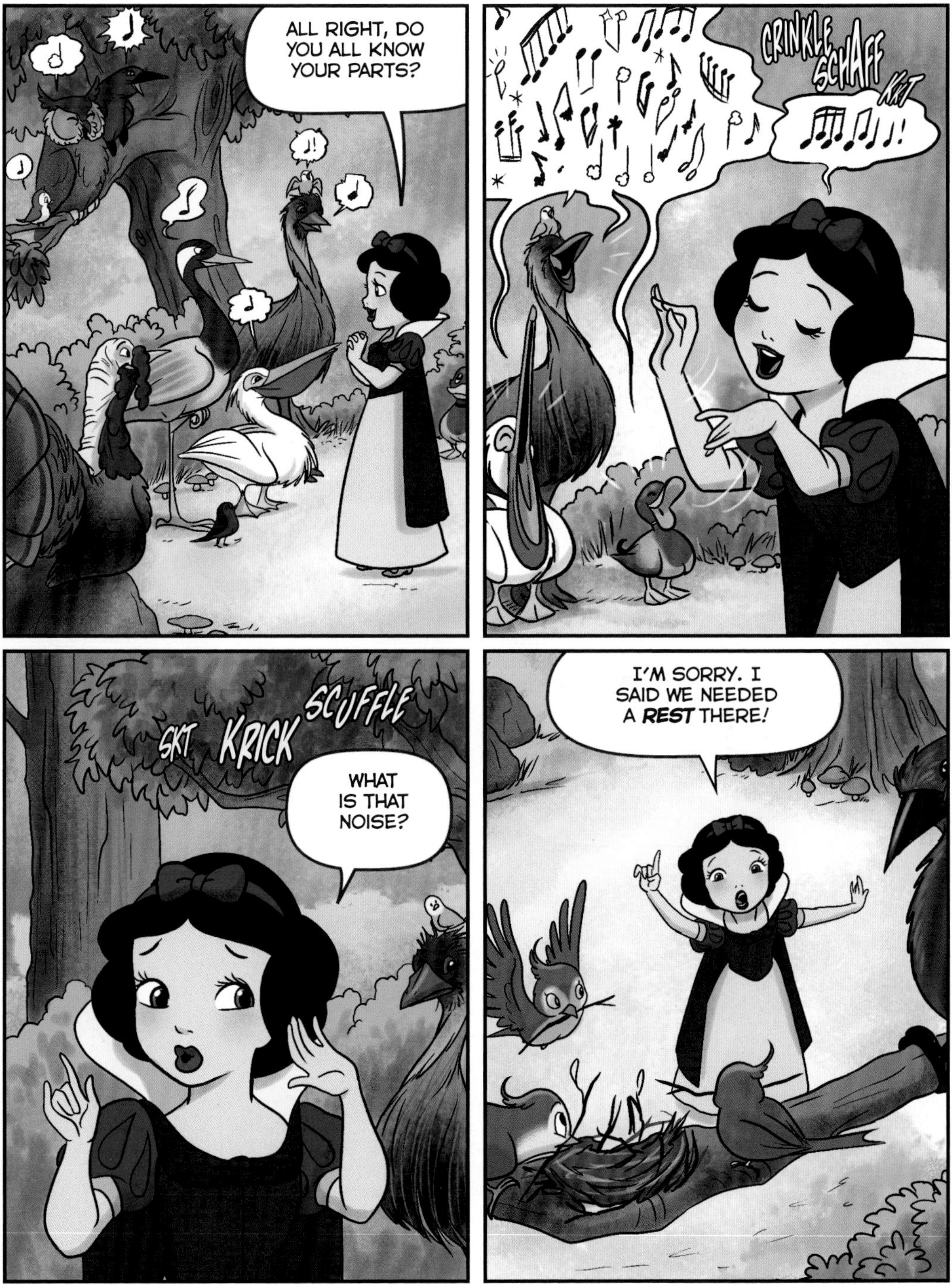
ALL RIGHT, DO YOU ALL KNOW YOUR PARTS?
CRINKLE
SCHAFF
KRT
SKT
KRICK
SCUFFLE
WHAT IS THAT NOISE?
I'M SORRY. I SAID WE NEEDED A **REST** THERE!

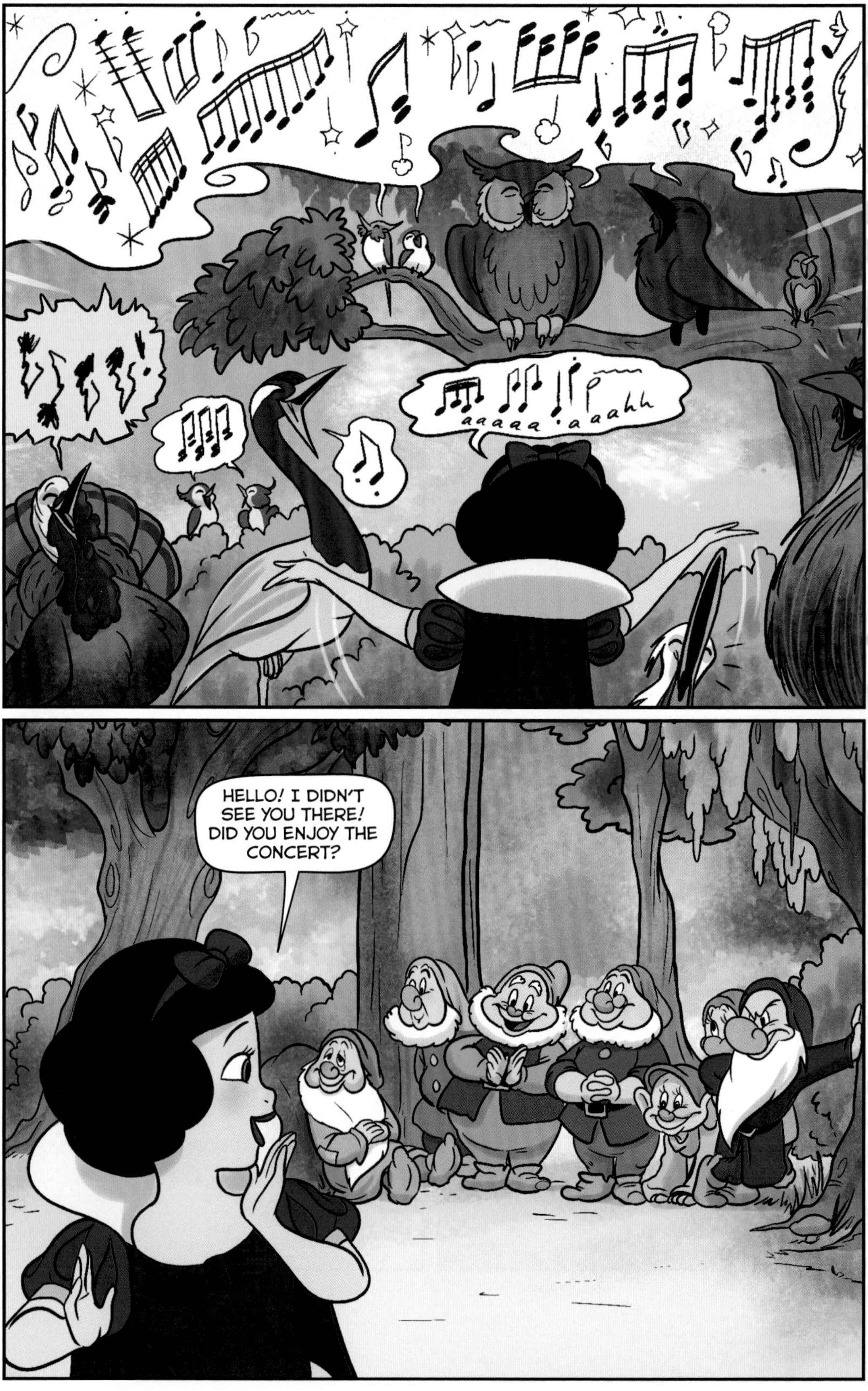
aaaaa aaaahh
HELLO! I DIDN'T SEE YOU THERE! DID YOU ENJOY THE CONCERT?

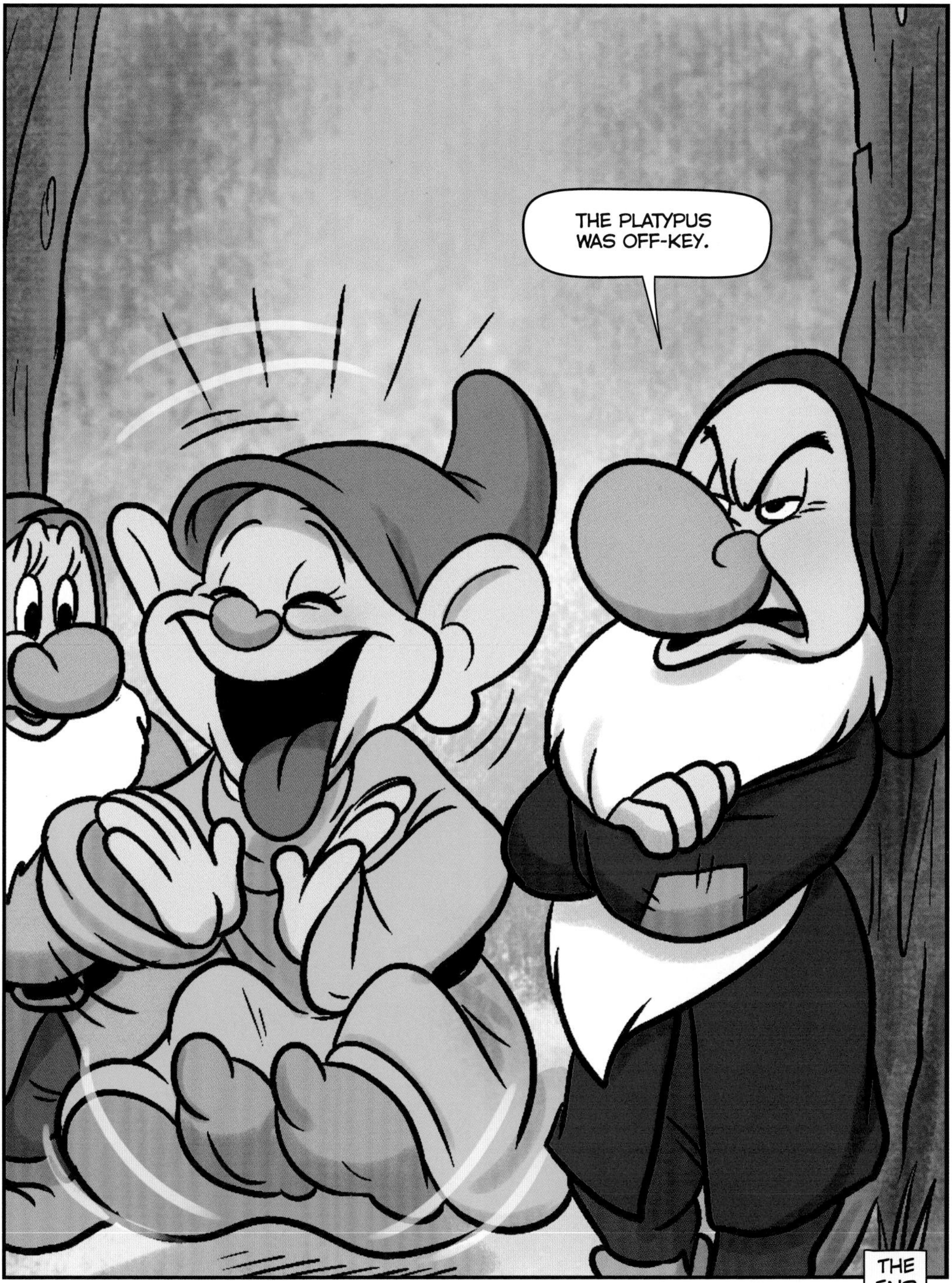
THE PLATYPUS
WAS OFF-KEY.
THE
END

# "LATE NIGHT READS"

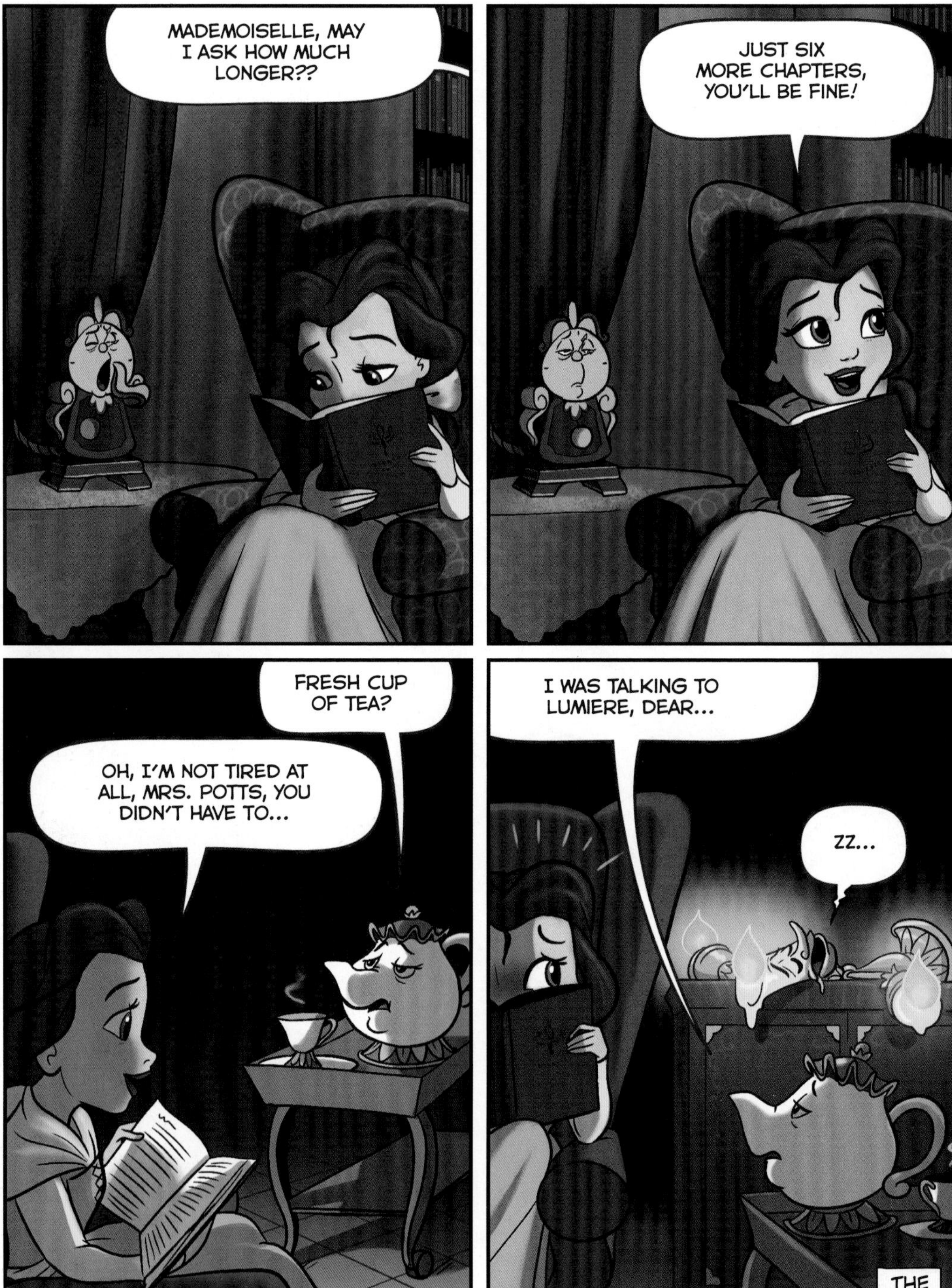
MADEMOISELLE, MAY I ASK HOW MUCH LONGER??
JUST SIX MORE CHAPTERS, YOU'LL BE FINE!
FRESH CUP OF TEA?
OH, I'M NOT TIRED AT ALL, MRS. POTTS, YOU DIDN'T HAVE TO...
I WAS TALKING TO LUMIERE, DEAR...
ZZ...
THE END